CLOAKS
AND
VEILS

Published by Thomas & Mercer
P.O. Box 400818
Las Vegas, NV 89140

ISBN-13: 9781612183572
ISBN-10: 1612183573

CLOAKS
AND
VEILS

J. C. CARLESON

THOMAS & MERCER

CHAPTER ONE

AUGUST

She never imagined that she would ever actually miss wearing a burqa.

The tent-like blue garments hid the weathered beauty of Afghan women, turning them into azure ghosts, each indistinguishable from the next. Only the most intense scrutiny revealed tiny differences: a scuff on the tip of a shoe peeking out from underneath the voluminous fabric or a small tear to a tattered hem.

And for Dara, that was precisely the point of wearing a burqa. Disguise. Concealment. Still, each time she pulled on one of the suffocating cloth prisons she suffered from a sort of vertigo—an intense, nagging feeling of claustrophobia. The sensation of being erased.

She did have to admit that the garments were effective at covering her from head to toe, though. Wearing a burqa had allowed her to breeze through several recent operations, peering undetected through the mesh eye opening of her disguise as she moved freely through the crowds of Kabul.

She used to curse the stifling garment each time she pulled it over her head, tensing as its billowing pleats and folds limited her movements and obscured her vision. But dressed in a burqa, she had been an anonymous blue blob. An inconsequential drop in a sea of faceless blue blobs. She had been virtually invisible. She had been safe. And she had been able to venture into neighborhoods that were off-limits to her male colleagues.

Now, dressed instead in the slightly less conservative hijab that was more appropriate for her present environment, she might as well have been marching through the streets in a string bikini. Her head covering was pulled down all the way to her eyebrows, and the loose-fitting cloak hid her weapon handily, but she still felt exposed. Her naked face felt like a beacon.

Thanks to Italian blood on her mother's side, Dara at least had the dark hair and dark eyes to carry off the veiled disguise. Sort of. But if anyone had looked—*really* looked at her—they would have noticed that her skin was a shade too fair and that the shape of her eyes was more Sicilian than Syrian. The difference between a burqa and the system of cloaks and veils that she wore today may have been only a few inches of uncovered skin, but it was more than enough to get her killed.

Fortunately the men in this neighborhood—one of Jordan's poorest and most densely populated—were distracted. The decrepit buildings housed a huge and ever-growing number of Iraqi refugees, and today's protest against their squalid living conditions and lack of work permits was the angriest one yet. Dara kept her face down as she wove through the shouting mobs. The chanting was growing louder—and more enraged—by the minute. She had been in similar crowds enough times to know that violence was inevitable. Someone would throw a brick or a rock. And then someone else would shoot—into the air at first, and then maybe at a window or a car. And from there it was all downhill.

She hoped that she could get out before the shooting started. But even if she didn't, she would be fine. She had done her homework. She knew what to do. She had memorized a half-dozen routes out of the neighborhood, and she knew where the road-blocks would go up, if things went that far. She also had a variety of hide sites picked out and a contact who could give her shelter, albeit grudgingly and at great risk to himself. She didn't want to rely on a backup plan, though. As far as Dara was concerned, any deviation from the original plan was a mistake, and mistakes always came with consequences. Still, she always made allowances for the unexpected. Just in case.

Getting out alive wouldn't be the hard part. Getting *in* had been the hard part.

Dara lowered her head even further, painfully aware that she was one of very few women left in the streets. The rest had gathered up their children and sought the scant safety that their meager dwellings offered. Dara picked up her pace, trying to slide through the crowd without drawing attention to herself. She couldn't afford to stand out in this neighborhood. She was surrounded by people whose lives had been torn apart four times over: first by invasion, then by sectarian violence, then by flight from their homeland, and now by the impoverished limbo of their refugee status. And there was no one they blamed more than the US government. Had anyone guessed who Dara was—who she represented—she would have been torn apart by the angry mob. She wasn't frightened so much as she was just…aware. The danger was simply a fact—a variable—to be recognized and respected.

Finally. She recognized the makeshift storefront from the satellite imagery. Her target. The front door was locked, but she had expected that. There was a small, street-level window on the back alley side of the building, just big enough for her to climb through. Barely. As she lowered herself into the darkened building, she whispered a small word of ironic thanks that she was still gaunt after her most recent bout of intestinal parasites—this time compliments of an undercooked ceremonial dinner with a Sudanese tribal chief. "Ah, giardia. The gift that keeps on giving." Five pounds heavier and she wouldn't have fit.

She relaxed as her eyes adjusted to the darkness. The layout of the room was just as her source had described. Hopefully his description of where the data was hidden would be equally accurate. Dara could be in and out in less than a minute—exactly the way she liked to conduct operations. Particularly operations that required walking into neighborhoods full of people who would very much like to see her dead.

But just as she was about to sweep aside the carpet to look for the hidden floor compartment that her source had described, she heard the doorknob rattle. She froze in place, her right hand automatically reaching for her gun. She hoped that the flimsy lock would deter whoever it was, since there was nowhere to hide in the small room.

No such luck.

She stepped behind a small table in the corner of the room as she heard the unwelcome sound of a key turning in the lock. It wasn't big enough to hide behind, but at least it offered a margin of cover.

The dark-haired man who slipped in obviously expected the room to be empty; he didn't even bother to look around as he quietly pulled the door closed behind him. His eyes were still adjusting to the dim light when Dara spoke, and he whirled around when he heard her voice.

"You had a goddamn *key*?"

His hand jumped for his weapon, but he stopped himself as Dara yanked the veil off of her head. He at least had the courtesy to look embarrassed as he recognized her.

Dara's eyes narrowed as she stared at Tariq Bataineh, the very same officer from Jordan's General Intelligence Directorate who had ordered her to stand down on all operations in Iraqi refugee sectors. He had stubbornly refused her request to reconsider, even when she explained just how critical the data she was after was. He hadn't seemed to care that there were lives at stake. And yet here he was.

"This was *my* operation, damn it. My source, my information, my op. I only told your service about it as a courtesy and to make sure that your people wouldn't get in the way." Dara's voice came out as a hiss. She wanted to yell, but she couldn't risk attracting attention from outside.

He didn't respond. His eyes were too busy scanning the room, looking for the same computer drive that Dara was after.

She smirked. At least she'd known better than to divulge *all* of her source's information. Only she knew the exact location where the data storage device was hidden. She was figuring out how to grab the thumb drive and get out quickly when the gunshots started.

Dara and her unwelcome companion both instinctually dropped to a crouch. Fortunately the store's front windows had long since been boarded up, either because the owner hadn't wanted prying eyes to see what was going on inside or because the glass had been broken in previous neighborhood skirmishes. Unfortunately, it sounded as if the protests were erupting into violence just on the other side of the door.

Tariq crept over to the uncovered window in the back of the room and peered out cautiously. Dara used the opportunity to scoop the thumb drive out of the small compartment hidden underneath a loose floorboard. She tucked it into the folds of her robe and silently replaced the carpet as he assessed the size of the small opening. "Trust me, you won't fit," she advised him, taking in his broad shoulders. "I barely managed."

He pulled back from the window as the sound of running footsteps echoed through the alley. "We might be stuck here for a while, then." He spoke for the first time, his words cloaked in an accent that gave away both his Arabic mother tongue and traces of his British prep schooling—the mark of a privileged upbringing.

"Speak for yourself. I'm out of here as soon as the alley is clear." She knew that she wasn't being fair, but she was angry. "Just tell me one thing before I go. Did you try to steal my op because I'm a woman? Or because I'm CIA?"

He watched her as she replaced her hijab, dropping to a crouch again as the sound of broken glass and then another gunshot rang out. The crowd out front wasn't moving, and the flimsy plywood covering the front windows wouldn't offer much protection against bullets or flames. "Actually, I thought I was doing you a favor. I had been warned that today might be a bad day to pay a visit to this area, so I decided to get the data myself. I would have presented it to you, with pleasure, if you hadn't decided to go it alone. After I officially denied your request to come here, I might add. Besides," he held up the key, "you're not the only one with sources in this neighborhood."

Dara ignored him as she pulled herself up through the small window. For the moment the alley was deserted. She turned back just long enough to poke her face into the room. "You'll be waiting here a long time, dressed like that."

A dark expression crossed his face. Panic? Or anger? It was hard to tell. Dara didn't have time to worry about it as she darted away.

The alley was still empty, and a quick glance around the corner revealed that she had a relatively clear path out of the most chaotic part of the neighborhood if she headed east instead of the way she had come. *Now or never,* she said to herself, and then… stopped.

She stomped her foot in frustration. *I don't owe him anything!* She debated with herself for a moment, all the while watching the crowd surge and circulate. There were definitely a few weapons visible, and she watched as men picked up rocks, bottles, anything they could get their hands on. This was going to get ugly, fast. But if Tariq was good enough to get a key to the front door, then surely he had contacts in the area who could get him out safely. Right?

"Damn it!" she said out loud and then whirled around to hurry half a block west. If something went wrong on this operation, no one would be able to say that it was her fault.

It only took her a minute to find what she was looking for and then to return to the back entrance of the target location. She pushed a bundle of cloth through the window and then climbed back into the room where Tariq was still trapped. "That was close—it's heating up out there. Good thing today seems to be laundry day for the neighbors. Here, I brought you something." She pulled at a variety of dark garments that she had grabbed from a clothesline. "I don't think they make these big enough for your size—what are you, six foot two? But I grabbed a few, and we can improvise."

The man's face fell. "You want me to wear *that*?"

"It's the only way we're going to get you out of here safely. And, hey—we're supposed to be on the same team, *right*?" She wondered if his English language skills were good enough to pick up on sarcasm.

From his withering glance, she guessed that he understood perfectly. But to his credit, he didn't hesitate. Together he and

Dara fastened a makeshift hijab that almost rivaled a burqa in disguise coverage.

"You'll have to crouch down a bit as you walk so that you look shorter. And it would have been nice if you had shaved a little closer. There aren't many women walking around here with a five-o'clock shadow." She showed him how to pull the side of the veil across the bottom half of his face, ostensibly for modesty, but in his case, to cover up the strong jaw and the faint trace of dark stubble.

He was an attractive man, Dara noted, but he made for a terrible-looking woman. "Stay behind me, and keep your eyes down. I'll get us through the crowd, just stay close to my back."

She assumed that he would be mortified—a tall, handsome Middle Eastern man, and a senior Mukhabarat officer, no less, forced to dress as a woman and let an American CIA officer lead him to safety while on his own turf. To her surprise, though, he appeared more amused than anything else, and his eyes sparkled with humor. Before she turned to walk out the front door—a route that most definitely would not have been her first choice—he winked at her.

"I hope you're taking this seriously," she hissed and then stepped out into the mob.

It took longer than Dara would have liked to get through the crowds with her new companion shuffling blindly behind her, but they made it out.

Once they reached the nearly deserted road that circled desolately back to Amman, they finally relaxed. And Dara exploded. "Now that I've saved you one hell of a long and dangerous wait back there, I'm going to ask you one more time why you crossed my operation. Is it because I'm a woman or because I'm CIA?"

she asked. "Because your inability to trust me nearly cost us that op. *My* op."

He grinned at her. "I will admit that I seem to have made a mistake. I haven't spent much time working closely with women *or* with CIA officers. Perhaps I need to reexamine my stereotypes." He spoke so gently, so sincerely, that Dara struggled to maintain her fury. "Besides, the operation was a success, was it not?"

She clenched her jaw. He hadn't seen her take the computer drive, so how could he know?

"You said that I had 'nearly' cost us the op. I presume that means that you were successful? All the more reason for me to be impressed. And grateful." He pulled the veil away from his face. He really was attractive, Dara noticed.

"May I invite you to dinner, to thank you for your assistance?"

Dara stared at him. Was he serious? Was this man, Tariq Bataineh, one of the most senior intelligence officers in his country, seriously asking her out? She had been on the receiving end of a variety of proposals from rival spies, but never a…date.

And yet she found herself intrigued. It was probably a tactic. Maybe he just wanted to make sure that she never told his colleagues about how he had escaped dressed in drag and escorted by a woman. But as Dara looked at him—looking past the ridiculous disguise, of course—she didn't think so. She only saw interest. From man to woman, not from spy to spy.

"Dressed like that, I'd hope that you at least know how to cook," she teased, letting down her guard slightly.

He raised his eyebrows. "Now look who's making sexist stereotypes," he teased back. "And actually I do know how to cook. Quite well. And it would be my great pleasure to cook for you. Tonight? Eight o'clock?"

To her surprise, Dara felt herself nod. *Why not?* she thought. Once he got out of the costume, he really was quite handsome. She'd keep her defenses up—she always did. What could possibly come of one dinner?

CHAPTER TWO

FEBRUARY

Dara's new office didn't even have a window, much less a proper nameplate. She didn't care one bit that her name wasn't on the door, though. She liked being hard to find. She would have appreciated a window, however—even one facing the interior courtyard. It was disconcerting to arrive at work before the sun rose and then to trudge out of the building well after dusk, never once having seen the light of day. She might as well be in Alaska during the perpetually dark days of winter. In fact, she'd probably prefer a hard winter in Alaska to her current assignment: desk jockey, paper pusher, headquarters weenie, whatever you wanted to call it. She had spent her whole career in the field cursing the ineffective bureaucrats back home, and now she was one of them.

Some well-intentioned admin had printed out a temporary sign for her door: "Dara McIntyre, Counterintelligence Referent." She had torn it down on her first day. The very sound of her new title made her hostile; what the hell was a "referent" anyway? Judging from her recent experiences with other similarly titled new coworkers, it meant someone who spent her days interfering in field operations, generating useless paperwork, and generally being a counterproductive pain in the ass.

Dara had been told, repeatedly, that she was lucky she hadn't been fired or even brought up on criminal charges. After two weeks on the job, though, she wasn't so sure. A jail cell was probably bigger than her drab office—probably cheerier too.

She hadn't bothered to bring in any personal effects to decorate her office. For one thing, she didn't *have* a husband or kids, much less a family portrait to display. And a picture of her parents would just raise questions that she didn't feel like answering. Besides, bringing in personal effects would feel like an act of surrender to her new life. She had no intention of settling in here.

An unwelcome figure darkened her door. Dominic Cahill had never spent a day of his life in the field, but he took pleasure in sneaking around the halls, shamelessly eavesdropping and startling people with his silent approaches. There were quite a few people like Dominic at CIA headquarters—administrative employees unqualified to work as undercover officers overseas who nevertheless adopted some of the sleazier tricks of the spy trade to use against their own peers.

"Dara. Long time no see!" Dominic's feigned cheerfulness grated on her nerves, but Dara forced herself to offer a tolerant smile. Dominic was what CIA employees called a "legacy." His father had been one of the architects of the American espionage strategy early in the Cold War, and his grandfather had been one of the original OSS officers. This legacy of his had permitted Dominic to rise to a position well above what his experience or intellect should have allowed, and he wielded his unearned authority like a weapon.

"By the way," he continued. "I never knew that Dara was short for Sundara. Very unusual. What kind of name is that?"

Dara gritted her teeth. He'd been looking through her personnel file—the one place where she hadn't managed to purge all traces of her given name. That file, which contained extremely sensitive information, including the transcripts of her last series of humiliating polygraphs, was supposed to be inaccessible to all but the highest levels of agency management. *Be careful*, she reminded herself. Dominic may have risen even farther up the CIA food chain than she had realized.

"It's the kind of name that hippie parents like. It was either Sundara or Sunshine Bliss; fortunately Sundara won the coin toss," she answered flatly and then tried not to grimace as she watched him do the math: hippie parents equal liberal upbringing, and liberal upbringings run counter to CIA mindset. "Hence the shorter version."

Dominic laughed off her explanation, but she had seen his eyes narrow as he mentally filed away this new bit of knowledge. Yet another fact he could use against her.

"What can I do for you, Dominic?" She gestured at the stacks of paper covering her desk. In truth, there was nothing urgent or even mildly important on her to-do list, but she didn't want Dominic Cahill to know that. She just wanted him to go on his sleazy way.

But Dominic was not one to take a hint, particularly from someone he felt was below him in the agency's pecking order. He leaned against her doorframe leisurely. "Actually, Sundara—I mean Dara—I do have a small favor to ask." He paused, clearly expecting Dara to agree without even knowing what he was asking. He frowned when she didn't, and then continued. "We have a junior employee who has been having some…performance issues. She's bright enough, and did reasonably well in training, but lately she's been struggling. I thought maybe you could take her under your wing, show her the ropes."

Dara shook her head; she had no patience for this sort of thing. "Don't dump your problem children in my lap. I don't have time to babysit. Just fire her if she's not performing."

"It's more complicated than that." Dominic fidgeted.

Dara waited, eyebrows raised.

"Oh, hell," he sighed. "You'll find out soon enough. She's Jonathan Wolff's wife. Well, she *was*, anyway."

Dara may have been new to her CIA headquarters role, but even she knew that bit of information changed everything. "Ah, right. We can't go firing the American hero's widow, now can we?" She exhaled loudly. She was about to give in, if only to get Dominic out of her hair, until she realized that there was something suspicious about the request.

"Dom." She knew that he hated it when people shortened his name, but fair was fair. "Let's be candid here. You and I both know that I'm not exactly considered mentor material these days. Aren't I supposed to be hiding out in shamed anonymity here or something?"

Dominic winced at her bluntness. "Don't worry about that, Dara. This organization has a short memory. You'll see. Plus, we want to get her back out into the field as soon as she's ready, and you may have noticed that we don't have a lot of field-qualified officers roaming the halls here at headquarters."

I noticed, Dara thought.

Dominic lowered his voice and inched farther into Dara's office. "Look, we all know that she's pretty much guaranteed employment for life because of what happened to her husband. We just need you to assess whether there's anything left in her that we can use in the field before we throw her into some menial job in the headquarters dungeon."

"A job like mine, you mean," Dara said coldly. But she nodded in resigned acceptance. "Fine. Set up a meeting. I'll talk to your inconvenient, grieving widow."

"Be nice to her, Dara," Dominic warned. "This is a sensitive issue."

"Yeah, yeah," she waved him off and sighed.

Alaska in February would definitely be better.

CHAPTER THREE

Dara, as Dominic now knew—much to her irritation—had been born Sundara Rain to two well-intentioned hippies who had taken longer than most to discover that a mortgage and two kids really spoiled the buzz. Growing up just outside of Berkeley, California, she'd been taught, as were all children in Berkeley, to question authority as thoroughly and frequently as most kids were taught to brush their teeth. Ironically, she was convinced that this had helped her become a better spy. After all, it was hard to break international laws if you didn't first regard them with a certain amount of disdain in the first place, right? In Dara's opinion, it was the law-and-order robots marching around the halls of Langley who kept the CIA stuck in the Dark Ages.

Walking through the windowless corridor toward the conference room where Caitlin Wolff was waiting for her, she smiled at the idea of a liberal CIA. How different a place the world would be. Then she imagined her father, cheerful activist and grizzled yogi that he was, sitting cross-legged and barefoot while conducting an interrogation of a prisoner dressed in a tie-dyed jumpsuit. Nope. It definitely wouldn't work. Maybe a little moderation, though.

She entered the conference room and shut the door behind her. "I'm sorry about your loss," she started, feeling awkward.

If the young woman sitting at the oblong table heard Dara's words, she didn't acknowledge them. She smiled stiffly and stared straight ahead, looking as if she would rather be just about anywhere else.

The first thing that Dara noticed about Caitlin Wolff was that she looked like hell. Underneath the dark circles around her eyes, the raw cuticles, and the gnawed fingernails, she was pretty enough, in an all-American, shiny-blonde-hair sort of way, but she had clearly had better days. Now she looked exactly like what she was: a young woman who had just lost her husband. But despite the obvious toll that her husband's recent death had taken on her, she seemed to be managing to hold it together reasonably well. As she finally introduced herself, she gripped Dara's hand as firmly as a man and held direct, almost aggressive eye contact. Her voice was soft but steady. She still wore her wedding band, but she did not strike Dara as someone who wanted or needed pity.

Dara didn't know if Caitlin's confidence was real or feigned, but in her opinion, it didn't make a difference. Given that they were both in a profession in which acting the part was ninety percent of living the part, she suspected that Caitlin had the makings of an excellent field officer. She still had some fight left in her, even after what happened to her husband.

"I don't know what you've heard about me," Dara began as soon as she sat down. She shook her head and held up her hand to cut Caitlin off before she could lie about whether she had heard the rumors. "But since we're going to be working together, we might as well just get it out there on the table before we discuss anything else. I was the second in command in Amman, and I was sleeping with a senior Jordanian intelligence officer. I've never tried to cover it up. Tariq was an official liaison contact, and we developed a personal relationship. Unfortunately for me, there are a lot of people here at headquarters who assume that if you're sharing a bed, then you're also sharing classified information. Some of those same people think that if you're sleeping with someone with a name like Tariq, then you're obviously sleeping with a terrorist. Tariq has done more to combat terrorism than any single American I've ever met, but some people just can't get past the fact that he's an Arab." Dara caught herself falling back into the trap of defending Tariq, even if she had long since stopped trying to defend herself. *Don't bother*, she reminded herself.

"I digress. Long story short, in spite of the many colorful rumors floating around about me, I have never been formally accused of disclosing classified information, working as a double agent for the Mukhabarat, or—my personal favorite charge, apparently compliments of an anonymous tip—supporting terrorism. But I was yanked back to a headquarters assignment because some people will always believe the worst, and because it is apparently impossible to erase even ridiculous accusations from people's memories. So there you have it: the abbreviated version of my sordid tale. No need to tiptoe around it now."

Dara gave her disclosure bluntly, with no emotion. By now she had grown used to the scarlet letter that had been affixed to her file—to her reputation. She'd been made to repeat her version of events so many times that it no longer felt personal, anyway. Now it felt as if she were reading the lines from a script written *by* someone else, *for* someone else. She didn't particularly care what Caitlin's reaction to her little speech would be, then, but she was surprised anyway.

"*Tariq*," Caitlin said wistfully. "I'm picturing someone tall, dark, and handsome. You know, don't you, that your story sounds like a modern-day version of *Romeo and Juliet*? Star-crossed lovers and all that. *Très romantique.*"

Caught off guard, Dara grinned. After several long months of being made to feel like a traitor, a slut, a fool, or all three together, it felt nice to have someone react almost as a…friend. "Well, it wasn't quite as dramatic as it sounds, but Tariq certainly does fall into the tall, dark, and handsome category," she admitted, stifling a laugh. She and Caitlin shared a conspiratorial smile and then got down to business. "Let's talk," Dara said gently.

By the time their meeting was over, Dara had come to the conclusion that Caitlin would be fine. Or at least as close to fine as circumstances allowed. She was sad, distracted, and vague about her future career plans—anyone in her situation would be. But she was also sharp and determined, and she seemed resilient enough to make a comeback, given enough time. So when Dominic popped his head back into her office just as she was shutting down her computer and getting ready to leave for the day, Dara couldn't stop herself from snapping at him. "Jesus Christ, Dominic, what do you expect? The girl's husband—a fellow officer, no less—was yanked off the streets of Cairo by terrorists, held hostage and tortured for six weeks, and then assassinated on a gruesome video that she had to watch over and over again on the evening news. Are you really going to give her grief for being a little spacey on the job, or not putting in enough hours? Cut her some slack! It hasn't even been two months."

Dominic chewed on his lip. "It's a little more than spotty attendance, Dara," he started, but then seemed to catch himself. "No, you're right. She probably just needs more time. Just keep an eye on her, will you? That's all I'm asking. Bring her in on some of the cases you're working, keep her busy, that sort of thing."

Dara stopped him as he turned to leave. "Dominic, is there something else that I need to know here?"

"Nope," he said with a perfunctory shake of his head, whistling as he walked away.

"*Liar,*" Dara whispered. It didn't matter. She knew she'd find out soon enough.

CHAPTER FOUR

Travis Park hit the gym hard. The weather outside was as foul as his mood, so he had resorted to punishing the treadmill in the garishly mirrored cardio room. He didn't need to see his reflection to know that he looked like a lunatic. He'd been running at a maniacal speed for over half an hour, and sweat was flying off his body with every stride. His nostrils flared with each labored breath as he increased the machine's incline even further. A prim, middle-aged woman wearing headphones climbed onto the treadmill next to his, but then paused as she was hit in the face with a fleck of Travis's sweat. She cast him a disgusted look as she wiped her cheek and then moved to a machine on the other side of the room.

Travis gave it one more mile before he adjusted the setting to a cool-down pace. His head finally felt clear enough to think things through.

Earlier that morning he had put on his best suit, along with the tie that his ex-girlfriend had bought him for his birthday. He was pretty sure that everyone in the Counterterrorism Center knew that he was dressed up for a job interview—the overpaid contractors who kept the place running tended to go for a look that could only generously be called business casual—but he didn't care. His interview was scheduled for one o'clock, and he hadn't wanted to take the time to go home and change. *Let them think whatever they want*, he figured. It wasn't as if anyone was going out of their way to make him want to stay on staff at the CIA. His career there had stalled before it even began, for reasons Travis still couldn't figure out, and it had taken him weeks of effort to land this meeting.

He hadn't received the voice mail message until he was already en route to the interview. Cell phones aren't allowed in CIA facilities, so Travis, like everyone else, left his in his car while he was at work. He was pulling out of the compound gates when he thought to check for messages.

"Travis, this is Ronda McMillan, Mr. Truesdell's assistant." The woman's voice had a chilly quality. "Mr. Truesdell asked me to call you to cancel your lunch appointment. There is no need to reschedule. Good-bye."

Travis pulled over so that he could listen to the message again. He was baffled. Figuring that there must be some sort of misunderstanding, he pulled out the direct number that Jim Truesdell had given him when they spoke just a few days earlier.

Jim answered on the first ring with a cheery hello.

"Hi, Jim, Mr. Truesdell, um, this is Travis Park. We were scheduled to have a lunch interview today?" Travis stammered.

"Yes, I know who you are." The cheerful tone had vanished. "Or rather, I suppose I should really say that I don't know who you are at all. Did you really think that you'd get away with it? Do you think I'm an idiot?"

Travis's mouth opened and then closed again several times as he searched for a response. "I...I don't understand."

"Mr. Park, if you had done your homework, you would have learned that my sister-in-law is the undersecretary for Global Affairs at the State Department. When I mentioned to her over dinner last night that I was interviewing a young star from her organization, she offered to check you out. Imagine her surprise—*my* surprise—to find out that you don't work there at all, and you never have."

Travis rested his forehead against the steering wheel, feeling like the air had been knocked out of him. "I realize it looks strange, Mr. Truesdell, but…"

"But *what*?"

It was Travis's last chance to salvage the opportunity, and he knew it. This was Washington, DC, for God's sake, not Moscow. What would be the harm in revealing where he actually worked? It was against the rules, but he sure as hell wasn't having much luck following the rules. He was still considering it when Truesdell spoke first.

"A word of advice, Mr. Park. At a certain level, Washington starts to become a very small town. Cross the wrong people, and you'll find out very quickly that there's no room at all for you here. Don't let me hear your name again." The phone clicked.

Travis set his phone on the seat beside him and closed his eyes, still leaning against the steering wheel. He sat in that defeated posture until someone rapped sharply on his window. Travis jerked upright to see a uniformed officer glowering at him, his hand on his holstered weapon.

Travis had recognized the CIA security officer's uniform immediately; a quick glance at the discreetly marked sedan with flashing lights behind him confirmed it. He rolled the window down and flashed his ID badge. "Don't worry, I'm one of you," he said wearily.

"All the more reason you should know why we can't let anyone loiter this close to the facility. Ever heard of Mir Aimal Kasi? Move out. Now." The officer turned on his heel and stalked back to his vehicle.

Travis had rolled his eyes at the attitude, but he knew that the officer had good reason to treat him as a threat. In 1993, Mir Aimal Kasi had opened fire on CIA employees stopped at a traffic light just outside the headquarters facility, killing two and wounding three more. Travis guiltily realized that the attack had happened only a few yards from where he had pulled over.

He cursed at himself as he pulled back into traffic. "I can't get *anything* right these days," he roared out loud. He didn't know what to do with himself. He no longer had an interview—he no longer had any decent job prospects *anywhere*—but he didn't feel like going back to the office, either. Instead he drove to the gym.

Now, having sweated out his anger and embarrassment, Travis felt like he was thinking clearly for the first time in months. His crappy cover job didn't make him an attractive candidate for recruiters, it was true, but he also felt, deep down, that he wasn't having any luck finding a new job in part because his heart wasn't in the search. Maybe it was for the best that he'd been given such a bullshit résumé, forcing him to masquerade as a low-level staffer in one of Washington's anonymous bureaucracies. Seriously—did he *look* like a program assistant in the Office of Ocean and Polar Affairs?

No—Travis had joined the CIA because he wanted to be a spy. He believed in the mission, and he wanted to do the job he'd signed up for. Trained for. Sacrificed for.

He showered quickly and started to change back into his suit before he thought better of it and stuffed the tie and jacket back into his duffel bag. No more dressing up for interviews. It was time for him to rattle some cages and do the job he was hired to do.

And he knew exactly where to start.

CHAPTER FIVE

The next morning Dara sat in her parked car, staring at the enormous CIA headquarters building. Several football-field lengths of dirty slush lay between her and the entrance. She had spent her career prying secrets out of statesmen, getting close to world leaders, and stealing classified data, but she couldn't seem to figure out how to get her hands on a coveted parking pass for the covered garage. Instead she was stuck circling vulture-like every morning for an unassigned space in the general lot, which filled up ridiculously early each morning.

Her reward for clomping across an acre of slush was an Orwellian job that involved signing off on computer-generated spreadsheets documenting discrepancies and petty errors made by officers in the field. *Joe in Kuala Lumpur spent a statistically improbable amount on a train ticket!* screamed her spreadsheets. *Linda in Pretoria has taken the same red-eye flight the last four times she left the country! Andrew in Lima used his personal cell phone to call a source last month!* And it was Dara's job to nag, cajole, and wheedle the excuses and corrections out of the people who had once been her peers.

The algorithm-based audits had been designed at great expense by an outside consulting firm, probably by some computer genius living in his mother's basement. She didn't even pretend to understand the mathematics behind the system, but she did know that the system blindly reported anything out of the norm. Just the other week, for example, the automated system indicated that one unit in particular had generated a statistically improbable number of intelligence reports. Personally, Dara thought that the unit should be rewarded for accomplishing this, but the computer interpreted it as a counterintelligence red flag. She had duly investigated the flag—meaning she had walked down the hall and asked the unit chief what was going on, after first congratulating him off the record, and learned that the group had recently gained the services of a much-needed Urdu interpreter. They were suddenly able to process the data pulled from a half-dozen or so computer hard drives that had been confiscated in raids across Pakistan. The data had been sitting around CIA headquarters for months, but no one had been able to read any of it. Now, with the help of their new interpreter, the unit was putting out dozens of intelligence reports every day.

In Dara's opinion, this was just one demonstration of how a multi-million-dollar computer system could screw up something that one person could sort out with a ten-minute conversation. She had marched back to her computer, overridden the red flag, and moved on to her next thankless task.

"Welcome to your new life," Dara muttered to herself. "You're a goddamn hall monitor."

In Amman she had felt like she was part of something significant; world politics played out around her every day. Before that she'd been in Paris, living a glamorous life, hobnobbing in the diplomatic community. Working the "cocktail circuit," they'd called it. Her assignment before that, in Karachi, Pakistan, hadn't exactly been glamorous, but she'd had a driver, a villa, a weapon or two, and a job that she loved. Every previous assignment had

had something different, something uniquely exciting or challenging. Now she had a nondescript townhouse in the suburbs, a forty-five-minute commute on the beltway, and a job that made her feel very much like the proverbial hamster in a cage.

And she missed Tariq, more than she liked to admit to herself. She'd asked him not to contact her, and he had so far honored her request. The bastard. It was probably better this way, but it still stung. *He's moved on, and so should you*, she told herself.

She needed something to help herself reconcile with her new life. Maybe she'd light a ritual fire and burn all of her cocktail dresses and gun holsters. Or perhaps she'd start reading self-help books and adopt a few cats to complete her new spinster persona.

That's good. Keep your sense of humor, she lectured herself. Steeling against the cold wind, she climbed out of her car and trudged in to work.

Dominic Cahill was waiting in her office. Sitting in her chair, no less.

"I haven't had any coffee yet," she warned as she glared at him.

"Well, get some, because you've got work to do." Dominic sounded every bit as grumpy as she felt. "I thought you'd be able to handle Ms. Wolff."

Dara tossed her coat and purse onto the one chair in her office that remained unoccupied. "What, did she show up late for work this morning, or something equally catastrophic? Why are you even involved in low-level personnel matters, anyway?" She folded her arms across her chest and stood, looming over him, hoping he'd take the hint and get out.

He didn't take the hint. "It's a little more serious than show-ing up for work late, Dara. And I'm involved because the director personally asked me to be involved. Her husband's murder got a lot of publicity. As we speak we have nearly a hundred federal officers kicking down doors all over Egypt trying to find the kill-ers, and that's putting some serious strain on our already shaky diplomatic relations in the region. But whether we like it or not, Jonathan Wolff has become the poster boy for the CIA's involve-ment in the war against terror. A golden-haired patriot getting beheaded by terrorists gets a lot of attention from the media, so we're getting a lot of heat from all sides. And while we obviously want to make sure that we're doing the right thing with his fam-ily, we need to have some limits. And this morning the poor, grieving widow Wolff was caught attempting to destroy highly sensitive data that she had no business accessing."

"What kind of data?"

"Ask her yourself. She's waiting for you in the confer-ence room next door, and she says that she'll only talk to you." Dominic stood up and left without another word.

Dara decided that whatever was going on with Caitlin could wait until she got a cup of coffee. She trekked through the marble cor-ridors of the main hallway toward the in-house Starbucks. It still boggled her mind that there was a Starbucks located inside the world's most secure building. And judging from the perpetual line, the intelligence community appeared to have one hell of a caffeine addiction.

She walked into the conference room with two double lattes and was surprised to see that a glum-faced Caitlin was being watched over by a uniformed security officer. "You can go," Dara dismissed the officer, who looked at her doubtfully but left the room to wait in the hall.

"So what's this about?" she asked, tossing a sugar packet over to Caitlin.

Caitlin looked like even more of a wreck than the last time Dara saw her. Her eyes were red and swollen, and she had been using her sleeve as a tissue, leaving wet traces of smeared mascara on her white blouse. She fidgeted and twitched so much that Dara made a mental note to check on the dates of her last drug test and psychological screening. The CIA was nothing if not thorough in its intrusiveness into employees' lives.

The young woman took a sip from her cup of coffee but didn't say a word.

Dara sighed. "Look, Caitlin. I'm not interested in playing bad cop, or best friend, or mommy figure, or whatever it is you need to make you talk. You've gone through the same interrogation training as I have. If you're not going to talk to me, then I have better things to do. I'll just call the security goon back in and get back to my in-box. You're going to have to talk to someone, sometime, and I really don't care whether it's me or somebody else." Dara pushed away from the table and headed for the door.

Before she got there, Caitlin spoke. "Why do you stay?"

She asked the question so softly that Dara almost thought she'd heard wrong. "What?"

Caitlin asked again. "Why do you keep working here? You don't seem happy. Why don't you leave? Find another job somewhere else?"

Dara started to snap at the younger woman—it was none of her damn business, after all—but then stopped herself. It was a valid question. Asked by someone whose personal life had been ripped to shreds by the job even more viciously than her own had been. "I…" Dara wasn't even sure that she had an answer to give. "I guess that I used to love my job. Before things got so…complicated. I keep hoping that I'll get back there. Back to the place where I'm judged for my work, not my love life." She shrugged. "Or maybe I'm just not sure where else I'd go. This job tends to take over your life, you know."

Caitlin's gaze remained downcast as she nodded. "I know what you mean." She paused for a moment, chewing on her lip, and then looked up abruptly, locking eyes with Dara. "I'm pregnant," she announced.

Dara tilted her head, confused. It was about the last thing she'd expected Caitlin to say. "Um…congratulations?"

Caitlin broke into sobs.

Once again Dara fought the urge to snap at her. Her first and only female boss at the agency had given her a bit of advice that she never forgot: "Every tear that your male colleagues see you shed represents a five percent decrease in the amount of respect they have for you." That same officer, who proudly displayed a coffee mug on her desk emblazoned with the words *Battle Axe*, had added that *her* level of respect for a teary colleague decreased even faster. "You come crying into my office, you might as well find yourself a new assignment." Dara had never respected a supervisor more.

But today she bit her tongue. She waited until Caitlin had calmed down before she spoke again. "I'm glad you told me," she started—her voice sounding saccharine and forced even to her own ears. "Losing your husband and going through a pregnancy alone has to be incredibly difficult. I'm sure that everyone will understand if you need to take some time off. With pay, of course. Plus, there's a generous fund for the children of officers killed in the line of duty…"

With a brittle laugh, Caitlin seemed to transform. In the time it took her to sit up and pull her hair back from her face, she went from sobbing little-girl-lost to hardened cynic. "They didn't tell you what they caught me doing, did they?"

Dara shook her head.

"I was trying to delete all electronic records of this." Caitlin shoved an unlabeled folder across the table. "And then I planned to destroy the paper copy."

Scanning through the folder's contents, Dara was initially mystified as to why it would be important. It was just Jonathan Wolff's medical file, the bulk of which consisted of the extensive vaccine records that all CIA officers accumulate. It was a perfectly reasonable thing for an officer's widow to have in her possession, and nothing in the files jumped out as unique or compromising. Like the rest of his colleagues, Jonathan had been prescribed more than his fair share of Cipro and antimalarials by agency doctors—medication for the usual occupational hazards. Finding nothing controversial, Dara flipped back to the first page and then realized why Caitlin was trying to destroy the data.

"Blood type A positive. DNA sample on file in case remains need to be identified—standard protocol." She nodded, understanding. "Everything you'd need for a paternity test." Dara closed the folder. "He's not the father, is he? That's why you wanted to destroy the records? In case anyone ever starts asking questions."

Caitlin must have realized that her crying had had a counterproductive effect, because her eyes now remained dry as she met Dara's gaze. "It's complicated. Isn't that how you described it? *Really* complicated. Can we talk about this somewhere else? Somewhere outside of work?"

Dara hesitated. The last thing on earth she wanted was to become Caitlin's personal confidante. She'd learned the hard way to keep her personal life separate from work, and frankly, she just didn't have the energy to get sucked into someone else's drama. Especially the kind of drama that involved her young new protégée sleeping around and then trying to destroy CIA data to cover it up. "Caitlin, it's really none of my business—"

But Caitlin cut her off. "Please," she said simply and firmly. "Do you know the new bar that just opened off of Dolley Madison Boulevard? Can you meet me there tonight after work?"

Dara raised her eyebrows at the choice of venue but nodded. "Fine. But under one condition. I want you to leave the building and take a personal day. I don't have time to babysit you to make sure you don't steal anything else today." Caitlin looked offended at this, but Dara didn't really care. Without another word she stood up and left the room, wondering what the hell she was getting herself into.

The security guard was waiting outside. "She's free to go," Dara said, gesturing back at the conference room.

He tilted his head, unconvinced, trying to decide whether to trust her authority on the matter.

"She's my problem now," Dara snapped. "She's not a security risk. Besides, she's leaving the building now."

Absolved of responsibility, the uniformed officer shrugged and walked the opposite way down the hall.

For the briefest of moments, Dara hesitated. Perhaps she should have at least had the security officer walk Caitlin out of the building. She shook off the fragment of doubt, though, and strode off toward her office to tackle the tedious mountain of computer reports awaiting her signature. Dara knew better than most how even unfounded accusations had a way of becoming permanent in people's minds, and she didn't want to burden Caitlin with the same public humiliation that she had suffered. Caitlin was a mess, but she wasn't a threat. Dara felt nearly sure of it.

CHAPTER SIX

Travis shifted his weight in the hard plastic chair, keeping his eyes on the two men who had followed him into the run-down bagel shop a few blocks from the headquarters building. They sat down next to him, uncomfortably close. The man on Travis's left—the one who smelled like stale cigarette smoke—leaned in even closer, forcing Travis to slide his chair backward with a loud screech of plastic against linoleum.

No one spoke.

Was this some kind of test? Some kind of ritual to establish who was the alpha dog?

Travis assumed that the two men were his contacts. There was no one else in the deli except the white-haired woman unenthusiastically slicing vegetables behind the counter.

"So," he finally started, his voice scratchy. "How does this work?" He'd hoped for a warmer reception. Or at least a less awkward start. They were supposed to be on the same team, after all. "Do I tell you about myself? Or do you guys want to start?"

The two men smirked.

The one on the right glanced behind him to make sure that the woman behind the counter was out of earshot before he answered. "We already know about you." He spoke robotically, as if reading from a mental checklist. "Travis Park, age twenty-eight. Unmarried. Triathlete, good grades, blah, blah, blah. The goddamn all-American dream, but with a few extra languages and an ambiguous ethnic appearance coming from a Korean father and a Mexican American mother." He paused and then grinned for the first time. "Is it true that you used to claim to be an Eskimo?"

Travis blushed. "Stupid college trick. Not exactly politically correct, I know. My roommates used to dare me to come up with crazy stories to pick up girls. Otherwise they made me buy the next round of drinks every time a girl in a bar asked me where I was from." Sensing that the meeting was warming up slightly, he continued. "Sometimes I'd go with Polynesian. Or Tajik. Anything exotic, you know. Worked like a charm."

There was no reaction. The guy on the right wasn't grinning anymore; obviously he'd just baited Travis into babbling like a fool.

Idiot. Travis silently cursed himself. This wasn't the impression that he wanted to give them. He wanted them to take him seriously. "Stupid college trick," he repeated, trailing off.

The awkward silence returned. The two guys seemed to be enjoying it. Enjoying making him uncomfortable.

Screw it. What did he have to lose? "Look, guys. Sorry, I don't even know your names—"

"We're Jeff's friends. That's all you need to know. For now."

At last. An opening. Not much of one, but Travis grabbed at it anyway. "Okay, Jeff's friends. Well, if you're Jeff's friends, then Jeff probably told you what's going on. That I'm interested in working with you. That I'm sick of sitting behind a desk sifting through mountains of intercepts and trolling Jihadist websites. I'm done being passive. I'm ready for action. Jeff can vouch for me. He was my mentor during training. I finished at the top of my class—"

"The only thing Jeff knows for sure is that you weren't interested in working with us a few months ago. And that lately you've been wallpapering the private sector with your résumé, looking for a new job."

Travis slumped in his seat. "I didn't realize it was a one-shot deal." He stopped talking as the woman stepped out from behind the counter to adjust the window blinds near their table. He waited until she headed back to the kitchen before he continued, grateful for the interruption. He needed a moment to decide how much to say. He took a deep breath before continuing. "Jeff approached me the day I finished training. A year of training, as I'm sure you both know, that involved constant fucking with my head, physically grueling exercises, social isolation, and sleep deprivation. After a year of that shit, I was just *tired*. My girlfriend broke up with me halfway through the training—said she hadn't signed up for spending her life living with a zombie. She changed the locks, so I had nowhere to live. My car was totaled from a countersurveillance training exercise gone bad."

Travis raked his fingers through his hair, frustrated by the whiny note creeping into his voice. "I'm not complaining. I'm just trying to put things in context. When Jeff pulled me aside and asked me if I wanted to work on a few 'side projects'—that's all he'd say, by the way—you can hardly blame me for turning him down. I mean, I respect Jeff. He's a legend. But I just wanted to spend some time getting my life in order. Doing my job just like everyone else. Hell, I just wanted to catch up on my sleep."

The guy on the left pulled back a little and nodded. He was listening.

Travis wished someone else would say something, but the stage was apparently still his. He shrugged in defeat. Might as well go all in. "I don't know what happened. But my career just never seemed to get started after that. Every application for a field assignment has been rejected. I can't get promoted. My training classmates are all running circles around my career path, and I can't figure out why. I don't know what I did wrong."

Travis stared down at the table as a customer walked into the deli, waiting until the man placed his order for a dozen onion bagels to finish. "I'm ready to get started."

Finally the two men—Jeff's "friends"—responded. The smoker extended his hand. "You've made the right choice."

The guy on the right shook Travis's hand next. "Welcome."

CHAPTER SEVEN

Dara didn't see Caitlin anywhere when she walked into the bar that evening. She was actually glad to have arrived first, since it gave her a chance to grab a stool at the bar and catch up with the owner of Red Mercury, McLean, Virginia's newest hot spot.

"You have a sick sense of humor. You know that, right?" Dara greeted the woman behind the bar with a smile as she pointed to the name of the tavern, emblazoned on the menu above a crude rendering of a skull and crossbones.

"What's wrong with Red Mercury?" Naomi asked innocently and then broke into a wide grin. "Half the people who come here think it's some weird reference to my hair color." She pulled at one of her bright orange corkscrew curls. "Come to think of it, if someone were to put this color in a bottle, Red Mercury would be a great name for a hair dye."

Dara knew that the name of Naomi's bar had nothing to do with hair color. It was actually an inside joke for the CIA employees who flocked there for a convenient place to meet for drinks after work. Red mercury was a fictional substance that popped up frequently in nuclear weapons scams; someone, somewhere, long ago had started a persistent rumor that it was a key ingredient in nuclear weapons and that the US would pay top dollar for it. At least once a week, the CIA was contacted by some shady source offering to reveal the location of a cache of red mercury being stockpiled by terrorists. Demands varied, but the last Dara had heard, the asking rate was approaching four million dollars for a vial, barrel, or bunker full of the substance, depending on the scammer's creativity and chutzpah. The CIA knew, of course, that there was no such thing as red mercury, but a decision had been made that all claims needed to be investigated nonetheless.

"What if some illiterate sheep farmer stumbles onto a bunker full of weapons-grade uranium and doesn't know any better than to call it red mercury, since that's all he's ever heard it called?" This was the rationale that had employed Naomi Macek for the better part of the previous decade. Naomi had been what agency insiders affectionately called a "digger." She was part of a team that was dispatched to dig up, analyze, and dispose of any reported explosives, toxins, chemicals, or radioactive substances encountered by CIA officers in the field. It was dirty, labor-intensive, and dangerous work, and Naomi was the only female digger Dara had ever encountered. At five foot ten and nearly two hundred very solid pounds, though, no one had ever mistaken Naomi as being too delicate for the job.

Naomi had quit working for the agency to open her bar, but souvenirs of her previous job were on display everywhere.

"I can't believe they let you keep that stuff." Dara pointed to a glass display case full of nuclear scam memorabilia.

"They always told me to just get rid of the harmless materials," Naomi winked. "So I did. I put them all in my attic. I had a feeling they might come in handy someday. Remember that one?" She was pointing to a rusty metal container about the size of a lunch box.

"Of course I do. It damn near melted my fingerprints off!" Dara laughed as she examined the box. You could still see the sloppy white lettering that had been painted on: *Very very dangreus. Nucleer bom. No touch.*

"They tried to warn you," Naomi scolded.

Dara had first met Naomi in pursuit of that very metal box. She had been running a Turkish source who had a mixed record of providing useful intel. Most of his information was garbage, but once or twice he had been right. So when he reported in 2003 that one of his cousins had a friend in Iraq who had found radioactive material, she had no choice but to dutifully pass the information along to headquarters. The source knew, of course, that the US was searching frantically for its smoking gun in Iraq, and he wanted to make a quick buck. He provided next to no detail, demanded an exorbitant payment upfront, and everyone involved agreed that he was almost certainly lying. It didn't matter, though. Dara was ordered onto the next military transport plane into Baghdad. Just in case he *wasn't* lying this time. That's how desperate Washington was to find something—anything— to vindicate the invasion.

The cargo plane had no actual passenger seats, so Dara had found a spot on the floor, her feet pressed up against the wheels of a Humvee that was tethered precariously in place. Because of the threat from rocket launchers on the ground, all incoming aircraft had to do steep, spiraling descents into the not-quite-secure Baghdad airport. Dara knew the drill—this was her fourth trip to Baghdad in the last year alone. She had closed her eyes to try to grab a quick catnap, but she had been jolted out of her restful state by the sound of wet retching. She looked up in disgust at the army colonel who was splattering everything in his vicinity. As she turned away, she caught the glance of the one other woman in the transport plane: Naomi. Something about the fiery red-head's broad grin and belly laugh was contagious, and soon Dara was laughing too. The colonel glared at them viciously, but with the specks of vomit covering his lapel, he was hard to take seriously, and the two women laughed all the way through the rough descent. They'd been friends ever since.

"Who puts hot coals in a metal box, anyway?" Dara asked, still remembering the sound of her skin sizzling as she naïvely picked up the box without protective gloves.

"Anyone who's ever heard that nuclear material is supposed to be hot," Naomi countered, filling a wineglass for her. "They were just trying to convince you that you were getting the real deal from them. They wanted to make it worth your while."

"Good times," Dara said sarcastically, raising her glass to Naomi. She looked around the bar and saw quite a few familiar faces. As usual, the CIA employees had segregated themselves by occupation. A raucous group of logistics specialists was celebrating someone's retirement with a round of shots. Half a dozen analyst types were quietly debating a newspaper clip that they were passing around. A cluster of newly minted clandestine service officers had commandeered a table in the corner; they had moved the chairs so that no one in the group had his back to a window or a door. Military detailees had split themselves into two camps: clean-cut, uniformed officers sitting rigidly in one booth, and grizzly-bearded Special Forces types sporting Oakley sunglasses and desert-stained cargo pants slumped in another booth on the other side of the room.

Dara tensed as she spotted an unwelcome acquaintance. Melanie Oakes sat at a table with several other people who Dara assumed were also polygraphers. Yes—she was sure of it. It was obvious from the way they kept to themselves, not so much as waving at anyone else in the crowded bar. They were all drinking steadily and cheerlessly, barely bothering to feign conversation even within their own group.

Polygraphers were the pariahs of the CIA community. Intelligence officers all duly noted the importance of the polygraph as a tool, of course. That did not, however, mean that they had to like it. Or that they had to like the inquisitors who sat, inscrutable and stone-faced, behind the polygraph's computer screen, judging them. All CIA employees were required to regularly submit to the ominously titled "lifestyle polygraph." This meant that employees' personal lives, belief systems, relationships, financial health, and assorted addictions, vices, and flaws were all fair game for the polygrapher.

"Mind fuckers." That's what one of Dara's colleagues in Pakistan had called them. "They get off on it," he had claimed. "They like hearing everyone's dirty secrets and using your thoughts against you." He was biased, of course. Several years earlier he had been accused of financial misdealing after a polygrapher had assessed that he "showed hesitation" when questioned about his expense accounting. Ultimately he had been cleared after an exhaustive audit, but by then it didn't really matter. Everyone already knew that he had been placed on administrative leave for over six months while he was investigated for *something*. His career had never recovered, and he was left bitterly counting down the years until he could retire.

Dara didn't necessarily feel as strongly as her embittered colleague did about polygraphs in general, but she did intensely hate one polygrapher in particular—the same hawk-faced woman who now obliviously nursed a beer across the room.

Dara grimaced as she recalled how the polygrapher's eyes had bored into her as she asked the same questions a dozen different ways until she got the answer she wanted.

"What classified information have you discussed with Tariq Bataineh?"

Dara sighed heavily. "I've answered that question repeatedly. I have only disclosed information that I was explicitly authorized to share with him."

"So you admit that you have given him classified information?"

"He is an official liaison contact in the Jordanian government. The United States government regularly shares information that is of mutual concern. I was acting in official, sanctioned capacity whenever I disclosed sensitive material." Dara tried to control her anger, but it was gaining on her.

"So you have shared classified information with your lover, Tariq, on more than one occasion?" Melanie jotted something in her notebook.

"Yes, but—" She stopped herself. She'd already explained it enough times.

"Dara, do you cry out during sex?"

"What?" She couldn't hide her anger any longer as she stared, appalled, at the polygrapher.

"Okay, I'll ask a different question. Do you talk in your sleep?"

Dara counted to ten before answering. "No, I do not believe so."

"So you aren't certain?"

"Well, seeing as how I'm asleep while I'm sleeping, I can't be one hundred percent sure that I don't talk in my sleep, can I?" She willed the sarcasm out of her voice too late; the interrogator was *typing something into her computer again. "What are you writing now?"*

With a triumphant look in her eyes, Melanie read her latest entry: "Subject admits that it is possible that she may have inadvertently disclosed sensitive data to a foreign national while in a compromised state."

"You fucking bitch." Dara was already pulling the monitoring cuff off of her arm when the supervisor burst in to intervene.

"Quit glaring at that group," Naomi hissed as she passed by with an armful of empty pitchers. "They're some of my best customers."

"Yeah, I'd drink like a fish too, if I were one of them." Dara turned away in disgust.

"They're just doing their job," Naomi called over her shoulder as she disappeared into the bar's small kitchen.

Dara didn't agree with her. For her, it was a very personal matter.

She drained her wineglass and was considering another when Caitlin walked in. The young woman scanned the room, nervously assessing every person in the place until her eyes met Dara's, and then she jerked her head at one of the empty booths on the far side of the room, silently inviting Dara to join her.

"And here we go again…" Dara muttered under her breath as she rose from the barstool. She wasn't even entirely sure why she had just thought that, but something about Melanie Oakes's presence in the bar seemed like a bad omen, and she couldn't shake the feeling that she was about to be sucked yet again into something thoroughly unpleasant.

CHAPTER EIGHT

"This is a strange choice of locations if you want to speak privately away from work," Dara said as she joined Caitlin in the booth she had chosen on the quieter side of the bar. "You do realize that ninety percent of the customers here are agency employees, right?"

Caitlin nodded. "I know that. But it looks normal enough to be meeting my new mentor for a drink after work, right? I mean, more normal than if someone saw us meeting in a car or on a park bench. Hiding in plain sight, they called it in training."

Dara watched Caitlin's eyes dart around the room yet again. *She's acting as if she thinks someone is watching her.* Dara had heard of several cases of new CIA officers cracking under the pressure, becoming paranoid to the point of being mentally unstable. Clandestine service training instilled a constant state of vigilance and awareness, and sometimes, if you looked hard enough, long enough, through that carefully cultivated lens of heightened suspicion, even the most benign surroundings could start to seem threatening. Dara wondered if Caitlin was losing it. Not that she would blame her—the young woman had watched her husband's murder being played over and over again on television and Internet news sites.

"And honestly?" Caitlin continued in a lower voice. "I really, really needed a drink. For a few minutes, when I suggested this place, I forgot that I couldn't have one." She gestured at her stomach.

Crap. Dara had forgotten about the pregnancy too, and she had asked Naomi to bring a couple of glasses of wine over when she had a moment. She glanced around, hoping that she could signal to Naomi to forget the drinks. Too late.

Naomi hurried over with two wineglasses filled to the brim. "Generous pours for you ladies. Don't take this the wrong way, but you both look like you could use it."

Dara winced as Naomi set the glasses down and hurried off. "Sorry, I guess I forgot too."

"It's fine," Caitlin said. "I'll just pretend to sip it. I haven't told anyone else, so this will help me hide my little secret better anyway. If I do something obvious like order club soda, it'll just make everyone talk." She took a deep breath, then exhaled loudly. "Okay, I know you didn't exactly volunteer to help me out, but I don't have many people I can talk to, so you're it. Plus, you need to know exactly what you're getting into. So here goes."

Caitlin took a sip from her wineglass—Dara suspected that it wasn't just a pretend sip—and started to talk. She looked down at the table as she spoke; her voice was jagged and strained. "It started three years ago. The chaos after the 9/11 attacks had finally died down, and it was already obvious that we were doing more harm than good in Iraq." She looked into Dara's eyes pleadingly, as if already making excuses.

"Enough with the rehearsed speech. You sound like you're reading from a script. Just tell me what's going on," Dara said firmly.

Caitlin began to talk, and Dara quickly forgot everything else.

CHAPTER NINE

Dara sat alone in the booth for a long time after Caitlin left, polishing off both of their glasses of wine. Frankly, she needed something even stronger after what she had just heard. Naomi came over to check on her once, but Dara waved her away.

Caitlin's story was mind-boggling, and Dara was struggling to figure out just how much of it she believed. On one hand, the young woman did seem to be unraveling a bit—understandably enough. On the other hand, it *was* possible that she was telling the truth, as incredible as her story was.

Dara folded and refolded a tattered paper napkin as she sifted through the details of what Caitlin had told her. Several people she knew from her assignment in Paris entered the bar and waved at her hesitantly, as if trying to decide whether or not it was a good idea to acknowledge her presence in public. Dara ignored them. Internal politics in the CIA were worse than they had been in Chairman Mao's China. Aligning yourself, even outside of work hours, with someone under suspicion of compromise meant that you, too, risked coming under scrutiny. Dara knew that she made people uncomfortable now, so she tried to spare her colleagues by isolating herself. Professional misfortune was highly contagious in the halls of Langley, and there was no need for anyone else's career to suffer the consequences of her actions.

Dara wondered if that was why Dominic had paired her up with Caitlin. Perhaps he thought that two ill-fated officers couldn't cross contaminate. But did Dominic think that Caitlin's misfortune was limited to the murder of her husband, or did he already know some of what Caitlin had just confessed?

At first Caitlin only hinted at what had happened—what she had done. When Dara first started to comprehend what she was hearing, her initial reaction was skepticism. "Wait a minute, Caitlin. Stop right there. That's not even possible. The agency doesn't use honey trapping." In the back of her mind, Dara began drafting a recommendation for Caitlin to undergo psychiatric evaluation. What she was claiming *had* to be a lurid fantasy.

Honey trapping was the term for clandestine operations that used sex as bait to lure unsuspecting targets. Plenty of other intelligence services around the world used it. Doe-eyed young women "mistakenly" knocked on the wrong hotel room door of unsuspecting conference-goers, pretty young things took the next stool at the bar and began aggressive flirtations with traveling business executives, or prostitutes simply slipped something into a client's drink. No matter how it started, the end result was the same: the target ended the evening minus some of the secrets he had been carrying.

Dara remembered that during her training, several of her classmates had seemed disappointed to learn that the CIA did not, as a rule, use sex as an operational tool. When asked why not, their instructor—a white-haired, kindly grandfather type—hadn't minced words. "It shouldn't surprise anyone in this room to hear that men are more likely to lie, exaggerate, or mislead while in pursuit of a one-night stand than under any other circumstance. We want to obtain facts, ladies and gentlemen, not hormonally charged fairy tales. Pillow talk very rarely reveals accurate versions of events."

Caitlin nodded in agreement. "I know that *officially* the agency doesn't do honey trapping. But there are some of us who believe that a lot of the old rules deserve to be broken." She looked right at Dara as she said this, obviously expecting at least a somewhat sympathetic response.

Dara refused to take the bait, though. She sat in skeptical silence while Caitlin described her first "operation."

"For years the CIA had been watching these two Saudi brothers roam all over the globe. They were real dirtbags, but they were from one of the big oil families, so they had enough money and high-level connections that nobody could ever touch them. We knew that they were involved in some pretty nasty stuff—drug trafficking, underage prostitutes, you name it. But they always made sure to keep it out of their own country. They'd hop on their private jet, party it up somewhere for a long weekend, and then go back to their proper Muslim lives. Somewhere along the line, though, someone in their circle ended up dead. We never found out exactly what happened—just that it was something they couldn't cover up as easily as before. The families got involved, and it was starting to look as if they might finally have to face justice."

Caitlin put her wine glass to her lips nervously. Dara gently pulled the glass away from her and moved it to the far side of the table.

"So, we were never able to get all of the details, but somewhere in the middle of all this the families brought in a religious advisor to mediate. This advisor turns out to be one of the more extremist imams in Saudi Arabia, someone the CIA has been watching for a very long time. He suggests that the brothers can atone for their crime by supporting 'the cause.' We all know what cause that is. The imam is affiliated with half a dozen supposed charities that are all known to funnel money to terrorist groups. So the brothers made a very healthy donation to one of these charities, and lo and behold, their little problem went away. In no time at all, they were up to their wicked ways again, only now all they had to do to remain clean in the eyes of Allah was to make occasional contributions to this imam's funds."

Dara was all too familiar with the dilemmas that stopping this kind of funding presented. Freeze the suspected charities' assets, and the US incurred public wrath for denying funds to Muslim widows and children, or whatever needy group the charities claimed to be helping. Let the money go through, though, and a sizeable percentage of it ended up buying weapons and supporting terrorist training camps. It was a no-win situation unless you could prove without a shadow of a doubt that the charities were in fact siphoning money to terrorists—a task easier said than done.

Caitlin's husband, Jonathan, had been assigned to the task force that was trying to shut down the terrorist funding mechanisms. And according to Caitlin, he got tired of watching the currency fly by unchecked. "He was just the kind of guy who didn't like to sit around and do nothing. Everyone was always teasing him, calling him Boy Scout, because he was so all-American and idealistic," Caitlin said. "And he was a natural leader—charismatic, you know? People listened to him, followed him. I know I did."

So he and Caitlin concocted a scheme. It seemed simple enough. Caitlin was blonde and cute—just the type that the Saudi brothers liked best. They liked their wives traditional and covered from head to toe, but they liked their girlfriends Western and dressed in miniskirts as short as possible.

It had been surprisingly easy.

Caitlin and Jonathan booked adjacent hotel suites at the Dubai resort frequented by the brothers, and then Caitlin planted herself in the nightclub wearing a next-to-nothing dress and too much makeup. The younger brother was drunk enough and arrogant enough that he wasn't the least bit suspicious when Caitlin approached him.

It took all of thirty minutes to lure him back to her room. "Not bad considering the fact that the agency had already spent several years and several million dollars trying unsuccessfully to get next to this guy, huh?" Dara cringed at the note of defensive pride in Caitlin's voice.

Caitlin had encouraged her target to undress in the suite's parlor before bringing him into the separate bedroom, where she proceeded to "entertain" him for the better part of an hour. While she distracted him, Jonathan crept into the parlor and retrieved the target's state-of-the-art cell phone. Using a small device that he had borrowed from work, it took him fewer than three minutes to mirror image the phone and all of its data—including mobile access to e-mail accounts, banking records, schedules, contacts, and data from the GPS tracking program. It was an intelligence gold mine. He returned the phone to the room and then went back to his own room to wait.

At the end of the hour, the brother swaggered out of his conquest's hotel room, found his phone exactly where he had left it, and headed back to the bar none the wiser that anything unusual had occurred. As far as he was concerned, it was just a particularly lucky night out on the town.

"And you?" Dara asked.

Caitlin shrugged. "It was no big deal."

Dara raised her eyebrows. "And Jonathan?"

Caitlin's eyes dropped to the table. "Jonathan didn't mind. For him—maybe for both of us—it was like an adventure. I think...I think he actually kind of liked it. I mean, I know he did."

Dara sat back, not sure how to interpret that statement.

Caitlin tried to explain. "You know, the people who recruit CIA officers think that they're looking for Boy Scouts. The perfect patriot who speaks four languages, ties sailor knots, jumps out of airplanes, and goes to church on Sundays. But you know what they really want? They want people who can cheat and lie and steal—and *then* go to church on Sundays without the least bit of remorse. They need people with a dark side. Well, in Jonathan, they got it. For him it was sexy and exciting, like being in a movie. Like being Hollywood's version of a spy, instead of... well, you know how it really is."

Dara was stunned and, frankly, disgusted. Jonathan Wolff, their CIA martyr and all-American hero had enjoyed listening to his wife have sex with a terrorist in the next room. She found herself half-expecting Caitlin to burst out laughing, to tell her that this was all part of an elaborate prank—some sort of joke being played at Dara's expense.

She didn't laugh, though. And there was nothing funny about the rest of her confession, either.

Jonathan and Caitlin had repeated their operation, each time refining their technique. Eventually Jonathan had taken to installing surveillance equipment in the hotel suite. "For security reasons," he had said, although neither he nor Caitlin believed it. He'd kept the footage.

Caitlin claimed that it didn't bother her. "The end justifies the means," she told Dara, who was still withholding comment, albeit with increasing difficulty. "We managed to collect a hell of a lot of intelligence that no one else had ever been able to get. We'd just slip the data in with reports from other sources. It was good stuff, and no one ever questioned how it got there."

Neither of them spoke for a minute. Dara's mind had been whirling with a thousand questions when Caitlin abruptly looked at her watch and then practically leapt out of her seat. "I need to go," she had said, her voice grim.

Dara knew that they had barely scratched the surface, but she was too stunned to stop Caitlin from leaving. She needed time to process what she had been told, anyway. She had waved Caitlin off and then reached for her mostly full glass of wine.

Now, sitting alone in the bar, Dara felt slightly fuzzy; whether it was from the three glasses of wine or the bizarre story, she didn't know. And if she was honest with herself, she also didn't know exactly how she felt about what she had just learned. Like all CIA officers, she was frustrated by the crippling bureaucracy that limited their ability to make progress against their targets. Part of her, then, was impressed by what Caitlin and Jonathan had managed to accomplish. They had made a difference.

On the other hand, Jonathan was dead, and Caitlin was pregnant with a child whose father may or may not have been a man who was plotting to kill as many Americans as he could. Sordid means to a cruel end wasn't anyone's idea of a victory.

Eventually, slowly, she stood up from the table. It was late, and there was nothing she could do tonight. Tomorrow, though, she'd have to do *something*. She hoped that between now and the morning it would occur to her what on earth she *could* do about what she had just learned.

CHAPTER TEN

He was waiting for her when Caitlin pushed her way out of the bar. She ignored him for a second, relishing the crisp night air after the last hour spent in the claustrophobic spotlight of attention in the bar. She saw the way people looked up at her as she walked by, heard the whispers. *Isn't that...? The one whose husband...? Poor thing...*

"It's done. I did what you told me to do. The seed is planted."

He hadn't asked anything, but she knew what he wanted to hear.

He barely reacted. With as much as he—as *they*—had on the line, Caitlin would have liked to have seen some sort of acknowledgment of the stakes. A smile, a frown, a tremor, a nervous tic—some sign that he was *human*, for God's sake. But, as usual, his expression betrayed nothing.

She hated him for his calm indifference. She hated him for a lot of reasons.

Finally he spoke. "Good. That seed you planted needs tending, though. Stay close to her. Just don't say any more than you have to."

"You've made it abundantly clear that I'm going to take the blame for this," Caitlin said bitterly. "I just kept my end of the bargain, now it's time for you to keep yours." She left without saying good-bye. They were long past the need for courtesies.

She took a circuitous route home, feeling uncomfortable driving Jonathan's car. Or, at least the car that she still thought of as Jonathan's. It was newer and in better shape than her own aging Toyota Camry, but she still felt guilty each time she slipped behind the wheel. As if she was profiting in some small way from his death.

It was dark and it had started to rain, making it difficult to be certain of car makes and models when all she could see were blurred headlights in her rearview mirror. She had been trained well enough, though, that it was all she needed to confirm her suspicions. She was being followed.

It had been happening a lot lately.

She itched to react—to swerve, to escape, or even to smash into her pursuers. But she did nothing of the sort. They knew where she lived; they knew where she worked. There was nowhere to escape to.

Besides, she knew that they wouldn't hurt her. At least not yet. She still had a role to play. A seed to nurture. Blame to absorb. And hopefully, if she played her cards right, it would all come to an end soon enough. She just had to play by their rules for a little while longer.

She pretended not to notice when the surveillance car broke off, speeding past her just before she turned left into her apartment complex. She forced her face into a neutral expression and took the turn leisurely, not wanting to give her pursuer the satisfaction of seeing her rattled.

She trudged up the stairs to her apartment, exhausted. Knowing that someone else could still be watching, she forced herself to stand up straight and add a spring to her step. *Everything's fine*, she needed them to think. *I'm playing along*, she needed them to believe.

She kept up the pretense until she had closed the door behind her and armed the burglar alarm. Not that the cheap, pre-installed alarm would do anything to stop them, but the beeps were reassuring nonetheless.

She had nothing else left to protect her.

She undressed quickly and headed for one of the few refuges she had left. When she and Jonathan first found the apartment, it had bothered her that the bathroom had no windows. The space had seemed dark and airless back then. Now, though, she spent more and more of her evenings in the room, immersed in bath-water as hot as she could stand it. It was the only place left where she could be certain that no one was watching her, waiting for her to make a mistake.

She'd spent countless hours since Jonathan died hiding in this steam-filled, windowless sanctuary, just floating in her thoughts. This time, as she stepped into the familiar warmth, it suddenly occurred to her that she'd read somewhere that pregnant women shouldn't take hot baths. *Great. One more reason to feel guilty.* She'd have to look it up, see if it was true, or if the thought was just her subconscious being punitive. No—she should ask a doctor. She should *find* a doctor. Make an appointment. It was yet another terrifying item on her to-do list. Finding a doctor would make it *real*—something she'd been avoiding for quite a while now.

The heat made her drowsy, and her mind wandered to the day that this had all started. She would need to tell Dara some of it—more of it. Her new mentor may be jaded, but she wasn't the apathetic burnout that Caitlin had been assured. She was going to start asking some difficult questions soon, and Caitlin needed to be prepared. The best lies, Caitlin knew all too well, came as close as possible to the truth. She'd have to be selective in what she revealed, though. There were certain lines that should never be crossed, and certain truths that could never be told.

CHAPTER ELEVEN

Dara set off at a brisk pace, but soon enough her lungs began to rebel. She slowed to a more moderate jog, grumpy about the concession. She hated running, always had, but damned if she was going to settle into a sedentary life without a fight. She may have been stuck in a desk job, but that didn't mean that she had to let it consume her.

She was only thirty-six years old, but she felt ancient. It came with the job. Every few years a new country, a new identity. CIA officers ended up living a cat's nine lives, and then some, by the time they hit forty. *No wonder so many people in this line of work retire early,* Dara thought, wincing as she tried to outrace a nagging cramp in her calf. Where the heck was that runner's high that people always talked about? The only thing running ever seemed to give her was blisters.

The knot in her muscle finally relaxed, and she picked up her pace enough to pass another runner on the trail. She knew that she wouldn't last long at the higher speed, but she'd always liked the feeling of breezing past other joggers—particularly when they were decked out in ridiculously flashy running gear, as this one was. She couldn't fathom what would compel a grown man to wear neon-green spandex, short of a gun to the head. She may have been the only one aware that they were racing, but as she blew past Mr. Neon she enjoyed the one-sided victory anyway.

The disproportionate satisfaction that she took from that brief moment of silly, competitive glory made her aware of just how much she had lost her edge in all other aspects of her life. She knew that she had been acting like a dog who'd lost a fight, slinking through life with her tail between her legs. She trudged every morning to her punitive headquarters assignment, did the minimum amount of negligibly important work, and then cursed her way through heavy traffic to her generic townhouse, which was all but indistinguishable from the several dozen other townhouses on her cul-de-sac. Her love life was so dormant that it may as well have been declared extinct, and she hadn't even bothered getting in touch with any of the few old friends who still lived in the area.

She'd spent enough time wallowing in self-pity, and she knew it. She increased her speed even more, forcing herself to ignore the pain, until she crossed the invisible finish line that she had set for herself. She was gasping for breath as she stretched cursorily and then limped to her car, but she didn't care. It was time to engage—in her relationships, in work, in everything. It was time to remember why she'd signed up for this life in the first place.

Dara showered quickly at home and arrived at work early enough to snag a decent parking spot. A good sign, she decided.

She didn't wait for Dominic to make his slithering rounds, either. She headed toward the conference room where the weekly all-hands meeting was due to start soon. While en route, she decided that her new, more positive attitude toward work definitely did *not* mean that she would have to start attending staff meetings—at least not if she could help it. This decision was reinforced when she noticed that nearly everyone heading into the meeting was carrying an extra-large cup of coffee, undoubtedly to help them stay awake during the tedious hour to come.

She intercepted Dominic before he made it to the conference room. He was chatting with a woman from the director's office whom Dara recognized but couldn't name.

Dominic greeted her more cheerfully than the early hour required, in Dara's opinion, but she forced herself to make polite small talk for a moment before getting to the point. "I just wanted to give you a heads-up that you were right—there may be more to Caitlin's situation than I first thought—"

She had planned to give him a quick rundown of what Caitlin had told her the previous night, but Dominic cut her off abruptly.

"I don't have time for this, Dara," he snapped, all pretense of cordial charm gone. "As you can see, the meeting is about to start. I had assumed that you were capable of dealing with this yourself. If you're not, then I'll be sure to find you a new position better suited to your abilities."

Dara was speechless. Even the woman walking with Dominic raised her eyebrows in surprise at his aggressive tone. Dominic was glaring at her, his jaw clenched.

What the hell? With every ounce of her being, Dara wanted to tell Dominic exactly what she thought of his little outburst, but she held her tongue. This tirade was way out of character. Dominic was a stab-you-in-the-back sort of guy, not a shout-you-down-in-public type. Something was definitely up, and Dara wanted to know what. With as much restraint as she could manage, she quashed all of the four-letter words that were mere microseconds from tumbling from her lips. "I just wanted to let you know that the issue will require more investigation," she said, her fingernails cutting into the palms of her hands.

"Whatever is necessary. Just take care of it." He started to walk past her, but Dara stepped subtly to her left, blocking his path.

Dominic clearly wanted to end the conversation, but Dara couldn't resist pressing her luck. In fact, she was kind of enjoying his discomfort, even if she didn't understand it. She chose her words carefully. "The investigation may require more resources than my office currently has at its disposal."

This was both an understatement and a dig. They both knew that Dara's position had no budget, no other staff, and no travel authorizations. And they both knew why.

"Goddamn it, Dara, I said deal with it!" Dominic's face was red with anger, but Dara maintained her placid smile. "Consider yourself authorized. Whatever you need. Just stop bothering me with the details."

The woman whose name Dara couldn't recall was shooting her a look to stop talking, but Dara decided to go for one last victory. In the same neutral tone, she warned, "It might require field investigation." She made sure to maintain a blasé expression on her face. If Dominic knew how badly she wanted this, he'd turn her down for sure.

Dominic looked as if he wanted to tear her head off, and Dara worried that she may have pushed too far, too fast. He knew Dara's field qualifications had been suspended—he was the one who had delivered that little piece of news, feigning reluctance and claiming that he had "no choice" but to ask her to hand over each of her various alias passports. He was probably the one who had signed off on the decision in the first place. But it was also clear he wanted very badly to get Dara out of his face at that moment. "Then do it," he hissed, whirling around on his heel and storming past her.

Dara exchanged puzzled shrugs with the other woman and then walked nonchalantly in the other direction. She waited until she was around the corner before letting the grin spread across her face. She had no idea why Dominic had reacted the way he had, but she didn't care. Neither Dominic nor Caitlin seemed to be telling her the truth about much of anything, but as of that moment, like it or not, Caitlin had a new best friend in Dara, and Dominic had a new field officer. Caitlin's subterfuge and Dominic's lies were going to get Dara back in the game. It was a mercenary tactic perhaps, but she had good reason not to feel very charitable these days.

Caitlin's misfortune, tragic though it was, had just opened the door for Dara to get her career back.

CHAPTER TWELVE

Dara's satisfaction with her partial victory was short-lived as she returned to her office and realized that she didn't have a clue where to start using her newfound freedom. She was all too aware that Dominic Cahill could yank her field qualifications just as quickly as he had granted them back to her if she didn't show results.

Plus she felt vaguely guilty about her own selfish motivations for tackling this case. To make herself feel like less of an opportunistic jerk, she vowed silently to do whatever it took to help Caitlin untangle the horrible web that she had created. Perhaps she was just feeling generous because of her newly restored field credentials, but she had decided that Caitlin deserved her help. And as much as she hated to admit it, she couldn't help but notice the similarities between their respective plights. They were two female officers in a rough-and-tumble boys' club who had both made the mistake of falling in love on the job. Dara wasn't blind to the fact that Caitlin had made some incredibly stupid mistakes, but she felt as if her heart had been in the right place. Caitlin had chosen the wrong path, but for the right reasons.

Besides, she'd already paid a terrible price for her actions.

Dara could give her a chance of getting out of the mess she had made, just as Caitlin had given Dara a chance to get out from behind her desk.

But not quite yet. Dara had a lot of planning to do before she could go anywhere. She sat down at her desk and swore under her breath, feeling slightly battered by the sudden turn of events. All she had ever wanted was to live her life the way she wanted and to do her job. She was a damn good officer, and she knew it. The problem wasn't *her*—it was the fact that the CIA seemed to breed a disproportionate number of self-important pricks. Some people could shut off the darker parts of the job when the work-day was over. Others seemed to internalize the seedier elements of the profession, letting the lying, cheating, and manipulating seep into their personal lives and relationships.

She thought back to the day when this lesson had come crashing home, compliments of Charles Welbourne, the CIA station chief in Amman. Dara had never had any problem with Charles, but some of the younger officers had chafed under his leadership. Charles was somewhat of a caricature; he had actually been in Dara's training class fifteen years earlier. Even back then, when he was in his twenties, he had cultivated the image of a pretentious dandy. He posed self-consciously as a man born in the wrong era; he set himself apart by wearing eccentric bow ties and seersucker suits, and he had an irritating tendency to recite poetry at inappropriate times. Dara remembered people's eyes rolling in annoyance at one particular embassy party as Charles insisted on loudly reciting "Jabberwocky" in its entirety after consuming a half-dozen glasses of champagne. He hadn't been well-liked during training, either. Several other people in their training class had mocked Charles relentlessly after he mentioned filling his car up with "petrol" on the way to work.

"Hey, Charlie-boy, I don't know where you come from, but here in the U-S-of-A we call that stuff gas. Gas-o-leen, if you want to get fancy, but *petrol*? What's the matter with you?" Their classmate had spoken in an exaggerated Texas accent to emphasize his point, and Charles had earned the nickname "Petrol Chuck" for the duration of their training.

What most of their fellow trainees had not known until later was that Petrol Chuck's daddy was a four-star general. That didn't make Charles a legacy in the CIA necessarily, but his father's well-known influence on intelligence committees had made their instructors treat him—and his eccentricities—with deference. And later on Charles rose high and fast in the agency, in spite of his quirks.

He had been wearing one of his ridiculous bow ties on the day he broke the news to Dara that she was the subject of an Inspector General report. At first she had thought he was joking. Just the night before, she and Tariq had been at Charles's spacious Amman home for a small dinner party. Dara had thought nothing of their dinnertime banter; in fact, considering the company, it had been a pleasant evening. Charles had waxed poetic about the origins of love and insisted that she and Tariq share stories of how they first became romantically involved. Charles's wife, Suchin, had teased Tariq about the stereotypes of Middle Eastern lovers, and Charles had acted like nothing so much as an approving friend. He and Tariq had smoked cigars outside while Dara looked at his wedding album with Suchin.

Too late, Dara realized the next day that Charles had set her up. His dinnertime probing ended up forming the bulk of the IG's report that was eventually submitted—the one with the official finding that Dara was involved in an inappropriate relationship with a foreign intelligence officer. "High probability of officer compromise," the report concluded, without ever giving any specifics about what secrets, if any, Dara had allegedly revealed. "Incompatible association" was the nonsensical jargon used to label her relationship. The report painted Tariq as an enemy spy—ironic, given the extensive and ongoing partnership between the CIA and Jordan's intelligence service.

Dara, according to the report, had demonstrated "poor judgment," "questionable loyalties," and—her personal favorite— "exploitable vulnerabilities" by becoming romantically involved with Tariq. There were no facts to refute—simply a long list of conclusions reached by a nameless, faceless panel.

Charles had called her into his office to break the news. It took a moment to sink in, partly because she was still in social mode with him after their gathering at his home the night before, but also because she was fixated on Charles's monogrammed cufflinks. *What kind of CIA officer wears monogrammed anything?* She was distracted by this thought while he spoke. *How are you supposed to conceal your identity when your initials are on your sleeves?* He was obviously more concerned with his wardrobe than his cover.

When she finally caught on that he wasn't joking, though, she reacted without thinking. "What do you mean I'm being removed from duty for having an 'inappropriate' relationship with a foreign citizen? Half—no, scratch that—three-quarters of the men on field deployments for this agency are fucking a different local woman every week! You met your own wife when you were serving in Bangkok!"

"Yes, but most of them are smart enough to sleep only with prostitutes or the spouses of other diplomats. Present company excluded, of course." He tried unsuccessfully for levity, fidgeting in his seat. "You, on the other hand, chose to get into bed with a known intelligence officer."

"Yes, Charles, the point being that he is *known*. He's our primary liaison contact. Our ally. This isn't the Cold War, you know. He's not trying to use me to get intel—we're two colleagues who happened to become close! You'd rather I pick someone up off the street, or sleep with someone else's husband?"

Charles sighed. "To be blunt, yes."

Dara started at her boss in disbelief. "This isn't right, Charles. I hope you know that."

He raised his palms in the air in a melodramatic posture of innocence. "Our critics don't say 'Intelligence is a misnomer' for nothing."

"Fuck you, Charles. Be sure to put that in your cable when you write this conversation up." Dara stormed out of his office and hadn't spoken to him since.

Dara shook off the unpleasant memory. *Lesson learned*, she chastised herself, determined not to let herself get dragged down by the past. She needed to focus.

She outlined what she knew already. It wasn't much. Caitlin certainly hadn't spared herself any blame during her confession, but Dara knew that there was bound to be much more to the story than the young woman had disclosed. For one thing, Dara doubted that two junior officers could have pulled something like this off on their own. There had to be more people involved.

Dara also wanted to get to the bottom of Caitlin's reasons for telling her any part of her story. All intelligence officers know to question a source's motivation for revealing information. Once you figure out *why* someone is spilling their guts, you can often figure out what they're *not* telling you. Dara didn't believe for a second that Caitlin had unburdened herself of any secrets for purely therapeutic reasons.

Realizing that she only knew a tiny piece of the story, Dara forced herself to back up. A lesson from a long-ago class on writing top-secret reports flashed through her mind: *Bottom line up front.* Caitlin's story was full of salacious angles, but the bottom line was that her husband had ended up dead. The world of espionage was a small one, and Dara had no doubt in her mind that Jonathan Wolff's death had something to do with his extracurricular operations. There was no room in espionage operations for coincidence.

Besides, the worse the scenario she uncovered, the better it was for her career. Ironically, that was often the way it went in the CIA. The closer you were to tragedy, by accident or by intent, the more opportunity you had to advance. One of her closest friends in the Tel Aviv office, a gregarious Montana native named Jack, had been nicked by shrapnel when he happened to be eating lunch with a source in a café next door to one chosen by a suicide bomber. It had been a mild injury, but as he put it when Dara bumped into him in the business-class lounge in the Charles de Gaulle Airport in Paris, "It was the best damn thing that ever happened to my career. A huge bump in pay, a helluva long vacation to recuperate from what was basically a scratch, and my choice of assignments from here on out."

Jack had been lucky, of course, but there did seem to be some truth behind the suspicion that the agency tended to reward misfortune and bad luck just as handsomely as it did genuine bravery. So if Caitlin proved to be involved in something far worse than it first appeared, then Dara was damn well going to pursue it to the bitter end. It was the right thing to do *and* the self-serving thing to do, and Dara had no intention of backing off.

But getting results certainly wasn't going to be easy. Jonathan's murder had been officially declared a terrorist act, and the FBI was in charge of the investigation. Dara briefly considered contacting her counterpart at the bureau to get more details, then thought better of it. She didn't share the same sense of rivalry that some FBI and CIA officers maintained, but neither did she want to get sidelined. Not now, just when she was starting to regain her career traction.

Besides, she told herself, she didn't have anything substantial to share. Yet.

Plus, she had access to something—make that *someone*—that the FBI didn't.

The phone number was written indelibly on her brain. She'd called it often enough that she couldn't forget it if she tried. And a good thing too, because now she would probably be denied access to the files. Files full of reports that *she* had written. She couldn't make the call from her office anyway, so it would have to wait. There was a lot to do first.

In the meantime she rose from her desk to go in search of her new protégée. Caitlin had a lot of explaining to do.

CHAPTER THIRTEEN

She'd come to think of it as the walk of shame. Caitlin dreaded walking through the corridors of headquarters. So many pity-filled glances and ill-concealed whispers followed her every foray through the building that she had taken to hiding out in the agency's rarely used library. She sank into one of the cracked faux-leather chairs behind a dusty wall of dated periodicals and glanced at her watch. Ten more minutes to kill before her meeting with Dara. But if she didn't leave now, she might run into the early lunch crowd.

She frowned. Better to get to the meeting early than risk running into someone she didn't want to see in a crowded hall-way. She pushed out of the seat reluctantly and headed out of the library with her head down.

Caitlin knew that she had no one to blame but herself. She was the one who had come up with the idea in the first place, although she had meant it as a joke at the time. Had she had any clue just how far things would go, she would've kept her mouth shut.

Jonathan had organized the meeting as an informal brain-storming session not long after he and Caitlin had gotten married. She was still starstruck by her handsome husband, still giddy from the intense, border-crossing, danger-tinged adventure that had been their courtship during their year of training. Theirs was never an ordinary relationship. Neither of them wanted ordinary. That's why they'd been drawn together in the first place.

Caitlin hadn't known exactly what he wanted to get out of the meeting; she suspected that he hadn't even thought that far ahead. It was just the kind of thing that Jonathan did. He was always bringing people together, for one reason or another. Just a week earlier he had organized the CIA's first Ultimate Frisbee tournament; the final game had been a team from the Directorate of Operations playing against a team from the Directorate of Science and Technology. The ops team won, of course. Jonathan's team usually did, whatever the sport.

The conference room had only been available during lunchtime, so everyone brought their own food into the meeting. Between the crunching and unwrapping noises, not one, but two dramatic soda spills, and the fact that not a single one of the ten or eleven meeting attendees had more than two years' experience, the meeting had seemed casual and amateurish. Jonathan hadn't been the least bit deterred by the fact that the people in the conference room were more or less the same people he ate lunch with in the cafeteria every day. He still took the meeting seriously, his pen and notepad out and ready to take notes.

There had been one person at the meeting whom Caitlin hadn't recognized. Jonathan told her later that she had in fact been introduced to Tony Alvaro once before, but she didn't remember him at the time. He had a plain, easily forgettable face, and he didn't say much. Jonathan had filled her in on his details. Tony, who looked significantly older than any of the other people at the meeting, had entered the military straight out of high school; he eventually became a Navy SEAL. After a few years of increasingly messy operations, he had gone back to school on the government's dime, earning, of all things, a degree in philosophy.

Jonathan had been excited that Tony came to the meeting. "He's one of very few people I've met at work who have truly walked the walk," he told Caitlin later that evening over dinner. "He's just as new to the CIA as we are, but he has incredible experience, and he's frustrated like the rest of us."

She had just smiled and refilled his wine glass. At that point, only a few short months into their marriage, she had been content just to spend time with her new husband. If his new little group made him happy, then she was happy. She had a hard time imagining Tony as a Navy SEAL with combat experience—he just seemed too ordinary—but Jonathan had been impressed. He'd seen Tony as a sort of behind-the-scenes mentor figure. Someone who could show him the ropes, but not steal the limelight. That last part was important. Jonathan liked the limelight. He liked being the leader—the star.

But because their lunchtime meeting had been mostly just Jonathan and his friends, Caitlin hadn't taken it seriously. Her ever-idealistic new husband had organized it because, as he put it, he was sick of listening to everyone bitch and moan about how ineffective the CIA had become. He didn't want to be one of the whiners—he wanted to come up with a plan to actually accomplish something. He wanted to reinvent the place from the bottom up, and he still had the enthusiasm that only someone who doesn't know what they are getting into can possibly possess. Halfway through leading the group through a brainstorming session on new counterterrorism methods, though, Jonathan started to get frustrated.

"Come on, you guys. We're coming up with a lot of good ideas, don't quit on me now. Let's look at this a different way.

We're sick of being reactive, of feeling like we're being hunted, so let's think like *hunters*. If we want to hunt down and capture terrorists, we need to have some kind of bait. What is it that *we* have that the terrorists want?"

There was an awkward silence. "Technology," someone finally said without enthusiasm. Everyone else was focused on their food. It was obvious that their hearts weren't in this; they had only come along because Jonathan had invited them. They would rather have been playing Ultimate Frisbee.

Jonathan shot Caitlin a pleading glance. He hated failure, and she just wanted to bring a smile to his face. Plus, she was the only woman in the room—a situation she liked to use to her advantage. "Tits," she said, grinning to let everyone know it was a joke.

Everyone in the room laughed, releasing the tension. Tony laughed along with them, but he also sat up and looked interested for the first time since he had entered the room and slumped into a seat.

"She's right," he said.

Jonathan, still laughing, didn't seem to know how to respond.

"Technology and tits. Two things in very short supply in terrorist training camps," Tony continued quietly, with no trace of humor. "And we all want what we can't have."

The awkward silence returned to the room.

They moved to another topic after the brief, uncomfortable pause, and the meeting disbanded not long after that. Something about Tony's tone had stuck with Caitlin after the meeting. After more than a year of training as part of a group in which men outnumbered women three to one, she was no stranger to crude locker room humor; she could give as well as she got when it came to bawdy jokes. Tony's comment wasn't crude as much as it was…creepy. *He* was creepy. There was something too clinical, too calculating about him.

The theme of bait had come up quite a lot in subsequent meetings too, although the later gatherings included only a few of the original attendees. The very same types of bait that they had discussed during the first meeting. Technology and tits. Science and sex. Nukes and knockers, some of the guys had started to joke. More than once Caitlin had wondered if it had really been *her* idea, or if someone else would have suggested it eventually.

As everyone had collected the remnants of their lunches and stood to leave that first meeting, Jonathan had stopped them. "Wait a minute, we need a name."

He was treating it like his Ultimate Frisbee games, Caitlin thought at the time. Jonathan had come up with the name for the ops group's Frisbee team; they were called the Smooth Operators. Cheesy as hell, maybe, but fun. She didn't fault him for this, either. She loved his boyish side. It was part of his charm.

This request from Jonathan succeeded in bringing some of the levity back to the meeting. "Operation Invisible Hand," someone said.

"Okay, we have a suggestion from the econ major in the back," Jonathan said, grinning. "Anyone else?"

"Operation Golden Mean." Tony spoke for only the second time during the meeting. Acknowledging the blank looks from everyone else, he explained: "The golden mean is the desirable midpoint between two extremes, excess and deficiency."

Caitlin chimed in, still trying to bring lightness to the meeting to buoy her husband. "It sounds like Goldilocks and the Three Bears. One bowl of porridge is too hot, one is too cold, and the third is *just* right." She had said it teasingly, but Tony nodded gravely.

"An appropriate contribution from the philosophy major. Operation Golden Mean it is. I'll send out an e-mail with the details for our next meeting." Jonathan dismissed the meeting, taking charge once again.

But there hadn't been any more e-mails about the group. They had very quickly moved past the point of wanting to leave an electronic trail.

Now, having slipped into Dara's office the morning after her big reveal, Caitlin was second-guessing herself. She had planned to tell Dara *some* of this background. She had spent hours deciding what she could and couldn't reveal, and when and if she should lie outright.

She also knew what not to do.

"Good morning," she mumbled to Dara as she sat down. She knew not to fidget, or to over-share, or to exhibit any of the other classic indicators that a person was lying. She tried not to sound rehearsed or nervous. She kept her voice low and relaxed, yet spoke with a level of formality appropriate for a conversation with a more senior officer. She didn't let her eyes wander, her voice waver, or her posture change. She knew how to lie.

But this conversation with Dara was turning out to be more difficult than she had anticipated. Dara was a skilled interrogator, and her questions were keeping Caitlin on her toes.

It wasn't that Dara was being unpleasant or aggressive. If anything, she was sympathetic and warm. But she barely seemed interested in the facts and details that Caitlin had so thoroughly prepared. Instead she kept asking about Jonathan. And not just about Jonathan's death, either.

"Where did you two meet?" Dara asked within seconds of starting their conversation. "Where was your first date?" Later she asked whether Caitlin spoke much with Jonathan's parents these days.

Is this an interrogation or a fucking slumber party? Caitlin wondered. It was almost a relief when the questions turned to Jonathan's death.

The topic was painful, but Caitlin had spent hour after hour talking first to CIA officials and then to FBI investigators. She didn't know why she was so rattled, then, when Dara started to ask some of the very same questions that she had already answered a dozen times before. It was just that when Dara asked about Jonathan *now*, she felt worse somehow. Guiltier. Maybe that's what Dara wanted, she realized. It was a good tactic. She didn't like it, though, and she wanted it to stop.

Finally she interrupted, eager to get back to the topics she had rehearsed. "Um, I don't mean to seem rude or evasive, but Jonathan wasn't on one of our...special operations...when he was killed. His death had nothing to do with our, uh, other activities."

"*Special* operations?" Dara's eyebrows rose. "I'd say." And then she returned to her list of questions about Jonathan.

Who had directed Jonathan to travel to Cairo? Which asset was he meeting? How much money was he carrying? Was he traveling in true name, or undercover? Had he called or e-mailed Caitlin from Egypt? Had he been there before? The questions were basic, standard, but they flustered Caitlin anyway.

"Why do you keep asking me about him?" she finally pleaded. "Don't you want to know about what I did? What I already told you I did?"

Dara shrugged her shoulders as if it made no difference to her. "We can start there and move backward for the rest later."

Caitlin was relieved. After the unexpected grilling about Jonathan's last days, she was happy to finally get to the questions that she had prepared for. But even then, even though she tried to leave Jonathan out of her answers as much as possible, she found references to her dead husband kept creeping into answers she hadn't intended to give.

Worse yet, she found herself blaming Jonathan for things that weren't his fault at all. It was bad enough to speak ill of the dead under any circumstances, so what did it say about her that she was maligning the very man she'd do anything—*anything* at all—to bring back?

But it was too late to protect Jonathan. Caitlin wanted to at least protect his memory, but she was failing to do even that. Sparing Jonathan blame would have meant drawing attention to the one person she now needed to protect at all costs.

"Who selected your targets?" Dara asked.

Here, finally, was a question that Caitlin had expected, had prepared for. But in the context of the last half hour of questions that she *hadn't* been expecting, she reacted badly. Caitlin shifted in her seat and looked down at her lap before she could stop herself. *A sign of hesitation.* Forcing her gaze up to meet Dara's, she nearly choked on the words. "Jonathan's job in the counterterrorism center meant that he could pull data on the potential targets. He liked to pick cases that he felt were being ignored or swept under the carpet while higher-profile targets sucked up all of the official resources."

It was a partially true answer. It was how things had worked at first, anyway.

"And how did you fund your little escapades?" Dara asked, not bothering to hide her contempt. "Jetting around the world in pursuit of bad guys isn't cheap."

"Jonathan arranged for the costs to be rolled into some of the bigger, ongoing operations. No one bats an eye over the cost of a couple of plane tickets when it's squeezed into a multi-million-dollar budget." Caitlin tried not to wince as she more or less accused her husband of financial crimes on top of everything else. It wasn't even true.

Dara didn't believe her, either. It was obvious from the way she frowned and sighed impatiently.

"I think..." Caitlin was venturing into dangerous territory here. She was improvising, deviating from the script. "I think that he may have found someone in his department, someone higher up, who...sympathized. Maybe that person helped cover up the money. I don't know. Jonathan never told me any details." Again, this wasn't true, but it made Caitlin feel better to pin the blame on someone else. Jonathan had borne enough blame already.

I'm sorry, Jonathan, Caitlin thought to herself. *I just need you to protect me a little while longer.*

Fortunately there weren't many more surprises. By the time they finished, Dara looked as worn out by the process as Caitlin felt. Still, she resented Dara. She blamed her for bringing Jonathan up in the first place, for rattling her with personal questions. Ultimately, though, she supposed that it didn't matter. It wasn't as if Jonathan could get into any trouble anymore. And she knew that he'd understand.

Caitlin left the meeting feeling mentally drained. Back at her workstation, she logged off of her computer and left for the day without saying good-bye to anyone. She was exhausted, and she couldn't shake the feeling that it was *Dara* who had planted some sort of seed, rather than the other way around.

CHAPTER FOURTEEN

Dara hadn't pushed Caitlin on the subject of Jonathan to intentionally rattle her, although that effect wasn't entirely unwelcome. Instead, Dara had probed about the death of Caitlin's husband to establish a sort of behavioral baseline. Dara knew that if she could get a sense of how Caitlin looked, reacted, and spoke when she was truthfully answering questions about an emotionally charged topic, then she could better determine when she was lying about other topics.

At least that was Dara's official explanation for her elicitation techniques.

She had always been good at getting the truth out of reluctant sources. And as long as she was getting results, no one ever questioned her on her methods. If anyone had ever listened in, they would have quickly discovered that Dara's techniques were a far cry from the methods taught during clandestine service training. In fact, she tended to ignore altogether the military-derived interrogation techniques. In her experience the coercive, forceful approach tended to yield grudging half-truths, distortions, and exaggerations more often than it yielded calm, cold facts.

Still, she would never in a million years—not under torture or duress—reveal the source of her elicitation techniques: Madam Zolna, "Fortune-Teller Extraordinaire" of Northern California.

Dara had spent the summers of her teenage years being dragged to her parents' quasi-professional summer stock theater performances. Bored out of her mind after watching *A Midsummer Night's Dream* for the hundredth time, she convinced Madame Zolna, née Margaret Hutchins of Fresno, California, to hire her as an assistant. Margaret was one of the many free-spirited entrepreneurs who set up booths outside the seasonal theater production; her tent could usually be found between Blu George's hemp clothing stand and Felicity Ross's dream catcher and turquoise jewelry stall. It had been Dara's job to chat up the customers before they went in for their appointment with Madame Zolna. The whole point had been to extract details and facts that would help Madame Zolna figure out exactly what it was each customer wanted to hear from her thrift-shop crystal ball—all without the customers ever realizing that they were being probed for information. Dara would then reach through a slit in the curtain to discreetly slip her fortune-telling boss a note listing the details she had managed to extract. *Newlywed, on a diet, mother-in-law visiting later this week, car needs repairs,* she would write. And from there, Madame Zolna would conjure up a reading to match.

Dara's two summers working as a fortune-teller's assistant trained her better than any Department of Defense interrogation manual ever did. Not that she'd admit it, of course; she'd be laughed out of the building.

So Dara knew that she had taken Caitlin by surprise when she deviated from what the younger officer had probably expected during their conversation. She'd asked questions about the beginning of Caitlin's relationship with Jonathan—about better times—to sneak past the hard, defensive shell that the young officer had built around herself. And apparently this strategy had worked, because after talking about how Jonathan had proposed via an elaborate treasure hunt that spanned three continents and ended with a diamond ring presented on bended knee in a Michelin-starred restaurant in Paris, Caitlin visibly struggled to transition to her clearly rehearsed answers pinning the blame for all that had gone wrong on Jonathan. The one person who couldn't protect himself anymore was the person Caitlin most *wanted* to protect.

But she hadn't protected him. She'd blamed Jonathan again and again. According to Caitlin, the operations had been planned by him, funded via his creative accounting, and covered up by his deceptive reporting. Caitlin didn't deny her role in the operations, but she did deny knowing anything other than what Jonathan told her, what she saw Jonathan do, and what she heard Jonathan plan.

She was lying.

Caitlin may have been a good liar, but Dara was better, and lying well usually meant recognizing lies equally well. It was a simple matter of experience. All undercover officers gradually became better liars over the course of their careers. At the start of a CIA officer's career, lying was a duty, an act of patriotism. Young trainees didn't *enjoy* lying to friends and family about where they worked, but they understood that it was a necessary evil. Then, once unleashed in the field, junior officers usually began to see lying as a sport. Each time a customs official blithely stamped a fake passport without a second glance, each time a target swallowed a sugarcoated half-truth, each time an alias name was guilelessly accepted was a small victory, a point won.

Dara knew that, eventually, lying became routine for those who did it enough. It lost its stigma. The act of lying ceased to be a moral issue. It became, instead, a neutral activity no different from driving a car or turning on a computer. Lying became nothing more and nothing less than the truth. For CIA officers, it was just part of the job.

Caitlin hadn't reached that point of detachment from the truth, though. Dara could tell that Caitlin wanted—no, *needed*—her to believe her version of events. Whether it was because of pride, self-preservation, or fear, Caitlin was only giving her a self-censored, diluted version of the off-the-book operations that she had run with her husband.

It was enough to get started, though. And it was certainly enough to get Dara back in the field.

Back in her office, Dara stared at the outdated map of the world that she had hung over her desk. She could have easily picked up a more current version from any supply closet, but she liked the old map that she had been carting around over the years. On her tattered, faded map, Myanmar was still Burma, Czechoslovakia was still one country, and "USSR" was stamped ominously across the better portion of two continents. Dara liked the reminder that the world was always in flux, with or without the CIA's help.

She wanted to jump-start her stalled career and get out of headquarters for selfish reasons, of course, but Dara's rush to the field wasn't entirely self-serving.

Mostly, perhaps, but not entirely.

Dominic Cahill had told her to take care of the Caitlin situation, and that meant that she had to understand what happened to Jonathan. She *wanted* to know what happened to Jonathan. If nothing else, he had been a colleague. Even though Dara had never met him, she felt that she owed him something for that fact alone, regardless of what he had done.

Besides, Dominic had told her to watch over Caitlin. Dara's opinion of the young woman continued to waver between sympathy and disgust, but one thing had become very clear to her: underneath the calm exterior she was struggling so hard to maintain, Caitlin was terrified. She was so terrified of someone, or something, that she was willing to let Dara believe the absolute worst about her murdered husband. And about her. Dara wanted to know why.

She stared at Egypt on her map. The FBI agents working there knew nothing about Jonathan's extracurricular operations; they were investigating his death as if it were a run-of-the-mill terrorist act, if you could say that such a thing existed. Dara was happy to leave the traditional investigation to them. She would stick to investigating whether Jonathan and Caitlin's activities had anything to do with his murder. And if Caitlin continued to refuse to give full disclosure about what she and Jonathan had been doing in the months leading up to his death, then Dara certainly wasn't going to learn anything else while sitting behind a desk.

Dara focused on the map and studied the last two places Jonathan had traveled before he was killed. He and Caitlin had traveled separately, using clean alias documents to get to Dubai for their last off-the-books operation. Two weeks later, Jonathan had traveled to Cairo on official business; for that trip he traveled in true name, using a diplomatic passport. He had been seen leaving his luxury hotel the morning after his arrival in Egypt; no one saw him again until Al Jazeera aired footage of his execution six weeks later.

Networks all over the world quickly picked up the story. The contrast between Jonathan's blonde, all-American good looks and his hooded, visibly blood-stained executioners seemed almost a caricature: a handsome Prince Charming, head held high until his last moment, slain by evil, masked ogres.

Dara had first watched the video on the news with Tariq. It was late in the evening, and they were in her Amman apartment after dinner, clearing the dishes with the English-language news channel on in the background. They simultaneously stopped what they were doing and turned toward the TV as soon as the reporter uttered the words "CIA officer executed." They both stared wordlessly as the image switched from the television studio to the homemade video that had been delivered anonymously to the news station. Dara hadn't recognized Jonathan from the grainy video, and she had looked away from the gruesome footage as soon as she was sure that it wasn't someone she knew. She didn't consider herself to be squeamish, but she couldn't just sit and watch a colleague die like that. It felt disrespectful, somehow, to watch the brutal event unfold as she sipped tea in the safety of her living room. Tariq had stared intently, though.

"Anyone you know?" Dara knew that Tariq had studied the world's terrorist organizations inside and out.

He shook his head. "No. This group is new." He leaned closer to the screen.

"How can you tell?" Dara asked. "They haven't identified themselves. Their faces are covered, and they haven't said anything at all."

"That's just it," Tariq frowned. "Normally you can't get fanatics to shut up. They want the world to hear what they have to say, since they sincerely believe that they are delivering a message from Allah. These guys, though, don't say anything at all. There's no message, just the killing. It seems more like a personal revenge this way—it doesn't fit the usual pattern." He paused, disturbed. "What's the message? What are they trying to tell us?"

he asked quietly, still staring at the screen, as if the television itself could speak up and provide an answer.

Dara forced herself to watch the footage as it was replayed. Tariq was right. Not one of the three masked terrorists uttered a single word. Somehow their silence seemed to make their actions appear even crueler than if they had been yelling and screaming the usual extremist rhetoric. They offered no explanations as they slit Jonathan's throat and let him fall to the ground.

Dara shook off the memory. Caitlin seemed to honestly believe there was no connection between Jonathan's off-the-books operations and his death. She might be right, but Dara had to start somewhere. Cairo was already crawling with FBI agents investigating the case, and Dara didn't want to risk her shaky field credentials by stepping on the toes of a territorial Fed.

Besides, Cairo may have been Jonathan's last official trip, but Dubai had been his last *unofficial* trip. Dara was willing to bet that, since he had traveled there in alias, the FBI investigators didn't even know about Jonathan's little side trip to the Emirates. Which meant that it was wide open for her to visit.

She traced the distance between Cairo and Dubai on the map, her finger slowing only slightly as it passed under Amman. "Dubai it is," she decided out loud.

She called the agency's central travel office to book her tickets, cursing headquarters' bureaucracy once again as she was put on hold. While she waited, she reviewed the notes that she had taken during her conversation with Caitlin.

According to Caitlin, the last time she had worked with her husband, Jonathan had identified their final target at the last minute. A CIA source working in a travel agency in Yemen had sold two airline tickets to Dubai to a ragged-looking man who paid in US dollars. The traveler had asked for assistance in finding a luxury hotel for a "vacation" there with a friend. Yemen being a place where luxury, vacation, and foreign currency are all but make-believe concepts for the average citizen, the source was alerted by the transaction, which he promptly reported to his American handler. Jonathan.

Fast-forward seventy-two hours, and Jonathan and Caitlin were in Dubai, checked into the same opulent hotel recommended by the travel agent in Yemen, and newly acquainted with the hotel bar where Caitlin positioned herself only a few minutes before the targets arrived. Jonathan hadn't been able to unearth much about the targets—they seemed to have been living off the grid for quite some time—but his gut instinct told him that they were worth pursuing. Besides, it had been a slow month, and it was apparent to Caitlin that her husband was eager for action. She'd sensed they were rushing things, but she kept quiet about her concerns.

The night had not started off smoothly. For one thing, Caitlin's usual targets were the types of men who were accustomed to luxury hotels. They were wealthy, educated, and arrogant, and not at all suspicious of a blonde Western woman throwing herself at them in a bar.

The Yemeni targets were different. They had made an effort to clean themselves up to better fit into the lavish surroundings, but they still stood out among the oil barons, business magnates, intelligence officers, and high-end smugglers who tended to patronize Dubai's higher-end hotel bars. They were nervous, visibly out of place, and very much unaccustomed to drinking alcohol.

Caitlin regularly used alcohol as a weapon during her operations with Jonathan. The Muslim religion forbade alcohol, but Caitlin had found that, once away from home, her targets were easily persuaded to imbibe. It didn't hurt that Dubai was sort of like the Las Vegas of the Muslim world. Although its many bars and nightclubs were technically only supposed to serve alcohol to non-Muslims, most were co-located with hotels that didn't refuse paying guests of any religious denomination. As long as you were just visiting, Dubai offered a wide variety of forbidden fruits. For Caitlin, that meant her targets were cheap drunks. Unaccustomed to drinking alcohol, they tended not to hold their liquor well. In Caitlin's manicured hands, a generous pour of scotch was as effective as truth serum.

The Yemenis were no exception. Unlike her previous targets, though, they were extremely wary when Caitlin first approached them. She knew that they assumed she was a prostitute working the bar for clients with more means than they possessed. Many of Dubai's bars were frequented by easy-to-spot Eastern European call girls, and with her long blonde hair and short, tight skirt, Caitlin fit right in—exactly as she intended. Unfortunately, neither Caitlin's fawning attention nor the drinks she plied them with seemed to do the trick with these particular targets.

Naseem, the older of the two men and Caitlin's primary target, winced as he downed his first whiskey. After his second drink he began to ramble about how very much he loved his "brother" and traveling companion, Ahmed. By the third drink he was slurring his words. The more the two men drank, the more inseparable they became. Naseem threw his arm over Ahmed's shoulder and professed that all he had in life was but for Ahmed's taking. Ahmed upped the ante by drunkenly professing that his very *life* was for the taking by his newfound "brother," Naseem.

Caitlin's strategy depended on her ability to divide and conquer the targets, but the more they drank, the more oblivious they were to her charms. Even worse, the two increasingly inebriated men were starting to attract attention from the other bar patrons, and Caitlin feared that hotel security would soon be called. In desperation, she excused herself to use the restroom so that she could confer with her backup. The men barely noticed when she left.

Dara saw the exact instant when Caitlin realized she had slipped. Up until that moment, Caitlin had maintained that she and Jonathan had acted alone. Her eyes widened as she realized that she had just revealed a third participant, since she had already told Dara that Jonathan was in place in the hotel room. Obviously *he* wasn't the backup who was waiting in a sitting area around the corner from the bar.

Dara watched in silence as Caitlin quickly calculated how to play the slip. To her credit, the young officer recovered quickly, and she had folded the third participant into the story as if he had been there all along. "Tony passed me a small container of powdered sedative to slip into Ahmed's drink," she continued. When Dara looked at her pointedly, pen poised to take notes, she added his last name in an innocent tone. "Tony Alvaro," she said, as if she had planned to tell Dara all along.

The team had previously rejected the use of sedatives in their operation because the lingering effects could alert targets that they had been drugged. The team preferred to conduct their operations in such a way that the targets left with no knowledge that anything out of the ordinary had happened to them other than getting unusually lucky with an attractive blonde.

Caitlin hesitated, but Tony had assured her that the sedative was mild enough that it would just make Ahmed want to take a little nap while she continued to entertain Naseem. "Get them up in your room fast, though, before it kicks in," Tony had warned her.

Dara struggled to maintain a neutral expression on her face while Caitlin told her what happened next. Every part of her was disgusted, ashamed by the depths that the young woman had sunk to in the name of their little operational games. She had acted like a whore, not a spy. But Dara didn't let her judgment show. She needed to hear the whole story—whether she approved or not.

Caitlin had told her the rest in an emotionless monotone. "I slipped the drugs into Ahmed's drink. They were both too drunk to notice. Ahmed downed the entire glass of whiskey and yelled for another. The bartender refused to serve him, though, since he was already a mess. He started getting aggressive with the bartender, calling him names, which actually was a good thing, because it helped me convince Naseem that we should get his buddy up to my suite before we all got kicked out of the hotel.

"By the time I managed to herd them out of the bar and up to my suite, the drugs were obviously starting to take effect. Ahmed could barely walk, and he wet himself while we were in the elevator. Naseem, who was only slightly less drunk, started yelling at him, telling him that he was a disgrace, that he wasn't a true brother, all sorts of things. I was trying to calm him down, to get him to stop yelling, when Ahmed's eyes rolled back into his head, and he passed out on the floor of my hotel room."

Caitlin smiled as if the scenario she was describing was somehow comical. Dara didn't return the smile. She didn't think there was anything funny about it.

Caitlin sighed. "Naseem went crazy. He wanted to call for a doctor; he was convinced that Ahmed was dead. I knew that if he used my phone to call anyone to the room, things would get messy, so I offered to call myself. I obviously didn't want there to be any trail linking me with the targets, so I called Jonathan, not the hotel lobby. He was in the next room, so he came right away and took care of the situation. We went straight to the airport and took the next flight out."

Dara narrowed her eyes. "What do you mean by 'took care of the situation'?"

Caitlin flushed. "Jonathan burst into the room and punched Naseem in the face. The guy was so drunk that it didn't take much—he went out like a light. We went through their pockets, but they didn't have anything on them except a handful of Yemeni rials and some cigarettes. They didn't even have cell phones."

Dara wanted to shake Caitlin. "So, not long before he was murdered, your husband shook down a couple of suspected terrorists—one of whom *saw* him right before getting punched in the face—and you seriously don't think that had anything to do with his death? You're either the most naïve CIA officer to walk the halls of Langley, or else you're leaving something out. Which is it?"

"No. No. I'm telling you, it wasn't that big a deal. Naseem was drunk, he only saw Jonathan for a split second, and we had been using clean aliases, which we dumped as soon as we got home. There's no way a couple of low-level nobodies from Yemen could have traced anything back to Jonathan. Give me some credit—I've replayed the scene in my head a million times to see if I missed anything. It was just a dead-end op." Caitlin's lip quivered.

"It wasn't an 'op,'" Dara said angrily, no longer able to hold back. "It was a dangerous game that some stupid kids were playing, and it may have ended up getting your husband killed."

Dara caught herself. She needed to keep her anger in check for what she had to say next. The question that she had to ask was definitely not one to be asked in a confrontational manner. It was a question she didn't want to ask at all. But like it or not, Caitlin's answer might impact Dara. There were reports to be written and plans to be made, and Dara just wanted to be prepared. "Listen," she started in a calmer tone. "I don't want you to take this the wrong way, and ultimately it's none of my business, but..." *God, this is awkward*, she thought. "Have you considered your, um, options with this pregnancy? I mean considering..." She trailed off self-consciously. "I wouldn't even ask, but I need to know how you plan to play this when questions become... unavoidable."

Caitlin closed her eyes and leaned back in her chair. "Abortion. You're talking about abortion." She said it so softly that Dara barely heard. When she opened her eyes, they were filled with tears. "Of course I've thought about it. I've thought about it a lot. More than a lot. I've even picked up the phone a few times to make an appointment. It would make things much simpler, wouldn't it? But..." She took a deep breath and seemed to be fighting for composure. "What if it's his? What if the baby is Jonathan's? There's a good chance of it, and it's all that's left of him. It's all I have." Caitlin broke down and started to sob.

Dara stood up and rested her hand gently on the crying woman's shoulder for just a moment, and then slowly left the room. She wasn't going to get anything else out of Caitlin today. She had enough to get started.

It was time to get on a plane.

CHAPTER FIFTEEN

Travis had to keep reminding himself to stop grinning like an idiot. He was finally doing what he had been trained to do, and it felt fucking *great*. He felt like a goddamn rock star. But he needed to look serious. He needed a certain amount of gravitas to pull this off. Nobody would believe him if he looked like a smiling half-wit.

So much had changed in such a short time. The meeting in the deli had been just the start. He'd played his cards right, apparently, because he'd been contacted almost immediately to start working on a new project. A black project so off-the-books that even now, in the middle of the op, he wasn't even sure who was running the show. Not that he really minded. He finally had a chance to show what he was capable of.

Yesterday he had left his apartment as Travis Park, bored government employee. Today he was Jae Hyun-Jin, Korean gray arms dealer.

He'd protested at first that he didn't speak Korean well enough to pass as native-born, but his handler had brushed aside his concern. "Don't worry about it, man. The guys you're meeting are from Chechnya. I guarantee that they've never even heard Korean spoken before, so they won't know the difference.

Just speak English with a heavy accent, and don't wear anything too American."

"Where can I buy Korean clothes?" Travis had asked, causing the other men in the room to snicker. He still didn't know their names—"compartmentalization through anonymity" they claimed—and their laughter annoyed him.

"No, no. Don't make this more complicated than it needs to be," one of them reassured him. "I just meant don't show up wearing a Yankees sweatshirt or something crazy like that. These guys are so desperate to get weapons that they're not going to question you about anything. They'll just be grateful that you showed up at all. The only thing you need to do is find out where they want their guns shipped. Tell them that you can get whatever they want. Make like fucking Burger King—have it your way, you know? They'll be so excited when they hear that, you could stand up and sing 'The Star-Spangled Banner' in a pair of Stars and Stripes boxer briefs, and they still wouldn't ask any questions. The only thing you need to worry about is getting the point of delivery. Find out where the guns are going. Don't let them string you along and give you some middleman delivery address. Find out where the guns will end up, and we'll take care of the rest."

Travis resolved to perform well enough on this op that he'd be invited to participate in the back end. After months of being bored out of his mind, he was looking forward to doing something high risk, high reward. *This is what I'm here to do*, he told himself. He had wanted in, and this was most definitely in.

The fact that his handler wouldn't tell him anyone else's name made sense to Travis, even if it was slightly insulting. He'd earn their trust in time.

His meeting was in Bratislava. The more modes of transportation he took, the harder it would be to trace back his travel, so Travis flew into Austria and paid cash for a train ticket to Slovakia. Once in the capital, he went straight to a car rental agency, feeling quite pleased with himself for successfully crossing his first borders in alias. His hand shook slightly as he signed the credit card receipt, though. He had started to write a *T* for Travis, catching himself only in the nick of time before he blew his whole operation because he couldn't manage to sign a lousy piece of paper with his fake name. He took a deep breath before climbing into the comically compact rental car, reminding himself that it was the little things that could expose his true identity.

Adrenaline pumping, he drove the route that he had memorized, his car wheels slipping occasionally in the snow that dusted the streets of Bratislava. He found the coffee shop easily enough, and after watching it from across the street for fifteen minutes, he entered. His contact was sitting at the table in the back corner, a red duffel bag sitting prominently on the chair beside him as promised.

"I have a bag very similar to yours," Travis said, channeling his grandmother's heavy Korean accent. "Where did you buy it?"

The man looked up from his newspaper and scanned Travis from head to toe with heavy-lidded eyes. Travis panicked briefly. Was anything out of place? Was anything about him suspicious? Should he have mangled his pronouns to sound more foreign?

After a quick moment of scrutiny, the man's face cracked into a wide grin. "I buy this bag at store in London." A flash of panic showed in his eyes before he corrected himself. "A bookstore. Yes, a bookstore in London." The Chechen looked jumpy as he said the prearranged phrase. Travis wondered if this was his first clandestine meeting too. The thought that this guy might be even more anxious than he was gave Travis the confidence to step into his role and take charge.

"Let's keep this brief," he said, looking over his shoulder as if someone was watching them. He wanted the Chechen to stay nervous—the better to maintain control over the meeting. "Let me see your list."

The Chechen pulled a wrinkled, typewritten list out of his duffel bag and placed it on the table. Travis scanned the list, furrowing his brow at certain items as if mulling over a difficult decision. He knew that it didn't matter what the list said. It was a list full of wishes that were never going to be granted. He took his time, though, enjoying the chance for showmanship. Finally he folded the paper and put it into his pocket, nodding gravely. "Yes. I can do it. But only if we can make the arrangements for payment and delivery right now. I don't want to have this kind of inventory sitting in trucks while your people scramble around to find the money." He spoke harshly, decisively. "And no middlemen."

The Chechen's eyes narrowed. Travis's gut clenched. Had he gone too far? Been too direct? Perhaps he should have finessed the situation more, teased out the delivery details. He was about to backpedal when the Chechen spoke. "What is...middleman?"

Travis smiled with relief. It was just a language issue. "I will only deliver to you. I won't deliver to someone I don't know or haven't worked with before. No trans-shipment." He tried to think of another way to make his point clear, but it wasn't necessary. The Chechen grinned broadly again.

"Of course, of course. Delivery to me. And you will be my guest. We will have party to celebrate the arrival."

Travis nodded in agreement, knowing that the Chechen's party would never occur. He wrote down the details for delivery to a remote address well outside of Grozny, named a date, and then pushed away from the table with a grunt of farewell.

He had to stop himself from doing a fist pump into the air as he left the coffee shop. He did it! The Chechen hadn't doubted him for a second, and now Travis was walking away from a meeting with a terrorist organization's artillery wish list that looked like something that should be sent to a Santa Claus in hell. And it was an easy assumption that the address scrawled in Travis's notes would lead the CIA—or more accurately, a few select officers from the CIA—straight to either a key weapons storage facility for the group or, even better yet, a terrorist training camp.

Finally. Travis had done something that would make a difference. Finally he was *in*.

CHAPTER SIXTEEN

Dara punched random buttons on her car's satellite radio, fruitlessly searching for a local news station that could tell her why traffic could possibly be at a standstill at eight thirty in the evening. She'd had a long, frustrating day at work, and at the very least she deserved light traffic. Not that she had anything—or *anyone*—to rush home to.

Her relationship track record was definitely less than impressive. Before Tariq, she'd had a few short-lived flings with other CIA officers; her travel schedule was too hectic to meet, much less date, "real" men, as Naomi called men outside of the agency. Unfortunately, she'd come to realize that, for all their swashbuckling, adventurous ways, more often than not CIA men craved at home what they lacked at work. They wanted an archetype—a cheerful, wholesome housewife who represented the honesty and stability that they lacked in their working hours. They wanted someone who wouldn't ask questions. Who didn't know, didn't need to know, and didn't want to know. They wanted someone, in other words, who was the exact opposite of Dara.

And then, of course, there had been Michael. Her last "real" relationship. Dara was embarrassed to admit even to herself how many years had passed since things ended with Michael. They'd had the textbook college romance. She had been a senior at Georgetown when they met; he had been in his second year of law school. He had been very...earnest. It may not have been the most romantic of qualities, but Dara found him adorable. "You're like a big, loveable Saint Bernard," she had teased him for his longish brown hair and strong, burly frame. Life with him had seemed easy and natural.

She hadn't expected him to propose when he did.

He'd brought her home to meet his parents in Pennsylvania, and while they were hiking in the woods outside the rural home where he had grown up, he dropped to one knee and pulled a ring out of his pocket. She couldn't think of a reason to say no, so she said yes. She felt calm when she said it. She felt happy.

That night, sharing a bed in his childhood room and still giddy from the champagne that his family had poured to celebrate, she told him the truth about where she worked.

At the time it was all still new to her, too. She had only been working for the CIA for two months, and she was still in the early phases of training. Most of her time had been spent in administrative or technical classes; she hadn't even been close to anything operational. And she had been dying to tell him. "Now that we're engaged, I can tell you a little secret I've been keeping," she started, grinning. "Are you ready? It's going to blow you away." She was so naïve. She'd thought he would be proud.

But after she told him, he sat up in bed, frowning. "You made me lie to my family."

"Yes, but...it's an okay lie. It's a white lie. It's harmless," she stammered, taken aback by his reaction.

"No. It's not harmless. I don't know that I can start a family with someone who believes on principle that it's okay to lie to family. It just seems like a pretty slippery slope to me. I need to think about this." He turned his back on her and turned off the light.

They were crammed together in the quilt-covered twin bed, but in spite of their proximity, there suddenly seemed to be a huge gulf between them. *He'll get over it*, Dara told herself. *He's just surprised. He needs time to process, but it'll be fine.* It took her ages to fall asleep, but when she finally did, at dawn, she slept hard.

She woke up a few hours later to find that Michael wasn't next to her. She pulled on a bathrobe and went downstairs, calling out a cheerful "good morning" to the family gathered around the kitchen table.

She was met with chilly silence.

Michael's mother pushed back from the table and busied herself at the sink, clanking pans more loudly than necessary. Michael's father glared at her over his newspaper. Michael's younger sister was staring at her as if Dara was a mythical creature. And then there was Michael. He had a guilty expression on his face, and he wouldn't look at her at all.

"You told them." She didn't need to ask. It was obvious.

"I won't lie to my family. I never lied to *you*," he said, his chin set stubbornly.

Dara went back upstairs to get dressed, and then she sat in the room, confused. She didn't know whether to pack, or go for a walk, or just go downstairs and pretend that everything was normal. Eventually Michael poked his head in the door and made the decision for her. "Pack up. We're leaving."

"So, what, your parents hate me now?" She said it lightly, trying to make a joke of it.

Michael didn't return her smile. Nor did he say another word to her during the awkward twenty minutes it took her to pack and then say a tense farewell to his family. He drove in silence, well above the speed limit.

She let him stew until they were halfway back to Washington. "I understand that you're upset," she started. *She* was angry— furious, even—but she was trying so hard to see it from his perspective. "But telling people what I do for a living is dangerous. For me, of course, but also for you. What if the wrong people found out and tried to hurt you in order to get at me?" He was a practical man—surely he would understand the need to lie if only from a pragmatic standpoint.

"And who else can get hurt by your secrets, Dara? You, me— what about my family? What about *my* job?" He had recently accepted a job with a prestigious K Street law firm; he and Dara had spent the previous weekend shopping for new suits for his first day. "And you know that I want to run for office someday. How am I supposed to hold a public position when I can't even tell the truth about where my wife works?"

"It's a sacrifice, I know, but..." Dara didn't know exactly why she was defending herself. Wasn't he supposed to support her in the same way that she had supported him? Besides, he hadn't even passed the bar exam yet, for God's sake; it would be years before he could so much as run for city council.

"It's not a sacrifice I chose to make. You made it on your own." His voice was cold, bitter.

So that's it, she thought with a small sense of relief. His pride was just wounded because she hadn't consulted him along the way. That was fixable. She took a deep breath and tried a different approach. "I'm sorry I didn't tell you sooner." She rested her hand on his shoulder, wincing as he pulled away. "I didn't tell you that I applied in the first place because I did it on a whim. Remember when I was so stressed out about finding a job after graduation?

I never even thought I'd make it through the selection process. And then, from the very first interview, they kept hammering on about how I wasn't supposed to tell anyone. *Anyone.* It was like a part of the test. And at each subsequent contact they'd ask, 'Who have you told? Who have you told?' Michael, I'm positive that I would have been disqualified if I had told you. Even telling you now, I'm bending the rules. You're not supposed to know until I get permission." She was pleading with him now; she hated the note of desperation she heard in her own voice. "I only told you because I don't think we should have any secrets between us when we get married."

He went silent again, gripping the steering wheel so tightly that his knuckles were white. He abruptly pulled off the highway at a gas station; as he got out of the car, he slammed the door so hard the window rattled. He took his time—too much time— filling up the tank. It was only a couple of minutes really, but they were the type of minutes that count more than most. Dara sat frozen in the front seat, knowing that something terrible was happening but not sure how to stop it. Not sure if she could—or even should—stop it.

When Michael got back into the car, he finally spoke. "I can't do this, Dara. I feel like I don't know you. Like I've never known you." His voice turned cruel. "Like I don't want to know you."

"It's just a job, Michael!" She couldn't believe this was happening. Surely he was overreacting. Surely he would come around.

But he never did. Looking back, Dara could see that their relationship probably wouldn't have worked anyway. He was too literal, too dogmatic. "He sounds like a mama's boy," Naomi had commented when she heard the story. Michael hadn't had any room in his thoughts or feelings for ambiguity, and Dara's life was nothing if not ambiguous. But it still stung.

Dara shook off the unhappy memory as she swerved to avoid what looked to be an entire car fender lying across one of the beltway's lanes. No need to rehash old problems—she had more than enough fresh ones to keep her busy.

In fact, petty work frustrations were at the top of her list of current problems. Today she had spent twenty minutes on hold with the agency's internal travel service until someone finally answered, only to realize that she hadn't given any thought to which alias name she would use for travel. She hung up abruptly on the travel agent and headed down the hall to the alias documents department.

For reasons Dara could never understand, the alias documents, or aldocs, department was staffed by a uniquely frustrating group of employees. "The tennis shoe brigade," as people called the department, employed a contingent of cranky, near-elderly women who seemed to take pleasure in denying requests simply because they could. These women scuttled about their domain in elastic-waist pants and tennis shoes, and never seemed to venture outside their tiny fiefdom. It had pained Dara tremendously to turn over her meticulously developed alias identities when she was recalled to headquarters. She had felt like she was saying good-bye to a group of friends as she handed over her carefully organized box full of carefully forged passports from various countries, driver's licenses, wigs, glasses, credit cards, cell phones, and various other cover-enhancing documents and possessions.

Elisa Brannigan, an identity that Dara had created for Western European operations, for example, kept her keys on a lucky rabbit's foot key ring and favored red lipstick. Leticia Mendez, meanwhile, had a passport enviably full of stamps from tropical locales—souvenirs stemming from Dara's pursuit of a jet-setting Nicaraguan politician. Stacia Robillard had a blush-worthy number of membership cards for private gambling clubs; in her guise Dara had spent an astonishing sum of taxpayer dollars on backroom card games while honing in on a financier with powerful connections to the leaders of several Colombian drug cartels. While operating as Stacia, Dara used to have her nails manicured with garish colors to keep her constantly on alert not to slip up during the high-stakes operation. Aesthetically, Dara thought that the acrylic talons were gruesome—nothing she ever would have opted for in her true life—but she had loved rhythmically tapping the nails on the poker table to psyche out her opponents.

The aldocs staffer had grabbed the box from Dara, throwing it with a distasteful expression into an enormous safe. Dara had felt numb as she watched the pieces of her history—pieces of herself, even—get locked away in the steel vault.

Knowing the department's reputation all too well, Dara entered the aldocs office that afternoon with her warmest smile and her friendliest greeting, hoping to cajole someone into helping her. Her attempt at charm got her nowhere, though, once the tennis shoe-clad aldocs staffer typed her name into the system. "You aren't authorized to travel. Your alias documents remain confiscated." She glared suspiciously, as if she had just spotted Dara's face on a Wanted poster.

The woman, who, true to form, was wearing a pair of lace-up Keds, refused to accept Dara's explanation that she had been recently reauthorized, refused to make any calls to seek higher-level approval, and generally acted like a prison warden, only crankier.

Dara had stormed off in anger, and eventually made her travel reservations—after another twenty minutes on hold, of course—in her true name. She hadn't traveled in her true name for so long that the thought actually made her a bit nervous. She wasn't used to being herself. In fact, her real passport had remarkably few stamps in it for someone who had circled the globe for a living for the last fifteen years. Her alias personas were the *true* adventurers.

Now, stuck in traffic, her thoughts drifted, as they seemed to more and more often these days, to the second relationship that she'd lost thanks to her job. Tariq. He'd given her a sad, sweet smile the day he drove her to the airport for the last time; neither one of them had felt much like talking. She had been too angry at the time to appreciate the strength of his arms around her as he embraced her once more, or the smell of him as he pulled her close—the masculine combination of his cologne and the exotic spices lingering from the quiet meal that they had shared. She'd been too busy railing against the unfairness of her expulsion to trace his handsome face with her fingers one last time, to memorize his eyes, or even to remember to tell him what she had never said.

"I love you, Dara." He had said it instead. "This isn't the end of us. I promise."

His words had only fueled her anger at the factors separating them, and she had walked away from him quickly. Too quickly, and without looking back. She hadn't been able to say what she should have said, and she felt the regret like a physical pain.

Sitting in beltway traffic, heading to her dark and empty townhouse, she replayed those last minutes with him. She wished that she could go back to that moment—to do things differently. The combination of time and distance had finally allowed her to savor his words, his smells, and his touch in her mind the way she hadn't been able to in person. He was the only man who had known who she was, what she did, and had still accepted her. Still loved her.

She glanced at her watch as she inched forward in the hateful traffic. Amman was seven hours ahead of Washington. Tariq was probably sleeping with his windows wide open, as usual. "The better to air out the mind and body from the day's pollution," he had explained when she asked on the first night they had shared. He slept noiselessly, without so much as a snore or a sigh, and he never used an alarm clock. As she pictured him in his silent, still slumber, Dara allowed herself to wonder for the first time whether he was sleeping alone. She knew that she had given up all claim to him, but she still hated the thought of anyone else feeling his hands or his lips...

She jerked the wheel sharply before she could talk herself out of it, waving an apology at the driver of the minivan she cut off in her last-second exit from the freeway. The driver, a frazzled-looking woman with a vanload of kids, flipped her the bird. For some reason that weary, irritable gesture cheered Dara immensely and added to her resolve.

The exit took her to a suburban area Dara didn't know well. Only a few years back it seemed as if you could find a pay phone at any strip mall, gas station, or park. Now that everyone had a cell phone, pay phones were few and far between. Dara had to drive around for ten more minutes before she spotted a hotel. She parked in a spot reserved for guests checking in and darted through the lobby, looking around hopefully. Sure enough, in a dusty corner near the elevators, she found a miraculously still-functioning phone booth.

As a condition of keeping her job, she'd been given strict orders to end all contact with Tariq. She couldn't call him from her personal phone, since it was undoubtedly being monitored, and she didn't have time to buy a throwaway phone before she lost her nerve. She pulled an international calling card out of her wallet. She'd bought it from a newsstand in the train station weeks ago, telling herself that it was "just in case" she ever needed to use a pay phone in an emergency.

She punched in the numbers and held her breath, half-hoping that Tariq didn't answer.

"Alo." His voice was rough with sleep. Just the sound of it made her heart race and her eyes sting.

Maybe this was a mistake. "It's me." It wasn't what she planned to say, but she hadn't exactly thought out the whole conversation. The phone felt slippery in her sweating hand, and her legs felt rubbery.

"Darling Dara." He said it in the same teasing, affectionate way he always had, as if weeks hadn't passed since the last time they spoke. He was the product of years of international boarding schools and spoke perfect Queen's English, but he always said her name in a heavy, slow accent that he knew made her smile. She could hear him moving, sitting up in bed. "I've been dreaming of your voice."

She let out her breath and leaned into the phone as a group of teenagers all wearing matching sports uniforms poured out of the elevator. "It's been awhile."

"And I still love you."

Dara tensed. That wasn't what she wanted to hear from him right now. It was too much. She couldn't do this—how was she supposed to face the realities of her present if she was still living in the past?

"How's work?" He backed off. He had always been good at reading her.

She laughed humorlessly, grateful to be back in less emotionally charged conversational territory. "I'm saving the world, one government form in triplicate at a time. And you? I realized that I never asked you before I left if dating a Yankee spy caused *you* any problems at work. It just all happened so fast…" She trailed off, hoping he would hear the apology in her voice.

"Quite the opposite. In fact, I think I'll get a promotion out of it. I'm a bit famous now around the halls—there haven't been many Mukhabarat-CIA romances. My colleagues are very impressed."

"Don't tease, Tariq. I'm serious."

"Darling Dara, so am I. Everything is always so black-and-white for you Americans. You don't see that gray is actually a very beautiful color. It has a little bit of everything in it. *My* colleagues can appreciate the value of gray, even if yours cannot."

She was silent for several moments. She didn't want to talk about work, but she didn't know what else to say. "I miss you," she said finally. *I love you*, she thought.

"When can I see you?"

"Tariq, you know I can't be in contact with you." She was already regretting the call, even as hearing his voice breathed life back into her.

"And yet you called."

She felt her face flush. He was baiting her.

"You don't have to do anything. Just tell me where you'll be, and perhaps fate will take me there as well. Your employer can't control who you bump into on the street, after all." His voice was soft, persuasive.

Dara bit her lip, trying to will away the tears that were threatening to come. "I need to go. I'm sorry." She hung up and nearly ran out of the hotel, wiping roughly at her eyes as she pushed through a tour group of sweat-suit-clad retirees unloading their suitcases from a bus.

Once in her car, she drove too fast toward the beltway, grateful to find that the flow of traffic had recovered from whatever mysterious force had been impeding it just a half hour before. She turned the stereo up too loud and accelerated even more. She didn't want to go home. She didn't want to be alone with her thoughts. She exited once more, this time in a more familiar area, and found a shortcut back to one of the last places she should have wanted to go. She just couldn't think of anywhere better.

CHAPTER SEVENTEEN

Federal workers are not generally a rowdy or late-night bunch, and the empty tables in Red Mercury reflected that fact.

"Quiet night?" Dara asked Naomi as she slipped onto a barstool.

"Now it is. But you should see this place at seven minutes past five o'clock every weeknight." Naomi leaned over the bar to give her a quick hug.

"Seven minutes past five?"

"You're a headquarters rat now—you should know the drill. Quitting time is five o'clock on the dot, come war, invasion, or plague. Take a minute or two to get to your car, and then head the five minutes down the road, straight into my parking lot. So 5:07 is when the party starts here. By eight, though, the place quiets down." She tilted her head at one of the few tables still occupied. "With a handful of repeat exceptions. In fact, I'm about to cut that one off and send him packing. Want to watch me do the honors? I've gotten pretty good at snatching car keys away from drunk customers before they even realize what's coming at 'em."

Dara glanced over to where Naomi had gestured. The lone occupant of the table did seem to have had a few too many. He was slouched almost obscenely in his chair, his legs splayed apart and his shirt wrinkled and untucked. He had the bleary, unfocused look of a man who had been drinking steadily and purposefully. He was neither belligerent nor in high spirits; he was just plainly, quietly, thoroughly drunk.

"Hold on a second." Dara stopped Naomi. "I recognize him. Let me take care of it." She caught Naomi's skeptical look. "I'll make sure he gets in a cab, or else I'll drive him myself."

Naomi raised her eyebrows. "Damn, girl. I know you're lonely, but surely you can do better than that drunken fool."

Dara rolled her eyes. "Naomi! It's not like that. Give me a break."

Naomi grinned. "Your choice. Call me if you need me."

Dara *did* recognize the man, but she had never actually met him. In fact, she had seen him only once before, sitting at the exact same table just a few days before. She hoped that her hunch about him was correct as she approached. She was fairly certain it was. He had that look about him.

"Hi," she said casually, gesturing to one of the empty chairs. "Mind if I join you?"

The man looked up, surprised; he glanced around as if he thought Dara must be talking to someone else. Seeing no one else in the nearly deserted bar, he shrugged apathetically and then sank his chin back into his chest.

Good, Dara thought. He really was nice and drunk. That would make things easier for her.

"So you're one of the polygraphers, right?"

The man groaned. "Oh God. I knew you were too hot to actually be hitting on me. Don't tell me. I administered your polygraph, and now you want to tell me that I'm an asshole, I was all wrong about you, and now I've ruined your career, right? Have at it; I've heard it all before." He raised his half-empty glass in a sarcastic gesture of cheers.

"Nope. Nothing like that. We've never met." Dara knew she'd have to get to where she was going carefully; the man was extremely defensive. She stuck out her hand. "I'm Dara."

"Jim." He shook her hand cautiously. His hand was steadier than Dara would have thought, given his apparent blood alcohol content. His eyes were unfocused, though, and his words were starting to slur. "I've seen you here before." He sat up a little straighter. "Yeah, I remember now. You were here with that widow, right? The woman whose husband got killed just a little while ago? I did his two-year retest poly not long before...you know. Before it happened." He slumped back, shaking his head at the memory.

Dara sat back in her chair, quickly recalculating her strategy. She had intended to take advantage of the man's drunkenness to get him to spill dirt on one of his colleagues. Dara was fishing blindly, but she had hoped that Melanie Oakes—the polygrapher who had single-handedly done more harm to her career than anyone else—might have some enemies within her own department, and that she might be able to encourage a little collegial gossip with her brand-new drinking buddy, Jim. Dara hadn't even considered the possibility of getting information about either Jonathan's or Caitlin's polygraphs. The transcripts were kept separate from other records, and only the most senior CIA officials could access another officer's polygraph details. Now, however, she may have stumbled across another way to get at that information.

She rearranged her face into a friendly smile and leaned forward. This wasn't part of a personal vendetta anymore. Now, unexpectedly, this was official business, and Dara was good at what she did. "Oh wow. How interesting. From what I hear, he was quite the officer." She kept her phrasing neutral, letting her target direct the conversation for her.

He was all too happy to take the lead. Dara had a feeling that not many people asked him about his job.

"'Quite the officer.' Yeah, that's what I hear now too. Not that you could tell from his poly." He took another gulp from his drink and laughed softly to himself, as if he had just thought of a joke.

Jim's glass was getting dangerously low, and Dara needed to keep him talking before Naomi kicked him out for trying to order another. She pulled her chair closer to his and rested her hand on the table near his arm. She wasn't flirting, exactly, but someone as drunk as Jim could certainly misinterpret the signals, and Dara knew it. It was a cheap tactic, but she wanted to hear what he had to say. Plus, if she played things right, she might also be able to steer the conversation back to Melanie Oakes. She shook off the uncomfortable thought that her attempt to charm information out of Jim was only a degree of magnitude different from Caitlin's honey trapping. *No*, she reminded herself. *There are lines that I'd never cross. Never.*

"What do you mean by that?" She asked her question quickly, before Jim could take another sip from his drink.

"Well, we're trained to look for certain things, you know. Not everyone realizes that being a polygrapher is a complicated business that requires a lot of skill. You have to be a cop, a shrink, a priest, and an engineer, all at the same time." He spoke with a drinker's bravado.

"I believe it. And you saw something odd when you did Jonathan Wolff's poly?" Dara steered him back on topic, trying to keep him on track before his drunken, defensive pride could derail their conversation.

He snorted. "That's just it. I didn't see anything at all. The guy barely seemed to have a pulse. Part of the poly is asking trigger questions to get a rise out of the person in the hot seat. We get you all wired in and then watch what happens when we ask you why you hate your mommy, or if you're cheating on your spouse, or if you like to look at Internet porn. We don't really care about the answers; we just want to see how you react."

Dara winced as he chugged the last of his drink and then glanced around to order another. She needed to keep him focused. "Why is that?"

He smiled smugly. "Everyone always thinks there's some universal sign that a person is lying. Like, people talk faster, or they look up and to the left, or garbage like that. None of it's true. Everyone is different. What does happen, though, is a person reacts consistently in some unique way. Maybe your pulse goes up when you lie, and maybe mine goes down. Maybe you fidget more, or maybe you fidget less. What the polygrapher is trying to do when he pushes your buttons is just to see how *you* react when you're uncomfortable. Like poking a puppy to see if he'll bite." He laughed inanely.

Dara knew most of this already, but she still didn't understand what Jim had meant when he said that he hadn't seen *anything* during Jonathan's polygraph. "So what was Jonathan's reaction?"

"Jonathan didn't react to a damn thing. I pushed him a dozen different ways. I even played the homosexual card. Guys like him usually react big-time when I accuse them of fooling around with other guys. Him, though? Nothing. Not so much as a blip. And that can only mean one thing." He waved his hand, trying to catch Naomi's attention. Luckily she had her back turned.

He sighed and continued. "Countermeasures. There are things you can do to try to trick the machine. And, no, I'm not going to tell you what they are. Polygraphers' code of ethics."

Dara refrained from rolling her eyes, but it was a struggle. There were entire books readily available that described how to fool a polygraph machine, but she wasn't about to mention *that* little fact, lest it be added to her file as one more piece of "evidence" that she was a liar.

"If someone in the hot seat doesn't react to anything at all, it's usually because he's using countermeasures. And *that's* a reportable finding." He muttered a few slurred obscenities.

"So you reported Jonathan for using countermeasures during his poly?" The conversation was starting to interest Dara more.

"Ha!" he shouted, louder than necessary. "I tried. It's standard procedure, but my supervisor shot me down." He slammed his fist on the table for emphasis. "Told me to drop the issue and ordered me to give the guy a pass. I got a little mad, asked her why. And guess what? She didn't even know. Said it was a decision made above her pay grade. So I saluted the flag and gave the guy a pass. That's never happened before, though. Usually they defer to the polygrapher. It kinda made me worry that they didn't trust my judgment anymore."

Jim, whose volume had been rising throughout the conversation, finally caught Naomi's attention with an exaggerated wave. She came striding over with a bad-tempered expression on her face.

Dara stopped her before she could lay into Jim. "Don't worry, Naomi. We're just settling up. I'm going to give Jim here a ride home."

If Jim was surprised to hear this, he was too drunk to show it. He took his jacket from Dara obediently when she handed it to him and stood up when she did.

"Seriously, Dara, I get that you miss your ex, but this one's really not your type. Are you sure you want to do this?" Naomi hissed in her ear.

Dara smiled and patted her friend on the shoulder. "It's not that kind of ride," she said, throwing a twenty down on the table and leading Jim out of the bar.

She stuffed Jim into her car awkwardly. The guy was in lousy shape and probably had seventy pounds on her. She barely managed to get a nearby address out of him before he passed out, snoring slightly and leaving a greasy forehead print smeared on the passenger window.

Dara swore. There went her chance for an intensive debrief session. Now she'd be lucky if she could get him home before he puked in her car.

Jim's house was in McLean, an area that was usually too expensive for public servants. His house was the shabbiest on the block, though. It was one of the rare remaining 1950s-era ramblers that hadn't been razed and replaced with a shiny, new McMansion. There were children's toys on the front lawn, and the porch light was on. Intuition told Dara that *if* someone was waiting up for Jim, that particular someone most likely wouldn't appreciate seeing him dropped off by another woman.

"Focus, Jim, focus!" Dara slapped his cheeks lightly until his eyes snapped open. "Ride's over, pull it together."

The unkempt man took a deep breath, rubbed roughly at his face, and then seemed to give himself a short, silent pep talk before opening the car door. Dara suspected that this very scene had played out many times in this front yard. Chances were high, then, that no one was bothering to wait up for Jim. Still, she didn't want to be any more involved than she had to be. She watched him weave his way to the door, stab unsuccessfully at the lock several times with his keys, and then finally manage to enter the house.

"Home sweet home," Dara muttered sarcastically as she drove away.

A dark blue sedan pulled out of the residential area with her. More out of habit than any actual concern, Dara turned into a strip mall parking lot that emptied on the other side onto a one-way street. It was technically a shortcut that allowed Dara to avoid the notoriously long red light at the next intersection, but Dara had made the turn to see if the sedan would follow her.

It did.

A discreet glance showed Dara that the sedan bore government plates.

"Seriously, guys?" Dara asked out loud in exasperation. "Don't you have any real bad guys to chase?" But as ridiculous and petty as the suburban surveillance was, her stomach still twisted into a knot. She hadn't noticed anyone following her when she made her pay-phone call to Tariq, but she hadn't really been looking very carefully. And she'd been distracted.

I would have noticed, she told herself, hoping it was true. "Assholes," she said out loud.

Her pursuers weren't even bothering to keep much of a distance. *They* knew that *she* knew they were following her.

She pulled into yet another strip mall; McLean had plenty of them. This one was empty, and all of the stores were dark. Once she saw that the sedan had pulled in behind her, she stopped her car abruptly and got out, slamming the door closed behind her. She stormed to the back of her car and faced down her surveillance with her feet planted firmly and her hands on her hips.

With the headlights glaring in her eyes, Dara couldn't see the driver's face. She knew that what she was doing looked ridiculous; she was essentially having a staring contest with a car. She wasn't about to budge, though.

Finally the sedan yielded. The mystery driver whipped the wheel around, and her pursuers left the way they had come.

Taking her lesson from the minivan driver she had cut off earlier that evening, Dara saluted the departing car with her middle finger.

Once back in her own car, though, her bravado wilted. It took several minutes for her heart to stop pounding in her chest. It wasn't from fear. It was anger. She had had enough.

CHAPTER EIGHTEEN

It was a stupid matter of pride. Chad, Travis's slack-jawed bureaucrat of a supervisor, had needled him one time too many about missing days of work, not getting his spreadsheets updated on time, or—and this was the final straw—not attending the mandatory computer training program for the very same computer program that he'd been using every day for the last three months.

"I don't care if you think you know everything there is to know about it, you report to me, and I need to make sure that all of my employees get the training. If I don't, then *my* boss chews *my* ass." Chad wheezed slightly when he got worked up, and his face turned splotchy. He didn't like confrontation, and Travis had noticed that Chad seemed to be avoiding him more and more the longer they worked together.

Travis slammed his fist on his desk in frustration. "If they wanted people to take the training, they should have offered the class *before* they installed the damn software. It's not rocket science here. How the hell can the government justify making its employees spend two entire days learning how to use a program that an eleven-year-old could master in twenty minutes?"

It was one more example of the endless stream of bureaucratic obstacles that prevented anyone from getting anything done. Worse yet, the training course was scheduled to take place the following Thursday, the same day that Travis was supposed to be flying to Mexico City for an overnight operation. It was his first team op, and he was eager to go. He'd proven himself on two solo ops already, and he viewed his inclusion in the group as a good sign. He'd planned to call in sick, since he'd already used up most of his vacation days for the earlier operations, and now his idiot supervisor was screwing up his plans.

"You know, it's possible—just possible—that if this agency stopped focusing on bullshit like this, people like me would actually be able to take down some of these bastards instead of sitting around with the rest of you just listening to them talk."

This pushed Chad too far. He was intimidated by Travis, anyone could see that, but now he was mad. "You seem to think quite a lot of yourself, Park. You may have gone through the ops course, but you're no better than the rest of us. In fact, you're starting to become a problem. You have a bad attitude, and your attendance sucks. You're not going to accomplish a damn thing if you don't clean up your act. At least the rest of us show up and do our jobs." He hitched up his pants and started to walk away.

Travis exploded. "You have no idea what I've accomplished! While you tap dance around these goddamn cubicles and explain away the threats that roll through here every day, I'm actually getting something done. And I'm doing it in spite of you paper-pushing buffoons!" He stopped himself as he realized that he had said too much already. He pushed away from his desk and stormed out of the building to cool off.

He paced out in the cold air in front of the side entrance to the building, slapping away the clouds of smoke coming from the people huddled outside. He was standing in the last refuge that CIA smokers had left; this was the final area not plastered with No Smoking signs. He glared at the small group. They were middle-aged, overweight bureaucrats who didn't have enough common sense or self-control to stop puffing on the cigarettes that were slowly killing them. *"Idiots!"* he muttered, startling a grandmotherly woman who had started to shiver as she took quick, guilty-faced pulls from her cigarette. *These people represent what's wrong with this place.* He kicked at a cigarette butt still smoldering on the ground. *Goddamn slobs on top of everything else.* He knew that he shouldn't have mouthed off to Chad, but he couldn't help it. The guy was just such a do-nothing, incompetent drudge that Travis hadn't been able to help himself. Besides, he told himself, Chad wasn't smart enough to decipher anything he had said. He hadn't given anything away.

In hindsight, Travis realized that he shouldn't have been surprised by how quickly everything came back to bite him in the ass. CIA officers are essentially well-trained gossips. It was their job to eavesdrop, pick up on hints and innuendos, and then spread the word. Still, two hours seemed awfully fast.

Each of the dozen or so cubicle dwellers who had seemed so focused on their work during Travis's confrontation with Chad must have been greedily soaking up every word, probably instant-messaging the conversation in real time to buddies throughout the building as the argument occurred. That was the only explanation for why his handler leaned into Travis's workspace almost two hours to the minute after the confrontation.

"This can't wait," his handler said, heavy tension in his voice. "We need to talk. Now." He jerked his head toward the door, gesturing for Travis to follow him.

"Not out with the smokers, dude," Travis protested as they headed outside. "My lungs can't take any more."

The handler didn't answer, but he walked them out farther, until they were strolling through the parking lot. He pointed to a shuttle bus stop and then walked away without another word.

Jeff, Travis's old mentor, was waiting for him in the deserted bus shelter. Travis hadn't seen him since training—their last contact had been the quick phone call that had set Travis up with his handler. Jeff didn't bother to greet him—he just stood and started to walk farther into the parking lot, obviously expecting Travis to keep up. "What the fuck were you thinking?" he finally exploded when they were far enough away from the building.

Travis winced. "Okay, I shouldn't have yelled at my boss. But I didn't say anything specific, I swear."

"'You have no idea what I've accomplished…I'm getting something done,'" Jeff said in a mocking falsetto. "You don't need to tell them anything specific, damn it—they can figure it out on their own if they start digging." He looked over his shoulder to make sure no one else was around. "Do you understand the position you've put me in? I vouched for you. You know my name. If *you* go down, *I* go down."

Travis put his hands up in mock surrender. He was confused. He'd screwed up, sure, but it wasn't *that* big a deal, was it? "Calm down, man. Look, worst-case scenario, I may have implied that I was involved in something. And I'm sorry for that, I really am. But honestly? I think you're overreacting a bit. I mean, we're all supposed to be on the same team in there." He jerked his head back to the CIA headquarters building. "Right? I know our ops are supposed to be compartmentalized, but everyone in that building has a top-secret clearance. And it's not like we've done anything illegal. Your buddies said that our ops were cleared from the top. So what's the problem?"

Jeff shook his head and looked up at the sky. He started to say something but then stopped himself. Finally, grim-faced, he spoke in a quiet voice. "You're right. Nobody knows any details. Just do us all a favor and try to keep your mouth shut, okay? Go to your training class; don't attract any more attention. We'll tap someone else for Mexico City. It'll be fine." He stalked away, leaving Travis in the parking lot.

What was that about? Travis wondered. He wasn't a complete novice—he hadn't leaked anything important. Jeff obviously had some anger issues, combined with more than a touch of paranoia. He'd get over it, though. Mexico City may be off, but Travis knew that there would be more ops. From what he had seen of the group so far, they needed all the help they could get. He'd have another chance to prove himself soon enough.

CHAPTER NINETEEN

Shit. Shitshitshitshitshit. Dara was enough of a pro to not reveal her distress, but she was pretty damn distressed. As soon as she stepped off the plane into Dubai's pristine airport, she and a dozen other travelers had been herded by a trio of armed customs and immigration officers to a queue designated for iris scanning.

Dubai had been using biometric technology on a selective basis for years; iris scanning had proven to be a quick and easy way to nab criminals and travelers using stolen or counterfeit passports. But Dara didn't meet any of the criteria that they usually used to select which travelers would be put through a scan. Trying her best to appear nonchalant, her mind raced. In all likelihood, she knew, she had probably been selected because she happened to have been in the vicinity of someone who *did* fit the profiling criteria.

Since she was traveling in true name, the iris scan wouldn't normally pose a threat to her. Unfortunately, Dara had been selected for iris scanning once before—while traveling in alias. She had been working a counterterrorism operation jointly with the Jordanian intel service. Tariq had paired her up with his biggest, burliest, most-likely-to-protect-her-just-in-case officer. Dara knew that the man was actually a quiet, gentle soul, but he had the face of a killer. Unfortunately, Tariq's protective instincts had backfired, and her burly travel companion's appearance had caused them to be selected for additional screening.

Dara knew all too well that once the details of a person's iris scan were recorded into Dubai's advanced biometric system, they were permanently matched with the name and identifying details from the traveler's passport. That meant that Dara's irises were about to tell the Emirati officers minding the process that her name was Chloe Smithson instead of the name on the passport in her hand.

There were only four people ahead of her in line.

Dara's mind raced through the possible options. *Flee?* Not possible in Dubai's well-monitored airport. *Feign illness?* Dropping into a faint or racing to a restroom would only heighten the attention on her. *Pull the indignant "don't you know who I am" routine?* She did have contacts in the Emirati intelligence service, but she couldn't drop their names without identifying herself as an intel officer. *Bluff?* She could try, but she knew that customs and immigration officers had heard all the excuses a hundred times; they tended to be a cynical bunch. *Bribe?* Anywhere else, maybe, but Dubai was a wealthy place, and the cash in her pocket wasn't likely to do much to persuade anyone to look the other way.

With only one jittery-looking elderly man in front of her, Dara decided she'd just have to face the consequences and call in her contacts from a jail cell, if it came to that. It wouldn't be her first time in a cell, and as a Western female, she knew she would have the luxury of being released none the worse for the experience.

It was humiliating on a professional level, though. Getting caught like this was for amateurs, and Dara should have known better. She did know better. One name, one airport. You simply didn't mix alias identities and border crossings; it was clandestine ops 101. She'd just been so damned anxious to get back in the game that she'd taken a stupid chance.

And now she was about to get caught.

Taking a deep breath, Dara squared her shoulders and stepped forward to the eye scan as the man in front of her was screened and waved along in a matter of seconds. She handed over her passport without a word and looked into the scanner.

Someone barked something at her and she froze, waiting for the other officers to swarm over. She knew that they probably wouldn't be rough with her, but she hoped that they would at least let her keep her carry-on bag when they put her in the holding cell.

The officer looked annoyed. He spoke again in English, this time sounding impatient. "Madam, please move along. We have many people waiting behind you."

Masking her surprise, Dara apologized and stepped away, unhindered, toward the regular customs queue.

She had been cleared.

Instead of feeling grateful, Dara felt suspicious. She was certain that her iris scan should have been flagged. Perhaps there was a technical problem with the biometric system? She'd heard of one instance in the US when it was discovered that airport metal detectors had inadvertently been left unplugged for days. Thousands of passengers had been waved through the nonfunctioning—and therefore non-beeping—machines. It could happen here too. If that was the case, she should catch the next flight out of the country. There was a chance that the results were only delayed and that the authorities would eventually see the discrepancy between the names.

But even as she acknowledged the possibility of a well-timed technical glitch, she had a sneaking suspicion that the scanner was working just fine. If someone had tampered with the information in the database, on the other hand, then her record would be clean, and she would be free to travel into Dubai again.

She knew just the person who might have done such a thing. And, far from being a good thing, it meant that her unwelcome "savior" knew exactly when and where she was traveling. Which meant that this clandestine investigation of hers wasn't quite so clandestine after all.

She hiked up the strap of her carry-on bag and headed toward the airport exit, fuming. She had some people to see right now, but she knew that she would have to deal with this new problem sooner rather than later.

CHAPTER TWENTY

Twelve hours later, Dara was exhausted. The luxury hotels of Dubai were frustratingly discreet. No one working at any of the bars where Caitlin had seduced her targets remembered anyone remotely resembling either Caitlin or Jonathan. They could have been refusing to divulge information in order to maintain their employers' reputations as places where wealthy men from the Gulf countries could frolic and sin in peace. Or, more likely, Dara realized as she looked around, Caitlin's antics had just looked like business as usual. At each of the bars she visited, Dara saw more than one coupling of an older Arab man and a younger foreign woman. And blondes definitely seemed to have more fun in Dubai—or, at least they seemed to be overrepresented among the young, female bar patrons. Caitlin would have blended in perfectly.

In spite of her better judgment, Dara found herself admitting that Operation Golden Mean was simple and effective. Sleazy as hell, but effective. She couldn't condone what Jonathan and Caitlin had done, but she was familiar enough with their frustration with the CIA's increasing impotence that she could at least grudgingly respect them for *trying* to get results. But what she still couldn't understand was how their actions, which, frankly, had the operational sophistication of a fraternity prank, ended up with Jonathan dead and Caitlin terrified—of what or of whom Dara still did not know.

Dara checked into her hotel, took a quick shower, and then debated which phone call to make first.

She chose the easiest. She was working on a serious sleep deficit, and the second call could be a long one.

She grabbed a bottle of sparkling water from the minibar and then made the call on a clean GSM phone that she had swiped from headquarters. CIA officers went through mobile phones like candy. She still remembered the number she had to dial, even though several years had passed since she last used it. She just hoped that Yousef would answer.

He did.

"*Assalamu alaikum*, you handsome devil."

Yousef roared with laughter as he recognized her voice. "I wondered if I would ever hear from you again, my iron-fisted angel."

Dara smiled. She'd always been fond of Yousef, even when he was being a giant pain in the ass. "Yes, it's been awhile. I need to see you, though. As soon as possible."

"For you, I'll hop on the first flight of the day tomorrow. The usual place, I assume?"

Dara confirmed, glad that Yousef had remembered to speak cautiously on the phone. He damn well should; she was the one who had trained him to use secure tradecraft. He was a happy-go-lucky guy, so the lessons hadn't stuck easily, but Dara had hammered away at him until he finally agreed to her "silly little codes and precautions." He may have been difficult to teach, but Dara noted with satisfaction that they had gotten through their entire brief phone conversation without once mentioning any names or locations. She also knew that if he said the first flight of the day, then he would actually be on the second.

Dara checked her watch. It was getting late. Yousef was coming from Doha, which was only a short commuter flight from Dubai, so he would be there early the next morning. She decided that her second phone call could wait another day or two.

She set an alarm and crawled under the duvet covers, smiling a little. It felt good to be back in the game.

CHAPTER TWENTY-ONE

Dara woke up early the next morning and treated herself to one of her favorite indulgences: room service breakfast. Still wearing her bathrobe, she happily dug into an omelet big enough for two hungry people. She wasn't normally a big fan of regular bacon, but she loved the turkey bacon that was served in upscale hotels in the Middle East as a compromise between Western visitors and non-pork-eating Muslims. As she cleaned her plate, she thought about her history with the man she was about to meet for the first time in several years.

In many ways, Yousef al-Kuwari was the perfect asset. He was eager to please, spoke a half-dozen languages, and was ridiculously easy to motivate. Yousef was highly susceptible to flattery; the thicker Dara laid it on, the better. He also liked money. Quite a lot, in fact, since he fancied himself to be an underfunded jet-setter. And Yousef was also willing to do just about anything in exchange for a steady supply of Jack Daniels, which, to his credit, he did not actually drink, but which he liked to pass out as gifts or small bribes in the course of his never-ending quest to play the role of an important mover and shaker. More than anything, though, Yousef seemed to think that working for the CIA was an amusing game. This, Dara knew, made him sloppy and careless, but eminently willing.

Yousef's access to valuable information stemmed mostly from his impossibly large family. He had what seemed to be an unlimited number of cousins, uncles, and nephews spread out all over the Persian Gulf states and beyond. Thanks in part to the Jack Daniels, or so he claimed, they were all clamoring to provide him with bigger and better secrets to pass along to his "contacts."

When she pressed about the exact nature of Yousef's connection to these sources, Dara had come to realize that many of them could only be considered relatives in the loosest, most indirect terms. There were friends, neighbors, and cousins of friends thrown into Yousef's grab bag of sources. Back when she was running him as an asset, Dara had very carefully researched and confirmed two of these familial connections in particular. For all of his dubiously credible tips and overeager reports, Yousef's real value to the intelligence world was very specific.

Yousef's main contribution to the CIA had been his ability to deliver full copies of the videos and voice recordings that groups linked to al-Qaeda provided to the Al Jazeera television news network. He was able to do this because someone, somewhere, had long ago identified him as a convenient middleman. He had a cousin—three times removed, according to Dara's research— who had briefly spent time in an al-Qaeda training camp before deciding that jihad wasn't for him. This cousin must have somehow left on good terms, though, because he was the one who delivered the "terrorist tapes," as CIA analysts called them, to Yousef. Yousef then passed the recordings to his sister's husband, who was a program director at Al Jazeera.

Yousef's willingness to provide copies of the recordings to the CIA was a more important contribution than most people realized at first. Intelligence agencies, as well as news networks all over the globe, depended on Al Jazeera to broadcast full and

complete versions of the threats, boasts, and various other dia-
tribes sent in by terrorist organizations. And while it was in Al
Jazeera's best interests to pass along as much information as they
received, there was invariably editing. Sometimes the terrorist
tapes were edited down for time, since certain groups in particular tended to prefer lengthy, verbose rants over pithy eloquence.
On more than a few occasions, the content was deemed—by
government officials more often than network honchos—too
inflammatory to release to a volatile public. Most often, though,
Al Jazeera would air the full content of the message but leave out
the messy beginning and end for no reason other than the two
minutes of the camera guy messing with the lens before the real
show started wasn't what viewers wanted to see.

For CIA analysts, these cutting room floor scraps were a
treasure chest of information. The actual speeches recorded on
the terrorist tapes were scripted and rehearsed. The scenes cut
innocently by news networks were the ones most likely to contain someone slipping up and calling someone else by his true
name or inadvertently recording some sort of detail that could be
used to identify the whereabouts of the people on the tape.

Yousef was able to provide the *complete* version of the al-
Qaeda communications. Several times he had even been able
to provide the original recording. In one of those cases, which
involved dated VHS technology, technical specialists in the CIA
had been able to extract earlier data that had been recorded over.
The terrorists had recycled a videotape that had been previously
used to record the martyr statements of several of the group's
members. The videotaped statements included the participants
speaking directly into the camera, undisguised, and stating their
full names for the record. The cameraman apparently thought
that recording over the old footage would erase it forever. In fact,

the information extracted from the earlier recording had given the CIA enough information to put together a raid that took down a major al-Qaeda safe house and averted a major attack.

But for all of his important contributions to the war on terror, Yousef ultimately proved himself to have one critical flaw that undermined everything else he did. He had, as Dara put it during a secure videoconference with headquarters, a "teensy problem with honesty."

Dara was convinced that Yousef didn't lie on purpose. He just tended to make promises that he couldn't keep, and he didn't like to disappoint anyone. So when Dara asked him questions, Yousef liked to provide answers, even if those answers were not always entirely accurate.

Dara had tried to defend Yousef during the videoconference. "His information may not be one hundred percent accurate, but when he does deliver, he delivers big. I think it's worth sifting through some junk reports to get to the good stuff."

She was overruled. The chief of the analytical group had conveyed headquarters' consensus: "If we know he lies to us sometimes, then we have to assume he's lying to us always."

Dara sighed into her coffee mug as she remembered those words. Tariq was right. Americans, or CIA officials at least, really did think in black-and-white. Personally, she thought it was foolish to have complete faith in *anyone*, but she'd had no choice but to terminate contact with Yousef. She had at least managed to talk headquarters into authorizing a generous payment as a parting gift. In her opinion, it was always best to have spies walk away happy. Now she was doubly glad that she had fought for the payoff—it meant that Yousef owed her a favor.

She finished the last of her breakfast and got dressed. They were meeting in a small café located on the outskirts of Dubai's textile marketplace. One of Dara's colleagues had recommended the spot because it was nearly impossible for surveillance to keep tabs on anyone inside without revealing themselves. Dara wanted to get there first so that she could watch Yousef's approach to see if anyone was trailing him.

As usual, Yousef arrived exactly nineteen minutes late. He had always been uncannily punctual in his tardiness, almost as if someone had taught him early in life that anything less than twenty minutes late was actually on time. Dara, who had been trained to use plus or minus three minutes as the maximum allowable time window during operations, had learned to adjust. It was just Yousef's way.

"Good morning, my beautiful drill sergeant, my favorite minder, my benevolent overseer." Yousef greeted her with a bear hug that drew glares from several of the more conservative patrons.

Dara used the embrace to scan the crowd over Yousef's shoulder, focusing on the two spots that she had earlier identified as the most likely locations for surveillance to set up. She didn't see anything suspicious.

"Yousef, my friend, you are looking better than ever. Life must be treating you well." Yousef preened in response to her flattery.

Several cups of tea later, and Dara got to the point. "So are you still playing delivery boy?"

Yousef sat back in his chair, pouting as he crossed his arms over his chest. His generous severance payment may have kept him on speaking terms with Dara, but he was still sore about losing his Jack Daniels supplier. "Yes, I am. And I probably shouldn't tell you this, but I will. Your people may not want what I have, but plenty of others do. I had a regular bidding war for my services, and guess who won?" He didn't bother waiting for Dara to guess. "The French. They don't pay as well as you used to, but they also don't mind if I freelance here and there when the price is right."

Dara knew that Yousef was playing a dangerous game by offering his services to anyone with access to cash, but she also knew that she couldn't stop him. He had always acted as if he were invincible. "Just be careful, Yousef."

He waved her off and lit a cigarette. She let him smoke and sulk for a few minutes before she started again, this time proceeding more cautiously.

"Have your new French clients had any luck tracing the tapes?" This had always been a sensitive subject. Yousef had no qualms about handing over the tapes, but he had always been protective of his cousin. He had refused to press for details about how he acquired the tapes. Dara had once asked if she could meet the cousin, and Yousef had laughed at her.

"That would be a very, very bad idea," he had told her. "He isn't a bad man or a terrorist. He's just…angry. And he hates Americans very much. Anything else, though, I will do for you. Anything at all. Just ask." He had changed the subject in a hurry.

Yousef's refusal hadn't deterred the CIA. Determined to trace the tapes back to the original source, they had located the cousin and put round-the-clock surveillance on him for the better part of a year. In spite of the fact that he had passed several tapes to Yousef during that period, though, they had never once been able to figure out who had passed the information to *him*. It was as if the tapes just magically materialized in his possession.

"You Americans are so competitive!" Yousef grinned at her now. "No, the French haven't had any more luck than you did. Nor will they. I told you that my cousin is very clever."

Dara suppressed a brief urge to gloat. Intelligence services *were* competitive, and it would have grated on her if the French had succeeded where she had failed. "Okay, Yousef, the main reason I needed to meet with you is to find out whether you can get me any details about a video that was aired first by Al Jazeera. We haven't been able to identify the group responsible, but we know it's not from any of your cousin's usual sources. I just thought that your brother-in-law might be able to provide information about how the network got the tape."

"Which video are you talking about?" He had a strange glint in his eye.

"The video showing Jonathan Wolff, the young CIA officer, being executed."

"Ha!" Yousef slapped his hands down on the table, grinning widely. "That was me!"

Momentarily stunned by his bizarre reaction, Dara didn't respond at first.

"I told you. I'm freelancing now. It wasn't from my cousin, but *I* still delivered that video to Al Jazeera." He winked at Dara. "Now aren't you starting to regret firing me?"

Dara stopped herself from tearing into Yousef. He was shallow, foolish, and unprincipled, but she needed him. Besides, he was, as he had always been, a naïve young man who seemed to believe that he was playing a part in a movie rather than engaging in very real and potentially very dangerous operations. She took a deep breath and forced herself to speak in a neutral tone. "Why don't you start from the beginning, Yousef."

Basking in the attention, he started to talk. "After you left, I needed a little extra cash. So I let certain people know that I had connections that could help them get their messages out to the world. My sister made her husband promise to help me out. He whined a bit, but she is a very stubborn woman, and eventually he agreed. So a few months ago I got a call from someone I didn't know..."

As Yousef spoke, Dara grew uneasy. Standing in one of the few vantage points outside the café was a man she was sure she had seen before. One of the rules of surveillance detection is that if you spot the same person multiple times over time, distance, and change of direction, then you are most likely being followed. Dara had spotted this man several hours ago, as she left her hotel on the opposite side of town. It *could* have been coincidence, but she didn't think so. In general, the people staying in the luxury hotels of Dubai were not the same sorts of people lingering around the textile market. That was one of the reasons she had chosen this spot in the first place. As she watched, another man joined the first one. The newcomer didn't look familiar, but from this distance she couldn't be certain. The two men stood without speaking, staring intently at the café.

She leaned forward across the table and spoke to Yousef in a low voice. "Do *not* react to what I'm about to say. Do *not* turn around, but I'm concerned that we may have someone watching us."

Yousef, being Yousef, whirled around instantly to look. The two men seemed to realize they had been spotted, and they both faded instantly into the crowd, disappearing as if they had never been there at all.

"I don't see anyone," Yousef said.

"Well, I don't like it." Dara's instincts were on fire. Something was happening—she could feel it. "We need to leave now. I'll go right and catch a cab at the corner. You exit left and then walk through the market to the taxi stand on the other side of the block. Get out of the area as soon as possible." She stood up to leave.

"Dara, wait, wait." He looked sheepish. "I didn't tell you, because I thought you might get angry. My nephew heard I was coming to Dubai, and he wanted to come along so that he could go shopping for his girlfriend. It's nothing—I swear. He just thinks the jewelry here is better quality and a better price."

"You said you didn't see anyone." Dara didn't like to take chances.

He hesitated. "I didn't, but I'm sure it's him. I told him to wait for me a few blocks away, but he's a stupid boy, and he never listens to me."

"What does he look like?"

Yousef hesitated. "Uh, he has black hair, medium build, average height. Looks a bit like me, but not too much."

Dara bit the inside of her cheek in frustration. Yousef had just described eighty-five percent of the men walking around Dubai. Including, she had to admit, the man she had seen watching them. She wanted to believe him, if for no other reason than she had a lot more questions to ask. But the voice of the chief analyst back at headquarters rang in her mind. *If we know he lies to us sometimes, then we have to assume he's lying to us always.* "But there were two of them."

Yousef shrugged his shoulders. "He has lots of friends."

After a brief moment of hesitation, Dara made up her mind, hoping she wasn't overreacting. "For your safety and mine, we need to abort this meeting." As a small concession to her lingering hope that she was just being paranoid, she thrust a pad of paper at him. "Quickly, write down everything you know about who gave you the video. Name, address, all of it."

He rolled his eyes at her, but did what he was told. When she glanced at his scribbled notes, she sat back in her chair. "But this address is in Spain. I don't get it."

Yousef flashed his trademark smile. "Yes, I guess I'm moving up in the world. They paid for me to fly to Barcelona, and even gave me some extra spending money so I could stay for a few days. Now *that's* a city where people know how to have fun."

Dara was surprised, but she knew she needed to get Yousef out of there. She'd have to piece together the rest of the facts on her own. She promised to be in touch soon, shooed Yousef out the door, and headed in the opposite direction.

"Dara, wait!"

Dara winced as he shouted her name and jogged back to her in full view of the crowds. "I forgot to tell you one thing. Maybe it's important?"

She gritted her teeth impatiently. She was already breaking operational security protocol left and right. "What?" she hissed.

"The guy who gave me the tape. He was an American."

CHAPTER TWENTY-TWO

Dominic Cahill was acutely aware of the fact that he was a victim of his own ambitions. He sometimes regretted that he hadn't been content to saunter off to a job at one of the investment banks when he graduated from Princeton, the way most of his friends had. No, he had insisted on joining the CIA, just like his father and his father's father. And, of course, being mulishly ambitious also meant that he needed to rise to levels higher than his forefathers, succeed where they had failed, and generally just show them up. His younger brother, who shared no such pesky ambitions, *had* shuffled off to the banking world, where at age thirty-two he was already a multimillionaire with a weekend home in the Hamptons and a wife who looked every bit the runway model she had been prior to being swept off her feet.

Dominic, on the other hand, was still languishing just south of senior management, collecting a government salary that was only now starting to resemble what his Princeton classmates had *started* at fifteen years before, and still smarting from a recent divorce.

It would all be worth it, though, if he managed to achieve his goal. He didn't need fame or fortune.

He just wanted to run the show.

He wanted to be the youngest CIA director in history. He wanted to control the strings of the organization that controlled the strings of the rest of the world.

He hadn't told anyone his goal—certainly never his father—because he knew how ridiculous it sounded. He realized that other people would dismiss him as a power-hungry megalomaniac.

That wasn't the case, though. He wasn't some caricature of a dictator-in-training. He didn't have any ulterior motives in striving for his goal, or any particular plans once he had succeeded. He simply believed that he had the unique combination of attributes that made his goal a valid possibility. For better or worse, those attributes included the ambitious streak that was now causing him considerable grief. Intelligence operations were in his blood. His grandfather and then his father had made their marks on the world's chalkboard; Dominic thought it only natural for him to achieve what they had, and then more. That wasn't hubris, he reasoned. That was evolution.

Still, he kept his mouth shut about his goal. He worked hard, he rose fast, and he became part of the inner circle. He had a long way to go, but he was on the right trajectory.

But as he had recently discovered, being the junior member of the inner circle wasn't always a desirable role to play. These days he felt more like a gofer or a lackey than he ever had, even during his first few years in the CIA straight out of college.

Today's task was no exception.

Today he had to go through the hoop-jumping exercise that passed for secure communications between several uniquely paranoid individuals. They had good reason to be paranoid, he knew, but that didn't make his task any less of a pain in the ass. He grumbled as he made his way down seven floors and then out to the parking lot.

Within the walls of the CIA's headquarters, you had to be even more careful than in the outside world. Big Brother was alive and well in Langley. No, scratch that—Big Brother was *created* in Langley. E-mails were monitored, phone calls were recorded, and there were cameras *everywhere*. You couldn't even hold a discreet car meeting in the parking garage anymore, after an infamous and recently retired deputy director had been caught *in flagrante delicto* in his car with a much younger staffer who bore absolutely no resemblance to his wife. A red-faced security officer had waited until he finished and then politely asked him to discontinue his backseat liaisons. Soon thereafter cameras were quietly installed even in the executive parking garage.

But there was always a way.

Dominic had initially thought himself quite clever for the strategy he had devised. It was designed, ostensibly, to maintain separation between the parties involved. More importantly, it had been developed to ensure that Dominic had access to every aspect of the operation. He was the man in the middle, the constant presence, the hub. He had clawed his way up to the top; there was no way he was going to risk being cut out of the loop. Lately, though, he'd been kicking himself for not anticipating the headaches that this role would cause him.

Fortunately, communicating with one of the parties involved was easy. It didn't require sneaking around at all hours and in all weather; there were no phones or other non-secure electronics involved, and there was no paper trail.

Dominic just had to step into his boss's office and close the door.

A closed-door meeting between Dominic, the newest special assistant to the director, and the director of Central Intelligence wasn't at all suspicious, of course. There was always a perfectly valid reason.

Today's meeting, for example, had been scheduled so that Dominic could brief DCI Abram Hendricks on an important budgetary matter. Hendricks pondered the documents Dominic had delivered, reached a decision, and dictated part of the response that Dominic would draft that afternoon. Anyone looking into the purpose of the closed-door meeting would find an abundance of related documentation, all dated and time-stamped appropriately.

But what they discussed next would not be documented anywhere.

"Status." Abram Hendricks had a commander's habit of giving one-word orders to anyone he perceived as beneath him, as if they didn't merit the extra breath a complete sentence would require.

Dominic knew exactly what he was asking. "We're making progress. Dara McIntyre has stepped right into the investigator's role. In fact, she's making connections faster than we anticipated. She was—*is*—a smart enough officer. She'll do what's necessary."

Hendricks frowned. "Don't make it too easy for her. The facts have to come to light in the course of a proper investigation, not because we dropped hints in her lap. She'll be suspicious unless she has to work for the information."

Dominic nodded and then started gathering his papers, assuming their meeting was over for the day.

"We're not finished here."

Dominic winced at the tone of rebuke in the director's voice and sat back down.

"This threat absolutely has to be contained. Soon. Do you know how bad it looks when officers under my command get executed? It makes me look incompetent. Like I can't protect my people." Hendricks pointed at Dominic as if he were already accusing him. "I hope you aren't limiting your options to one officer with a spotty record."

Dominic considered his response carefully. The fact of the matter was that it had been the director himself who had ordered Dominic to involve as few people as possible. Lining up a plan B or a plan C in case Dara didn't work out would have meant more people would have to have been brought in. Abram Hendricks, however, did not like to have his contradictions pointed out to him.

Dominic gave as diplomatic an answer as he could manage. "We don't have anyone else standing by, but we do have a variety of options available to us regarding Ms. McIntyre's level of involvement."

The answer seemed to satisfy the DCI. "Fine, but we're under serious time constraints. Take it up to the next level now. We don't want her to get...distracted." He gestured dismissively and turned to his computer.

Dominic nodded sharply, as if that made perfect sense to him. More often than not, though, he found himself at least slightly uncertain of what exactly Hendricks wanted from him. At first he had attributed it to his lack of field experience. During his first few weeks working for Hendricks, Dominic had gone home every day feeling as if he were missing something important that everyone else already knew, and that perhaps he wasn't smart enough or experienced enough to succeed. But little by little he had started to notice that other people—officials with far more years of service than he had—also tended to walk out of meetings with the director with looks of mild confusion on their faces. Finally Dominic had concluded that the DCI intentionally spoke in ambiguous, abstract terms whenever he was unsure about how to proceed, in stark contrast to his normal, bombastic way of ordering people around. The man could spend hours spouting minutiae about his own accomplishments, but change the subject to something less self-congratulatory and it was as if someone hit a mute button. The combined effect meant that equivocation mode replaced command and control mode whenever Hendricks was nervous. That way, if things went wrong, he could always say that he had been misinterpreted, or even disobeyed. Dominic actually sort of admired this, even though it sometimes made his own job difficult. Like today, when Dominic could have really used some clarity. But Hendricks was not a man who liked to clarify, even under the best circumstances. Moreover, the DCI liked to have the last word during every conversation. Asking questions was not the way to get ahead in this organization. So Dominic left, as many had before him, in puzzled silence.

Now, as he left the building in a foul mood, Dominic vowed to take more control over the next conversation on his agenda. He hated the fact that he always seemed to leave the DCI's office feeling like an idiot. The person he was contacting next also tried to treat him like a peon, but Dominic wasn't going to let it happen this time. After all, this was someone who, strictly speaking, never should have been permitted to take part in any kind of US intelligence operation in the first place. He was certainly not authorized to receive classified information, although Dominic had observed that above a certain level within the CIA, the rules governing classifications and unauthorized disclosures seemed to be viewed as optional.

The logistics required for the next discussion were not quite as simple as walking into someone's office, though, and Dominic first needed to concentrate on placing his call without making any careless mistakes. He wasn't field qualified and had never gone through any operational training, but you can't help but pick things up when you work for the CIA.

Dominic drove his car off of the headquarters compound and didn't stop until he was certain that his call would not be transmitted via the cell towers closest to the CIA's main building. It was a small precaution, but it would impede anyone trying to sort through phone calls made by CIA employees by focusing on the call's point of origin.

He removed the cell phone from his glove compartment and rummaged around for the battery. He had learned that phones could still be geo-located even when they were turned off, unless the battery was removed. He had purchased the phone with cash and then later bought a card with top-up minutes from a gas station, also with cash. He used this particular phone to call one person, and only one person. His call recipient had a similarly dedicated phone.

He wiped his perspiring hands on his pants, irritated. He didn't know why *he* should be nervous. These calls always seemed to set him on edge.

He pulled a slip of paper out of his pocket; on it he had written a phone number in his own rudimentary code. He'd given up trying to memorize the number. With several safe combinations, his multiple computer passwords, the pin number that allowed him to enter the building, plus the separate pin number for the executive offices, his head was too full of numbers already. On the slip of paper, each number he had written was one less than the number he actually had to dial. So when his notes said 2, he needed to dial a 3. It was simple, childish even, but it still took him several minutes to make sure that he had entered the numbers correctly.

The phone rang seven times before anyone picked up. Dominic gritted his teeth. It was just like the bastard to make him worry that no one would answer.

"Yo, Jeeves." It was him.

They had agreed never to use real names during their calls, but Dominic loathed the man's habit of using belittling nicknames. He cleared his throat and spoke. "The boss wants to see results soon. You need to pick up the pace. *Our* way this time." Dominic tried to emulate the director's ability to issue vague instructions that could be interpreted in several different ways if things went wrong.

The other man laughed at him. "The *boss* isn't really in a position to be calling the shots, now is he?"

Dominic grimaced. These calls never went as he intended.

The other man spoke again before Dominic could respond. "You know what, though, sport? I'm feeling extra cooperative today. Besides, I think this could get fun. You want me to pick up the pace? I can do that. But you know what I just realized? I just realized that there's a hell of a lot of room in your comment for interpretation. How about you be a pal and get a little more specific. How about you tell me *exactly* what you have in mind."

The bastard was baiting him, and Dominic knew it. He was almost certainly recording the conversation, and other people might be listening in even as they spoke. Dominic chose his words carefully. "We need to be sure that our newest team member stays motivated. We need her to finish the job she started."

The man laughed again, longer this time. "No problem, chief. I'll *motivate* our lady friend. Just leave it to me." He clicked off the phone.

Dominic removed his phone's battery, put it back into the glove compartment, and started his car, feeling nauseated. He had just delivered a message that he didn't fully understand to a man who seemed to take pride in intentionally misinterpreting *him*. He was setting things into motion, but he wasn't sure which direction they were heading.

But at least he was in the loop. He had worked hard enough to get here that he wasn't going to be pushed out by one dead-end operation gone wrong. He put the details of the phone call out of his mind and headed back to work.

CHAPTER TWENTY-THREE

Back in her hotel room, Dara showered quickly. She had completed an exhausting, three-hour surveillance-detection route after her meeting with Yousef. If someone had been following her, she would have spotted them as she traversed the city using a route designed to draw out her pursuers. But then again, if they already knew where she was staying, there would be no need for them to follow her. They could have just skipped the exercise and waited in the air-conditioned lobby of her hotel while she switched in and out of taxis, wandered through crowded markets, and entered and exited various parking garages, stairwells, and office buildings through different doors.

She hadn't detected any surveillance, nor did she recognize any of the faces she scanned in the hotel lobby. Still, her nerves were buzzing, and she was on high alert. Catching sight of two men who may or may not have been innocently waiting for Yousef didn't fully account for the suspicion she felt, though. Her decision to abort the meeting had been more instinctual than anything. She was a good officer, and she knew it. If her spidey senses were tingling, then she was going to act accordingly.

She had already booked a new flight out of the country, and now she had some time to kill before she had to leave for the airport. *Damn*, she thought. Plenty of time to make a phone call she wasn't looking forward to. She was out of excuses.

She dialed the number from memory, half-hoping no one answered.

"Alo." He answered on the first ring.

She didn't bother identifying herself; he knew her voice. "A funny thing just happened to me, and it made me think of you. I've just managed to travel into a country where I should, technically speaking, not have been allowed to enter. Any chance you might have had something to do with this?"

He laughed warmly. "A gift from me to you, darling Dara. How's the weather in Dubai?"

She felt her anger evaporating, and a smile edged at the corners of her mouth. She shook it off. This was serious, and she couldn't let him distract her. "You shouldn't have done that, Tariq."

"It was only fair. It was my officer who got you spotted by the immigration goons the last time you were there; they never would have pulled you out of line for iris scanning if you had been alone. Plus I recently cultivated a new...*friend* there who is quite handy with data, shall we say. I just made sure that you had a nice, clean record in the computer system there before you arrived."

"And how, may I ask, did you know I'd be traveling here?" Dara asked, even though she already knew the answer.

"My love, it was *your* government who provided us with the tools to monitor travelers throughout the Middle East. Your American analysts have never quite seemed to get the hang of keeping track of Arabic names. We're all named Mohammed Mohammed as far as they seem to be able to tell. My government offered to help out, and here we are. Or, more accurately, there *you* are."

Dara felt a juvenile impulse to stamp her feet in frustration. He was right. The CIA and the NSA had essentially outsourced some of their monitoring functions when they discovered that they simply couldn't keep up with the volume of data they were collecting as part of the war on terror.

"You aren't supposed to be using it against American citizens," she said angrily. "I seem to recall hearing you make that commitment with my own ears when *I* briefed you into the program." But even as she chastised him, she was also pleased—not that she'd ever admit it. His actions were highly inappropriate. But they were the highly inappropriate actions of a man who still cared.

"Mistakes happen, Dara. Sometimes we just stumble upon bits of information that turn out to be very useful later on." Tariq was teasing her. "So," he continued, "you can just go ahead and *tell* me where you're heading next, or else I'll simply have to rely on another 'mistake.'" His voice grew serious. "Dara, I know you are trying to do the right thing, but I am under no obligation to your superiors. I want to be a part of your life. Until *you* tell me otherwise, I plan to be. Even if I have to be...creative about it."

Dara bit her lip and felt her resolve weaken. She had been instructed, under no uncertain terms, to cease all contact with Tariq. Her job depended on it. More and more, though, her job was feeling less important. Less of a priority. Less of her identity. Plus, she reasoned, he *could* easily track her movements with just a few keystrokes. She sat down on the edge of the bed. "Spain," she said finally. "I'm going to Spain." She refused to let her mind wander to the possible outcomes of this revelation.

"I'm sure you'll enjoy your trip. In fact, I know a wonderful tapas bar just a few short blocks off of Plaza Catalunya," he said.

"They serve the best *gambas al ajillo* you'll ever eat." She could almost hear him smiling on the other end of the phone.

It took Dara a second to realize what he had said. Plaza Catalunya was a central location in Barcelona—exactly where she was headed next. "Damn it, Tariq, I didn't tell you I was going to Barcelona. I just said that I was going to Spain. I only made my flight reservations a few minutes ago!"

"Oh, is there a Plaza Catalunya in Barcelona?" His voice was full of mock innocence. "Just a lucky guess on my part. And will you look at the time? You'd better hurry to the airport if you want to make your flight."

"I'm hanging up now before you get both of us in more trouble than we're already in," Dara said with a smile before she put down the phone. "Good-bye, Tariq." She needed to be cautious. Tariq was playing games that could make her lose her job. But the mere possibility that he might just be crazy enough to show up in Spain was irresistible.

Is he worth losing my job over? Dara hadn't thought so when she left Jordan—or at least she hadn't allowed herself to answer the question truthfully. She hadn't even allowed herself to consider it. But lately she *had* started to consider it. And now she was less certain of the answer to this question every time she heard Tariq's voice. Seeing him in person would almost certainly destroy her resolve to be practical, to play by the rules. And, she was starting to realize, that might not be such a bad thing after all.

She grabbed her carry-on bag and slammed out of her room, cursing under her breath as she glanced at her watch. As crazy as his antics were making her, Tariq had been right about the time. She did need to hurry to the airport.

CHAPTER TWENTY-FOUR

Caitlin looked at her wrinkled fingers. She would have stayed in her lavender-scented sanctuary even longer if the water hadn't cooled off to a chilly room temperature. She debated adding more hot water but then convinced herself to get out. She'd been in the bathtub for ages already. She still hadn't called a doctor's office to ask about the safety of hot baths for pregnant women, or even to make a first appointment. It wasn't that she was in denial, she reasoned. She was just…waiting. Waiting to see what would happen next.

"Time to get moving," she said out loud, even though there was nowhere she had to be.

She had left work early that day—even earlier than usual. Dara wasn't in the office, and no one else dared to give her any projects. They all avoided her like the plague, as if her husband's bad luck might be contagious.

Even Tony had been scarce lately, when for weeks it had felt like she couldn't escape his constant hovering. *Could he know?* Caitlin wondered if Tony had figured out that she had dropped his name. Ratted him out. Tattled. It was possible. He always seemed to know everything before anyone else did. For all Caitlin knew, Dara could have already approached him—could have already started asking questions about him.

But Caitlin didn't think so.

If Tony knew what she had done, she'd probably be dead by now.

She shivered slightly, but only because the water felt cold. The idea of death—of dying—had lost its chill after what happened to Jonathan. When the alternatives to death were as bleak as hers, the threat of Tony or one of his lackeys murdering her lost a considerable deal of its previous deterrence.

But that didn't mean she was giving up just yet.

She actually hadn't intended to give his name to Dara. She had walked into the meeting fully intending to stick to her script. To absorb the blame. Well, to share the blame with Jonathan, that is. But she'd been rattled by Dara's off-topic questions, and she'd lost focus. She knew she had screwed up the second she mentioned that someone else had been with them in Dubai, and she had watched as Dara caught on immediately.

She could have covered up her mistake. She could have woven some story about Jonathan coming downstairs to check on her progress. She could have simply denied that there was any third person involved in the operation. But she hadn't.

It had been a split-second decision. As soon as she realized she had slipped, it had felt as if time stood still in the interrogation room. Options flashed through her mind: Truth or lie. Script or consequences. Herself or Tony.

She chose Jonathan. She chose to preserve some tiny part of his memory, no matter what it would cost her. And if she was honest with herself, she realized that she was trying to strike an impossible bargain with fate. If she did this one small thing for Jonathan, she thought—if she could honor his memory, honor *him*—then maybe the baby would be his. It could be his son. By giving Tony's name to Dara, she hoped desperately and illogically that she could give Jonathan's name to her unborn child.

Caitlin couldn't tell Dara everything. Not yet, anyway. She still had too much at stake, too much to lose. But by giving Tony's name, she gave Dara a thread that, if pulled, could unravel their whole charade.

She hoped like hell that Dara pulled.

Caitlin yanked the plug from the drain and let the water empty. She pulled on a bathrobe, stepped out of the humid bathroom, and then froze.

The apartment was silent, as it should be since she was alone, but a strange light flickered from the den at the end of the hall. The television was on, Caitlin realized. But she certainly hadn't turned it on—she didn't watch much TV these days. Nor did she have any pets that could have knocked the remote off the table; she and Jonathan had traveled too much to even consider owning a goldfish, much less a dog or a cat.

Standing motionless in the hallway of her apartment, Caitlin knew that she had to react—that she had to do *something*. "*Get off the X!*" the gruff voices of her overseas personal security instructors yelled in her head. The first rule of safety was to get out of the crosshairs, out of danger—to get off of the X. But as she stood there, damp in her ridiculous pink robe, she felt far more a scared girl than a trained CIA officer. She'd stopped thinking like a covert operative the day she heard that Jonathan was dead.

She snapped out of her mental paralysis. Jonathan had owned a handgun, but it was probably still on the top shelf of the closet in their bedroom—in *her* bedroom—which was right next to the den. No, better to leave the apartment and risk feeling foolish if the threat turned out to be nothing.

But as she turned to flee, she heard a voice call out. "In here, Caitlin. Join me."

She couldn't place the voice, but it was familiar. Fear turned to confusion mixed with anger. *Who?*

She walked reluctantly toward the den. *Get off the X.* The mantra of danger avoidance echoed again in her mind, but she brushed it aside as her anger grew.

As she'd thought, the television was on in the den, its sound muted. Caitlin stopped breathing as she took in the video that was playing noiselessly on the screen. Her unwelcome visitor was sitting on the couch, watching the TV with a smirk on his face.

"Tony." It was as if she'd conjured up his malevolent presence just by thinking about him.

He turned up the volume in response. "Wait, I like this part."

Caitlin's heart lurched as she watched herself onscreen. Her captured image tossed back her hair, laughing, and then climbed seductively onto the lap of a bleary-eyed, dark-haired man. The man slipped Caitlin's shirt off in one fluid motion, and Caitlin rocked her hips against his.

She had seen the video only once before, after she and Jonathan had returned home on separate flights, shared a bottle of champagne, and toasted one of their early victories. While Caitlin had been busy giving the man in the video a lap dance that he would never forget, her husband had been in the next room imaging files from the target's laptop computer. The data had contained confirmation of a senior Pakistani general's secret support of Taliban leaders hiding out in the tribal areas. It was a major success. On their own—just the two of them—they had managed to get a hold of the kind of information that could change foreign policy overnight.

It was also the first time that Jonathan had installed video equipment in the room before the operation. Safely back home, he had slipped the DVD into the player casually as they sipped champagne, saying something about wanting to check out the resolution. Caitlin had watched the scene play out, half horrified, half proud. It didn't feel like she was watching herself. It was her alias doing those things, not her. Thinking of it that way made it seem more like she was just watching someone act in a movie. Still, she had nervously watched Jonathan out of the corner of her eye when the scene heated up. He had encouraged her to do whatever was necessary to keep him safe while he pilfered the target's electronics, but this was the first time he was actually seeing what went on in the next room.

She didn't need to worry about him getting jealous, though. He was mesmerized. They had finished that bottle of champagne, plus half of a second, and then had some of the best sex of their marriage.

And now Tony Alvaro was watching the video. The video that Jonathan had kept in a safe buried in the back of the den closet.

Sure enough, the closet door was standing wide open.

Caitlin struggled to come to grips with the scene playing out in front of her. *How? Why?* There were so many questions, she couldn't even figure out where to start.

Finally, Tony paused the video. The still shot on the screen was a lewd moment, with the target pawing drunkenly at Caitlin's bare breasts.

Caitlin grabbed at the remote control, which Tony held just out of her reach. "You asshole!" she finally screamed.

Tony smiled at her condescendingly. "Now that isn't very ladylike of you, is it?" He glanced over at the TV screen and laughed. "But then again, ladylike is highly overrated." He turned off the video and patted the couch seat next to him.

Caitlin didn't move.

Tony sighed exaggeratedly. "Okay, I'm sorry. That was pretty low of me. I just needed to be sure that we're still on the same team. That you still understand what's at stake."

Caitlin met his eyes and answered him with undisguised fury. "You haven't let me forget for one minute what's at stake here. You and your buddies follow me everywhere I go. You break into my apartment, you threaten me...and you want to know if we're on the same team? Fuck you and your friends, Tony. Fuck your team. I've done everything you've asked me to, and now I just want out. Just leave me alone."

Tony was unfazed. "And Dara?"

For the first time, Caitlin smiled. "She's sharp. She's already figured out that you were in Dubai with me for the last op. I'm sure she'll be contacting you soon." She didn't add that it was only because she had revealed the information herself. *Let him figure it out on his own. Let him sweat.*

For a quick instant Tony's face showed such rage that Caitlin was afraid he was going to hit her. The look of anger disappeared, though, and was replaced by a calculating smile. "Actually, that's probably a good thing. It could come in handy soon. Well done." He'd guessed that it had been her fault. "But from now on stick to the script."

Caitlin kept her face blank. She didn't know why he would possibly be happy that Dara had linked him to Operation Golden Mean, so she didn't want to let him see her react. Tony had an uncanny knack for being one step ahead, and she didn't want to accidentally run afoul of whatever he was plotting now. She wanted to stay as far away from Tony and his plans as humanly possible. "Get out of my home." She said it slowly, almost a growl.

Tony stood up and walked over to her. "Hey, Caitlin, I really shook you up, didn't I? I'm sorry, I really am. I just had to be sure what was going on. C'mere." His voice was oily, gentle, and he put his arms around her as if he were giving her a friendly hug.

Caitlin stiffened under his touch, silently willing him away. He lingered, though, and his hands started to trace circles on her back. His touch grew firmer, and he pulled her closer to him.

Disgusted, Caitlin pushed him away from her as hard as she could. But he didn't release his grip. One of his hands tightened painfully around her right bicep as his other hand yanked roughly at the belt of her robe. "Come on, Caitlin. You'll fuck a bunch of jihadis, but now you won't let *me* keep you company? Jonathan's gone. Just let it happen."

Caitlin couldn't believe what was happening. She fought back, but he was much stronger than she was, in spite of his wiry build. Finally, desperate, she screamed out, "Tony, stop! I'm pregnant!"

He did stop. His mouth dropped open; it was the first time Caitlin had ever seen him look truly surprised. But then his face twisted into an ugly, contemptuous grin. "Surprise, surprise. So we'll be seeing a little Jonathan Junior soon? Or will it be an Abdul Junior? *That* would be a tough one to explain, wouldn't it, if your little darling came into the world bearing no resemblance to your fair-haired dead husband?"

She backed away from him wordlessly, pulling her robe closed to the neck.

He laughed cruelly. "I bet you don't even know who the father is, you stupid whore. You have no idea what you've done here. Do you know what kind of questions people are going to start asking if Golden Boy Jonathan Wolff's widow gives birth to a little Arab baby less than nine months after her husband's death? It won't be long before they realize that their all-American poster boy for the war on terror was up to something funny." He shoved past her, heading for the front door. As he opened it, he turned around, fury in his eyes. "Keep your mouth shut, no matter what happens. Understand?"

Caitlin nodded weakly as he left, slamming the door behind him. She fell to her knees, shaking, but no tears came. She had cried enough in the last few months for an entire lifetime. Crying time was over.

She had no doubt that she would be seeing Tony again soon, and the next time she wanted to be prepared. She stood up slowly, walked to the bedroom closet, and rummaged around the highest shelf until she found Jonathan's Glock handgun. He had always kept it unloaded, since it had no manual safety, but she found a full magazine next to it.

Caitlin worked the slide release several times and then dry fired, reacquainting herself with the gun. She hadn't particularly enjoyed the firearms portion of her training, but she had been a surprisingly decent shot. Plus, her instructors had made her drill with a handgun until shooting it was a part of her muscle memory.

She loaded the gun and tucked it into the pocket of her robe. *Locked and loaded.* She was glad that it didn't have a safety. She didn't need one. She was ready to fire.

CHAPTER TWENTY-FIVE

La Rambla, a long, tree-lined street with a crowded pedestrian mall down the center, was a terrible place to try to spot surveillance. Dara had been there once before, but she didn't remember Barcelona being quite so chaotic. Judging from the crowd, a teeming mob of tourists and locals alike, Dara had arrived during some sort of early spring break. Everyone in the city seemed to be outside, stepping in and out of the tapas bars, souvenir shops, boutiques, and attractions that lined the street, or else just ambling along at a frustratingly sluggish pace. The weather *was* gorgeous—it was an unseasonably warm evening—but Dara barely noticed. She elbowed her way past street performers, wide-eyed tourists, hustlers selling everything from maps to marijuana, and rowdy young men all wearing the blue-and-red-striped shirts of Barcelona's soccer team. The soccer hooligans were loudly and drunkenly celebrating either a recent victory or a pending match; it was hard to tell which.

Dara had been tense since arriving in Spain, and with her spy's natural aversion to crowds, she was positively jumpy in this throng. She gritted her teeth as she was jostled yet again, this time by a middle-aged woman who was somehow simultaneously smoking, carrying three enormous shopping bags, shouting in Spanish into her cell phone, and holding the hand of a wailing toddler.

It wasn't just the crowd that was making Dara nervous. She had a lot on her mind. For starters, she knew that, technically speaking, she should have headed straight back to Washington with the kind of information she had learned in Dubai. The fact that there were Americans involved in Jonathan Wolff's death had a number of possible implications, none of them good. CIA officers are trained to extrapolate and predict the worst-case scenarios, and Dara knew that the information Yousef had given her could mean that there was a terrorist cell with Americans involved, or even a terrorist cell operating on US soil. That was the kind of information that got law enforcement, the White House, and the intelligence community moving fast.

Even if the fact that Yousef had been given the video by Americans *didn't* indicate an American terrorist cell was responsible for Jonathan's death, Dara still had an obligation to report it immediately. At a minimum, the FBI was involved in a huge investigation that assumed Jonathan's murderers were Egyptian. Dara's information would turn their investigation upside down.

She didn't take this obligation lightly, and she fully intended to march back into Langley and force Dominic to listen to what she had to say. But…not right away. Yousef had given her everything he knew about the Americans, and it wasn't much. The Barcelona address where he had been told to go was all he had: no names, no contact information, and only the vaguest of physical descriptions. He had shown up, been handed a DVD and a fistful of cash, and been told to go enjoy the city. With a story as vague as Yousef's, Dara had a feeling that she knew exactly what would be done with the information: nothing. At least not yet. After all, not only was his information sketchy, but Yousef was a *former* asset terminated several years ago with a documented history of lies and exaggerations. He wasn't exactly what Washington considered a credible source.

And then there was the fact that Dara had met with him in the first place. She had contacted him without authorization, and in fact had met with him in spite of an explicit ban on future meetings—a standard rule for CIA asset terminations. She visualized a mental chalkboard with two marks on it. *Yup,* she said to herself, *that makes two—count 'em, two—charges of inappropriate foreign contact for Dara McIntyre.* These days she didn't have much more credibility than Yousef did back at Langley.

On top of everything else, Dara was facing the distinct possibility that Jonathan's death was a direct result of his involvement in Operation Golden Mean. Up until Yousef had dropped his little bomb in her lap, she had assumed that Jonathan's killers were his *targets,* not his *colleagues.* But if the man who had delivered the video to Yousef was an American, then that meant Jonathan's killer could be, too. And the only Americans Dara knew of who could possibly know about Yousef al-Kuwari's side business of delivering secret videos to Al Jazeera were the Americans who had access to the reports *she* had written. Highly classified CIA reports only accessible to CIA officers.

And nothing would make the trail that Dara was following into the clandestine world of her own brethren disappear faster than a bunch of aggressive FBI officers trampling onto CIA turf.

She had to pursue this on her own. At least for now.

If she had had anything—anything at all—that amounted to what the CIA called "actionable intelligence," meaning information that was specific enough to *do* something about, then she would have hopped on the next flight to Washington and reported herself without hesitation. But she didn't. She had enough information to scare her, to make her think that something seriously wrong was happening, but she didn't have enough to make anyone believe her or Yousef. She had to collect more information to make sure that the facts didn't get buried.

The crowd around Dara surged and then stopped altogether. Two of La Rambla's human statues—street performers who collected tips from tourists for posing motionlessly while wearing elaborate costumes—were about to come to blows over a turf dispute. A top-hat-wearing man covered head to toe in bronze paint was shoving a much shorter man dressed in ratty yellow feathers. The yellow man may have been at a size disadvantage, but his costume included long yellow claws that looked as if they might be able to do some real damage. Hundreds of people crowded around, and everyone who had a camera was using it. Bright camera flashes were erupting all around, further impairing Dara's ability to tell whether anyone was following her.

Not that she even knew who she was looking for. There were too many possibilities at this point.

Her heart raced as she inched through the throng of onlookers. For someone in a profession that depended on living a discreet lifestyle, Dara had an embarrassing number of people interested in tracking her movements. She had her own colleagues proving their lack of trust by trailing her back home—and possibly here, for all she knew; there were the two men who had made repeat performances in Dubai and who Dara still didn't fully believe were innocents just along for the ride with Yousef; and then she had Tariq keeping tabs on her using the very tools that the CIA had given him.

Speaking of Tariq…Dara peered over the top of the gridlocked crowd. She was within a block of Plaza Catalunya, the very spot in Barcelona that Tariq had mentioned when they last spoke. *He wouldn't dare*, Dara told herself. But she knew Tariq, and she knew that he certainly *would* dare to show up in Barcelona if he felt like it.

With a growing sense of uneasiness and impatience, Dara fought her way through the crowd. In doing so, she moved just enough to realize that someone standing behind her had his hand entangled in the straps of her purse, preventing her from going any further. Already on edge, Dara acted without hesitation. She whirled around and smashed the base of her palm forcefully into the would-be thief's face.

Her assailant fell to the ground, his nose spurting blood, and looked up at her with a look of absolute disbelief.

All around her, people turned to stare. The human statues were now engaged in a motionless stare-off, and the new confrontation was far more interesting.

"Damn it!" Dara swore aloud as she looked down at the boy she had just felled. He was just a pickpocket and looked to be no more than sixteen or seventeen years old. Dara knew petty crime was as common as bad paella in this section of town, and yet she had still overreacted. Now she had managed to draw even more unwanted attention to herself. She cringed as one of the tourists lifted his camera and snapped a picture of her.

She used the crowd's shifting attention as an opportunity to crash her way through. "Sorry!" she apologized as she nearly knocked over an elderly couple wearing matching caps bearing a cruise ship logo.

She had just made her way into a relatively clear area of the street when someone else grabbed her arm. She whirled around for the second time, barely keeping herself from striking out again.

"Whoa, easy there. I saw what you're capable of. The poor boy just wanted your wallet." Tariq eased his grip on her arm but maintained contact. "Hello, Dara."

Dara, who hadn't even realized that she had been holding her breath, exhaled deeply and felt herself lean into Tariq without even intending to. "Hello, Tariq."

CHAPTER TWENTY-SIX

"Join me." Tariq offered his hand.

Dara hesitated, but only briefly. She was eager to leave the crowds of La Rambla behind, and—if she was honest with herself—she was feeling almost overwhelmed with conflicting emotions. She had known that Tariq might show up, but she hadn't been prepared for the way his presence would affect her. She was way too rattled to be operational anyway; she might as well hear what he had to say. She *wanted* to hear what he had to say.

Without another word she took his hand and let him lead her away from the chaotic tourist zone and into the dark, maze-like streets of Barcelona's gothic quarter. The ancient streets of this area were too narrow to permit cars, so although there were plenty of pedestrians, everything sounded muted and hushed after the circus-like environment they had just left. It felt surreal to be walking hand-in-hand with Tariq, as if they were just another tourist couple enjoying a clear winter's night in the city.

Tariq turned down one crooked street and then another. "It's close, I promise," he reassured her.

"Then stop. Here. Now." She pulled him to a stop. At some point she had to go back to reality. She had to tell him to stop tracking her, to stop following her, to stop interfering with her operations—and with her life. But for now she just wanted Tariq to stop walking. Standing in the middle of the narrow street, she pulled him to her and reached up to turn his face toward hers. She just needed to look at him for a moment, to drink him in with her eyes and convince herself that she was really, truly standing there next to the man she thought she'd never see again. Slowly, as if he'd vanish if she moved too fast, she leaned toward him, tilting her head up and pulling him even closer until their lips met. She closed her eyes and gave in to the dreamlike state created by the combination of the crisp Mediterranean breeze, the hushed city noises, and his lips on hers. She allowed herself a singular moment to be unguarded and free in his embrace before pulling away. "I love you," she whispered, quietly enough that he couldn't possibly have heard.

The *gambas al ajillo* at the small restaurant Tariq led her to *were* fantastic. As was everything else—the food and the company. She reluctantly passed on the wine, though. She needed to stay sharp.

But as perfect as the night might have been had circumstances been different, their date, if that's what a covert reunion like theirs could be called, started off awkwardly. With so many subjects to avoid, their conversation was stilted. There were so many topics that couldn't be broached. Not yet.

Halfway through their meal and following yet another awkward pause in the conversation, Tariq finally pushed back his chair, stood up, and walked around to Dara's side of the table. Without a word, he leaned over and kissed her, as if in revenge for her alleyway embrace. It was the deep, knee-weakening, heart-thumping, unmistakable kind of kiss that had never failed to set everything right between them. Dara felt herself surrender to the kiss, to her feelings for Tariq, and she knew that she had made a choice. When Tariq finally rose and sauntered back to his chair, Dara felt her face flush.

"Don't be embarrassed," Tariq grinned. "Spain is an amorous country."

Sure enough, no one had even given them a second glance.

"You're trying to distract me." Dara had missed Tariq's mouth very much, and she ached for more.

"Yes." His eyes held hers captive.

Dara frowned. That answer was a little *too* honest. "Tariq, don't misunderstand me. I'm happy to see you. Happier than I should be, in fact. But besides the fact that this little rendezvous could get me fired, there are things going on that I need to take care of. Without you. I'm here on official business," she finished lamely.

"So am I."

Dara sighed. He wasn't going to make this easy. "Please, Tariq. Let me do what I need to do. I assume you already know where I'm staying. I'll give you my room key, and we can meet there later, when I'm done."

He waved her away as she started to dig through her purse for the key. "Keys are for amateurs." He reached across the table and took one of her hands in his, then drew it to his mouth and kissed it gently. "Do what you need to do, darling Dara. I'll be waiting for you. We'll talk more then. We have much to discuss now that we've finally broken the ice."

Dara hesitated. Now he was making this *too* easy. She was suspicious.

He saw her doubt and laughed. "Go on, don't worry. I plan to stay right here and finish off this bottle of Rioja that you refused to share with me."

She stood up and then kissed him good-bye, once more marveling at just how liberating it felt to act so...normal. He tasted familiar and wonderful.

"*Hasta pronto.* See you soon." He waved her off as he refilled his glass.

It was definitely too easy. Dara headed out the door anyway. She had bigger problems to worry about.

The address that Yousef had given her wasn't far away from the bright lights and touristy drama of La Rambla in distance, but it was light-years away in terms of ambiance and mood. The streets of Barcelona's Raval district were dark and narrow and reeked of backed-up sewage. Whereas Plaza Catalunya was dominated by fanny-pack-wearing British, American, and German tourists whose pasty skin bore patches of bright red sunburn, El Raval was home to a very different group of expatriates. The hardscrabble residents of this neighborhood, one of Europe's most densely populated, came from the world's poorest countries. Nigerian men standing in clusters glared suspiciously at Dara as she walked by; so did the groupings of Moroccan, Roma, and Tunisian men. Eastern European prostitutes ignored her in one alley; a separate group of West African prostitutes ignored her in the next alley. The various cultures seemed to live together in close proximity here in Barcelona's most worldly barrio, but they still maintained very separate lifestyles. In one block alone Dara noted an Asian grocery store, a halal butcher shop, a business offering cheap phone calls to Pakistan, a travel agency with flyers printed in Arabic, and a small dress shop that was selling a strange combination of flamenco skirts and saris.

The separate groups kept their distance from one another, but they seemed to be united in one thing: their belief that Dara didn't belong in their neighborhood.

Dara ignored hisses from one group of men and sidestepped another as several of them flanked out to block her progress, whether out of ill intent or simply boredom, she couldn't tell. *Damn it.* Why had she waited until after dark to check out the address Yousef gave her? She didn't need any kind of special covert action training to know better than to come to a high-crime neighborhood so late at night. Once again she'd let her feelings for Tariq cloud her judgment.

She finally found the street she was looking for. Fortunately it seemed to be deserted. Only a precious few of the buildings actually displayed street numbers, so Dara had to count from the corner to establish that a decrepit building at the dead end of the small street was the one she was looking for. The five-story apartment building looked ancient and sorely in need of foundation supports. Wincing at the smell of urine in the foyer, Dara stepped inside.

If there had ever been any internal hall lights, they weren't working now. Dara stood just inside the door for a minute until her eyes adjusted to the darkness. It was eerily quiet. Either the building was abandoned, or else its occupants all worked the night shift.

She picked her way up a rickety staircase, grateful that the apartment she was looking for wasn't on the top level. Debris crunched under her feet.

Dara could barely see the numbers on the doors, but she finally found apartment 3-B, which was as silent as all of the others in the grim building. In keeping with the rest of the building's condition, the apartment's door sat crookedly enough in its frame that there was a considerable gap between it and the floor. Any light at all in the apartment would have been easy to spot in the darkness of the hall.

Dara pressed her ear to the door. The warped wood was thin enough that she could hear the street noises outside. *A window must be open.* There were no other sounds. She did a quick mental review of the building's exterior. There had been no patios or terraces, just small, barred windows. She was willing to take a chance that no one was inside.

She stepped back, debating whether to enter now or to sit back and watch the apartment to see if anyone showed up, when a harsh light flared in her face.

She spun instinctively to put more room between herself and the door she had been pressed against. She needed more space to be able to defend herself or, better yet, escape.

The flashlight flicked off, though, and Tariq stood there, holding his hands up in a sign of surrender. "Dara, Dara, it's just me. I didn't mean to scare you."

Dara was furious. He'd crossed the line. It was one thing for Tariq to pursue her on a personal level, but now he was interfering with an operation. "Get out of here," she hissed at him.

"You didn't tell me that you were coming to this part of town. Late at night isn't such a good time for you to be wandering around here." He at least had the good sense to keep his voice low.

"It's none of your business where I go," she said, waving him away angrily. "This doesn't involve you."

"Quite the contrary, darling Dara. You are very much my business. Now, were you planning on knocking politely, or shall we go ahead and let ourselves in?" Tariq reached over and turned the door handle before she could answer.

To both of their surprise, the door opened. It was unlocked.

CHAPTER TWENTY-SEVEN

Tariq started to enter the apartment first, but Dara held him back. "Stay out in the hall," she warned him.

He shook his head. "It might not be safe, and you're not armed."

How did he know? She glared at him with unmasked suspicion.

"You took a commercial flight and failed to declare a firearm. I saw your travel records, remember? And I seriously doubt that you've had time to pick up a weapon from a source or from the black market; you only arrived a few minutes before I did."

She started to argue that he didn't know anything about either the apartment or whether she was armed, but thought better of it and just shoved past him. "Cut the macho bullshit."

There were definitely both pros and cons to dating a fellow spy.

Once inside the three-room apartment, she relied on the moonlight filtering in through the small, dirty windows to do a quick check of the rooms. Only when she was convinced that the apartment was empty did she turn on the light.

The apartment was not empty.

Dara's heart skipped a beat as she took in the scene in front of her. A man's body lay on a plastic tarp; the plastic sheeting had been arranged to contain the staggering amount of blood that surrounded the corpse.

Her training kicked in. She scanned the room methodically, taking mental snapshots as she went. Remaining risks? None apparent. Weapons present? None visible. Surveillance or other electronic equipment? Dara checked all of the likely locations but did not spot any computers or security cameras. There *were*, however, other cameras.

The room seemed to have been set up as a makeshift studio. Two video cameras set up on tripods were pointing at the gruesome scene. Tattered white sheets had been hung from the ceiling as a backdrop; the section of the sheet nearest the body bore copious splatters of blood.

Dara checked the cameras without touching them. Both were turned off, and she could see that neither contained a storage disc or memory card. Whoever had recorded the man's death had taken the footage with them.

Only after completing the physical assessment did Dara remember that Tariq was with her. She turned and saw that he was standing just inside the closed door, a hardened look on his face.

"We need to leave. Now."

Dara knew he was right, but she wasn't quite finished.

She stepped gingerly toward the body, making sure not to walk through any blood. The plastic sheeting had been bunched up and arranged around the man in such a way that the blood had collected deeply and tidily. It almost looked as if he were taking a leisurely bath in his own blood.

She studied the man, who was lying on his side facing the cameras. He could have been anyone, from anywhere. He was young—in his late twenties or early thirties—and fit. He looked like he could have put up a good fight, but Dara didn't see any bruises or injuries other than the gaping slice on his neck that extended from ear to ear. She didn't need to be a pathologist to know what killed him.

"Dara, this isn't your job. Let's go." Tariq was still standing near the door.

Once again he was right. CIA officers didn't deal with dead bodies. Spies were in the business of stealing secrets, and as the saying goes, dead men tell no tales.

Dara couldn't take her eyes off of the body, though. She had seen a few during her career, but only in war zones, where they came as no surprise. Here, in this shabby apartment less than a kilometer from Barcelona's tourist epicenter, it made less sense. And something was bothering her about the body, although she couldn't quite put her finger on it.

"I don't believe in coincidence." Dara spoke more to herself than to Tariq.

The dead man didn't look Spanish. He didn't quite look Arab either, although his hair and skin tone made her wonder. With his eyes closed it was hard to tell, but his face seemed to have at least some Asian features. Dara was usually good at reading faces, but she couldn't pinpoint this man's ethnicity. His clothes didn't reveal anything, either. He was wearing tan slacks and a blue dress shirt—the uniform of professional men worldwide.

"What the hell are you doing, Dara?"

She ignored Tariq as she bent down, leaning over the corpse as far as she could without coming into contact with the blood. Gingerly, she probed at the dead man's pockets, checking for a wallet or passport. Nothing. With her stomach roiling, she pulled at the back of his shirt. She recoiled in shock as she felt that the body still bore the faintest trace of warmth.

Was he still alive? She felt for a pulse, bloodying her fingertips as she did. There was no pulse. He was definitely dead. Recently dead.

She wiped her hands on her pants, grateful that she had worn black. At least the stains wouldn't show until she had a chance to get rid of the slacks. Steeling her nerves, she continued her mission.

Somehow she wasn't surprised when she saw that the tags of his shirt had been cut out. Holding her breath, she checked the waistband of his pants. The tags there were gone too.

It couldn't be a coincidence.

Cutting the tags out of clothing was a superstitious practice used by CIA officers since the days of the original OSS. The rationale was that it would make it harder for enemies to identify you as an American spy if they couldn't first determine that you were American. Removing the tags meant that your American brand names wouldn't give you away. In today's global marketplace it no longer made as much sense, but lots of officers still did it anyway. Dara scratched unconsciously at the back of her neck, where her own tagless shirt collar rested.

Then she realized what had been tugging at the back of her brain. His shoes. A good intelligence officer tries to blend into his surroundings, including dressing in local fashion. But even the best officers tend to stick to what is comfortable and familiar when it comes to footwear. Spies spend way too much time on their feet to deal with pinched toes from foreign shoes. And even covered in blood, Dara recognized that the man on the floor was wearing a popular American shoe brand.

He's one of us. Nothing that Dara could see proved anything, but she felt it in her gut. It was like Jonathan Wolff all over again.

"Dara!" Tariq's voice was sharp, urgent.

She finally stood up. There was nothing else she could do here. It was time to go.

CHAPTER TWENTY-EIGHT

"It's too soon, Dara. Maybe there will be something about it tomorrow."

Tariq waited patiently while she flipped through the TV channels over and over again. The hotel's cable selection offered news programs in Spanish, English, Catalan, and German; not a single one was reporting anything about a murder in Barcelona.

Tariq had called an old contact in the Spanish *Guardia Civil* to report their discovery. At his request, the information was logged in as an anonymous tip. Neither he nor Dara would be connected to the crime.

But Dara still felt uncomfortable about leaving the body. It felt like she was abandoning a colleague. Tariq had finally persuaded her that it was the best option. "You don't know anything about his identity, and the last thing you need right now is to become involved in an official investigation."

She knew he was right. Cops and spies were like oil and water. Police officers enforced laws; intel officers broke them. To make matters worse, the Spanish government did not look kindly upon CIA officers operating on their turf. Dara's presence at a murder scene would have raised a lot of uncomfortable questions and would undoubtedly have resulted in an official complaint through diplomatic channels.

Dara couldn't do anything to help the handsome young man lying in a puddle of his own blood, and her career would never withstand yet another complaint. So she had left, silently promising the dead mystery man to do whatever she could to figure out who had killed him.

Now, several hours later, she was sitting awkwardly on her hotel bed while Tariq lounged in the only chair in the room. With the television turned off, the tension began to grow.

Tariq broke the silence first. "So. This isn't *quite* what I had in mind for our first night back together."

Dara smiled wearily. "You sure know how to show a lady a good time."

The awkward silence resumed.

"I…" They both started to speak at the same time. He gestured for her to go first.

"Tariq, I don't even know what to say, really. Things are just so…complicated."

He smiled as he rose up from the chair and then sat next to her on the bed. "To the contrary, darling Dara," he said softly as he leaned over and kissed her neck. "It's not complicated at all." His mouth traced gently until it found her lips. He kissed her softly, once. "I love you. I want you. You're here. I'm here. Nothing could be simpler." He kissed her again, deeper this time.

She hesitated for only the briefest of moments until she gave in to him. She pulled him closer, returning his kisses, urgently now, and let his hands, his mouth, and his body erase the horrors of the day.

Several hours later, they lay naked, whispering and laughing together on top of the incriminatingly twisted bedsheets.

"Official business, my ass," Dara teased him. She shrieked as he flipped her over and groped her in jest.

"Why, yes. Your ass *is* my official business. I'll be expected to add a fully descriptive report to your file when I get back to the office." He leered at her comically.

"My file?" she said, still bantering. "You'd better not have a file on me."

"Of course we do." He pulled her back into his arms, nuzzling her neck. "You're a spy. A gorgeous, sexy, and dare I say, damn near acrobatic spy, but a spy nonetheless. We need to know your habits and vulnerabilities. And I, for one, would like very much to make a habit out of this."

Tariq was still joking, but somewhere, deep within, Dara felt a small seed of alarm sprouting. "And what does my file say about my vulnerabilities?" She tried to keep her tone light.

His fingers, skimming the curve of her waist, didn't seem to detect her growing tension. "There's a very handsome picture of me in your file. That's all anyone needs to know." He continued to trace her body with light kisses, and his voice was muffled. "In fact, I am quite proud to be your vulnerability."

Dara forced herself to laugh. It sounded as fake as it felt, but Tariq was distracted. "Let's check the news again," she said, pulling away from him and turning on the television. "And then I need to get some sleep. I'm flying out first thing in the morning."

"I know." Tariq stood and stretched languidly, then headed for the bathroom and turned on the shower. He hummed a slow song as he stepped into the water.

In the next room, Dara sat tensely upright on the bed, unsuccessfully trying to will away the doubts and questions that were starting to take hold in her thoughts.

CHAPTER TWENTY-NINE

"That does complicate things a bit, doesn't it?" Abram Hendricks stroked his chin and swiveled around in his chair.

Dominic watched him uneasily. The CIA director always turned to stare out the window when he was uncertain about how to proceed, as if he expected the view to somehow inspire him.

"We're sure that the baby isn't Jonathan Wolff's? It could actually be a good thing if it was, you know. Nothing gets more funding from Congress than a pregnant widow."

Dominic glared at the director's back. The damn fool believed that CIA analysts could come up with probability statistics for everything. "We don't know for sure. She told Tony about the pregnancy, but it doesn't seem as if she's told many others. We found no records indicating that she's seen a doctor yet, either."

"Good, good. Let's make sure no one else finds out about this." Hendricks stated this as an order.

The last I checked, the CIA had no control yet over either human biology or gossip, Dominic wanted to say. Instead he just nodded.

Hendricks wasn't looking. He was still facing the window, apparently not yet having found his answer. "If the paternity issue...goes the wrong way, it's going to raise some uncomfortable questions. We need to be ready to take action if it comes to that. How soon will we know?"

Dominic was losing the battle to control his frustration. Was he going to have to explain the birds and the bees to one of the most powerful men in the world? "Well, sir, unless you intend to strap her down and forcefully obtain a DNA sample from her unborn child, we're going to have to wait this one out. I doubt our paramilitary boys have brushed up on their amniocentesis skills recently."

The DCI turned slowly to face Dominic, his eyes narrowed and his jaw clenched. He did not often encounter either sarcasm or dissent in his office, and he didn't like hearing it now. "I suggested nothing of the sort." He let those words hang for a moment before continuing. "I simply want our mutual friend to stay close to the issue." He turned his attention to his computer, ending the conversation. "Close the door on your way out."

Dominic resisted the impulse to slam the door. He knew that he'd get nowhere by giving in to his frustration. But the fact was that he had started to lose confidence in Abram Hendricks.

He certainly wasn't the only one. The newspapers had been filled lately with speculation that the president was considering yet another shake-up of the intelligence community's leadership, and the director of Central Intelligence was an obvious target. After all, he had been appointed almost two years ago, and his results had been few and far between. Unless he managed to deliver al-Qaeda sliced and diced on a silver platter to the White House soon, Abram Hendricks wasn't long for the job.

It wasn't just journalistic speculation coloring Dominic's loyalties, either. Other people smelled blood too. During a meeting earlier that week, Dominic had witnessed the chief of Naval Operations flat out refuse Hendricks's request for military support for an upcoming operation. The navy official didn't even bother to give a reason; he had simply said no and moved on to the next item on the agenda. His failure to offer even the weakest of excuses sent an unmistakable message: Hendricks was no longer calling the shots. Hendricks had turned crimson with anger, but he hadn't raised the topic again.

Dominic, who was at the meeting to take notes as if he were a lowly secretary, had felt the power shift at that very moment in time. He saw that Hendricks felt it too. Abram Hendricks was losing his grip. He was getting desperate. Sloppy.

And yet, he was still here. He was still tossing out his vague, blameless directives, always confident that his subordinates would interpret his words in the darkest, most permanent way possible. By using this strategy, Hendricks had managed to stay above the dirty consequences of his decisions.

Perhaps, Dominic thought, *it's time for that to change.* At a minimum, Dominic had no intention of being Hendricks's puppet anymore when it came to Operation Golden Mean. What a stupid name for an operation, anyway. Tony had tried to explain what it meant during the second and final meeting when all three of them had actually sat face-to-face. Hendricks had loved it, the pompous ass. Dominic had no patience for philosophy. He preferred to think of himself as a man of action. Or at least as the man directing the action.

In this instance, though, Dominic had no intention of taking any action whatsoever. In fact, he hoped very much that Caitlin Wolff's pregnancy started showing soon. Her growing belly would represent a ticking time bomb for Hendricks's ridiculous plotting. A bomb with a nine-month fuse. Dominic grinned as he pictured an infant swaddled in a keffiyeh scarf. A little baby terrorist, raising questions that Hendricks definitely didn't want answered.

Caitlin's pregnancy was Dominic's leverage, and he intended to keep her safe so that he didn't lose the advantage. In nine months, Abram Hendricks would probably be long gone as a result of political shuffling, even if he was too arrogant to see it coming. In the meantime Dominic planned to use the director's remaining time to position himself favorably for the inevitable future.

He had to figure out how to keep Tony, who lately seemed to take great pleasure in doing the opposite of whatever it was he was ordered to do, from harming Caitlin—from harming his golden ticket. He smiled as he thought of Dara. He was very confident in her abilities. He liked her. Always had, even though he knew the feeling wasn't mutual. It was time to give her a boost, to help her along a bit.

And as for Hendricks? He didn't have time to dwell on Hendricks now. He was late for a friendly lunch—his treat, of course—with one Senator James Stadler. The very same senator whose name was being tossed around as one of the few emerging leaders in the intelligence world who had the confidence of both the Pentagon and the White House. Dominic definitely didn't want to keep him waiting.

CHAPTER THIRTY

"You've got to be kidding me." Dara said it out loud, even though there was no one nearby to hear her speak.

She had taken a cab home from the airport with the intention of stopping at her house only long enough to drop off her suitcase and grab her car keys. It was already late afternoon, and she wanted to get to the office early enough to report everything from her trip. Well, make that *almost* everything. They could catch her in the act with Tariq on their own, if they were so inclined. She had no intention of making it any easier for them to bust her again.

Her grand plan to rush into work came to a screeching halt, though, when she discovered that her front door was unlocked and slightly ajar.

The door hadn't been pried open, scratched, or forced in any of the ways you'd expect from a typical break-in. Nor was anything missing from inside the house. In fact, everything was largely intact. Everything but a few, critical exceptions.

One of the drawers of the file cabinets in her office had been left partially open. Her computer was pulled farther away from the wall than usual. A shoebox full of old photos had mysteriously fallen from a shelf in her closet, spilling its contents.

It definitely wasn't a burglary. Her TV, stereo, and a few pieces of semi-valuable jewelry were still there. But neither did it look like a professional job. Dara had participated in a few "room intrusion" operations, as they were called, accompanied by the agency's entry-op specialists. These were meticulous people who made their living by entering undetected, allowing the lead officer or technician to do whatever was necessary, and then leaving a room with no trace that anyone had ever been inside. They took photos of everything in the room before they even touched so much as a single sheet of paper so that they could be sure that, when they left, every last speck of dust was exactly where it had been before. They were locksmiths, alarm technicians, forensic experts, and world's best cleanup crew, all rolled into one. They were invisible.

No agency op would have been this sloppy. Not that Dara was particularly worried about what they might have discovered; she wasn't stupid enough to leave anything incriminating in her home. The only thing they would have found was a decade's worth of tax records, insurance documents, cancelled checks, and some old photos dating back to her college days.

She thought back to the car that had trailed her through McLean the week before. Whoever had been following her then hadn't exactly been subtle, either. But the surveillance car had had federal plates, so this had to be something official, even if it was ridiculously sloppy.

*Unless…*Dara thought of another reason for the careless surveillance and obvious home entry. In the intelligence world, there were several different forms of surveillance. One was discrete, invisible. Officers went to great lengths so as not to be detected by their target. Their goal was to watch without being seen.

The other type of surveillance was a form of harassment. It was crude, obvious, and intended to intimidate. The goal was to let targets know that they were being watched, monitored around the clock.

During the height of the Cold War, for example, American foreign service officers serving in Moscow and Havana had been subjected to harassing surveillance. Their cars were trailed so aggressively by their Russian hosts that the technique was referred to as "bumper locking." And when they left their cars parked somewhere unattended, they frequently returned to find their tires deflated or their windshields spray-painted. "Pig" and "Spy" were popular themes for the state-sanctioned graffiti artists. American officers' homes were entered freely and regularly, and their belongings were tossed around and scattered. Cigarettes were left smoldering in ashtrays, and petty items were damaged or taken. The message was clear: We are watching you, and we are in charge.

"Message received, assholes." Dara doubted that they had gone as far as planting listening devices in her home, but she spoke to them anyway.

As if on cue, someone rang her doorbell.

Dara flung the door open, half hoping to come face-to-face with whoever was harassing her. Instead, she found Caitlin.

Standing there hunched miserably in her doorway, Caitlin looked drastically different from the last time Dara saw her. There was no pregnancy glow surrounding this girl, Dara thought. She looked awful. Caitlin was shaking as if she were freezing, but she was drenched in sweat at the same time. Her clothes were filthy, and she kept looking back over her shoulder. If Dara hadn't known her, she would have sworn that the girl at her door was a junkie.

"I made sure they didn't follow me, but if they're watching you, then it doesn't matter what I do. They already know I'm here." Caitlin spoke in a hushed voice, as if she thought someone else was listening. "They know everything."

A week ago, Dara would have considered Caitlin paranoid, or even mentally ill. Now she was starting to believe that the young woman had very good reason to be terrified. She stepped aside and gestured for her to enter.

"Why are you here, Caitlin? And more to the point, what the hell is going on?" Dara didn't have time to play games or coddle anyone. She closed the door and pointed to the couch in her living room.

The young woman sat down heavily; she looked sickly and exhausted. Before she said another word, her eyes widened in surprise. "He's been here too."

Confused, Dara followed her gaze. She hadn't even noticed the manila envelope sitting on top of her coffee table until Caitlin reacted to it. She picked it up cautiously. Her name was handwritten in thick black ink on the outside of the envelope. Without even opening it, she could feel that it contained a disc of some sort.

"How did you know someone left this here?" Dara questioned her sharply. "How did you know I didn't put it there myself?"

Caitlin looked at her lap. "Because I've received a few of them myself. Same envelope, same handwriting. It'll be a video. Probably one you won't like."

Dara still didn't trust her. And she had no interest in sharing the contents of the envelope with anyone else before she checked it out in private. She put it aside.

"You don't trust me," Caitlin said, watching her.

Dara had had enough. She unleashed. "No, I don't trust you. I don't like you, either. You and your buddies got into something way over your heads, and I don't appreciate getting dragged into it. At a minimum, when people find out about you and your little bedroom ops—and believe me, they will—you're going to set women in this field back more years than you've been alive. But that's nothing compared to the fact that your stunts probably got your husband killed. On top of that, I think you've been lying to me, and I think you have something to hide. Considering how I feel about what I already know about you, I'm not sure that I even want to know what you're *not* telling me."

Caitlin didn't even flinch during the tirade. Instead she lifted her eyes to meet Dara's and spoke calmly. "You're right. About everything. I can't defend what I've done. I regret it every waking moment. But I do want you to know that Jonathan and I did what we did because we wanted to make a difference in the world. You can call us naïve, stupid, whatever you want, but the fact is that we *were* getting good results, even if you don't approve of our method."

It seemed as if everyone in her life was busy justifying the means to an end these days. "Shades of gray," Dara whispered.

Caitlin continued. "I did lie to you. I have been lying to you. But I plan to stop lying right now. You may not want to trust me, but if Tony has already delivered one of his envelopes to you, then you'll want to at least hear me out. We don't have to be friends, but believe me about this: we have the same enemy."

Dara raked her fingers through her hair, wavering between kicking Caitlin out of her house, picking up the phone to report her to the ops center, and listening to what she had to say. Finally, she sat down.

"Okay, back up. Tell me about Tony. Tell me about everything. And let's stick to the truth this time."

CHAPTER THIRTY-ONE

Caitlin started by showing Dara what her own video contained. She slipped a disc out of her purse and put it into the DVD player without bothering to ask for permission.

The video was poor quality. The image was shaky, and the sound was fuzzy. It was good enough to convey its message, though. It showed Caitlin wearing a sundress, looking relaxed and maybe more than a little bit tipsy. She was drinking a margarita, and at the beginning of the video, she clinked glasses with someone who sat just out of camera range. "Here's to my poor, kidnapped husband. Maybe by the time he gets back he'll have learned to do his own laundry. Maybe it takes a good hostage experience to make a man *really* appreciate his wife." She giggled, drunkenly. "Who am I kidding? He's going to come back fat from eating room service every day and tan from sitting by the pool. We should all be lucky enough to be captured by terrorists!" A male voice laughed along with her as the video cut off.

Dara felt sick. Everyone knew that Caitlin's husband had been snatched off the streets of Cairo, held captive, tortured, and ultimately murdered by terrorists. Having seen the horrible video of the murder herself, she couldn't understand how the man's *wife*, for God's sake, could possibly have been so cavalier about her husband's capture.

Then she got it.

"It wasn't real, was it? The kidnapping. Was it another one of your 'special operations'?" Dara's disgust turned into outrage.

Caitlin nodded miserably. "I wasn't involved in this one; it was the first of the operations he did without me. He wanted to branch out, as he put it, and do some jobs with some of the other group members. He was just supposed to hide out for a few weeks." She winced as she saw Dara's expression of fury. "Don't look at me like that. We had a reason. For the past year we had been watching operations in Egypt get shut down, one after the other. There are terrorist groups openly meeting and planning in Cairo—groups that have already targeted and killed a lot of innocent people. But since Egypt is supposedly one of our few allies in the region, nobody was doing anything to stop them. It was political bullshit. The Egyptian government says that there are no terrorists in Egypt, and the US just has to take them at their word, in spite of all evidence to the contrary, because it would be too 'politically sensitive' to accuse them of lying.

"Jonathan wasn't supposed to die," she whispered, her eyes filling with tears. "He was supposed to pretend to have been released on the day he was killed. They were going to rough him up a bit to make it look convincing, but no one was supposed to actually get hurt. The whole point was to get rid of the political barriers to taking out some really dangerous groups. It was a PR stunt, that's all."

"What went wrong? Who killed him?" Dara sat with her arms crossed over her chest.

"I don't know." Caitlin seemed to deflate. "I don't even know who else was involved, or even where they were keeping him. Jonathan took the whole compartmentalizing thing that Tony had been preaching seriously, so he only told me enough about the plan so that I wouldn't worry. And now all I know is that Tony Alvaro has a video of me making horrible comments about my husband being held captive, and one or more other videos showing me having sex with men who are well known to have committed murder and worse." Her voice dropped even more. "Don't you get it? He set everything up to look like *I* had Jonathan killed. He said he wouldn't show anyone the videos if I just played the quietly grieving widow and didn't ask any questions. And then, after I did that, he started asking for more."

"Such as?" Dara was shaking with anger.

"Such as setting *you* up."

CHAPTER THIRTY-TWO

Dara sipped on her second glass of wine. It was too late at night to go into work now, and besides, Caitlin's story made her wonder exactly *who* she could tell *what*. She hadn't offered Caitlin any wine, and the young woman was looking enviously at the Pinot Noir. "Here." Dara shoved a glass of tap water at her.

According to Caitlin, Tony Alvaro had transitioned from being a quiet participant in Jonathan's group to chief planner, and was now acting as the leader. "But everything is different now," she said. "He's different."

For starters, Tony had insisted that the participants in Operation Golden Mean borrow strategies from the very groups they were trying to infiltrate and destroy. The first change had been even more rigid compartmentalization. Tony had divided the group, which had continued to grow through word of mouth and recruitment efforts, into cells. Each cell was freestanding, and no one was allowed to know anything about any cell except their own. Tony was the only one who knew the true extent of the group now.

That meant Caitlin could tell her who was a part of the group up until the time Jonathan died, but not now. It could have doubled, or withered and vanished completely for all she knew. The only person she had contact with was Tony, and that contact was only when he had a "favor" to ask, as he put it each time he made a demand of her.

"He chose you because of your position," she explained to Dara. "It isn't personal, but he'll make it personal if he has to."

"My position?" Dara had to scoff. "I have no authority over anything. I'm in the penalty box, career-wise."

Caitlin shrugged. "I don't know. Something about audits."

A light went on in Dara's head. Among her other paper-pushing duties, Dara's position as counterintelligence referent meant that she processed the routine numerical audits that identified anomalies in CIA operations. It wasn't much in the way of actual responsibility, but if Tony's activities were triggering audits, then she would be the first to see evidence of them. It didn't seem like much to Dara, but she supposed that if Tony were cautious enough, or paranoid enough, he could see her as a threat.

Or an ally, even if an unwilling one. She would be able to cover up the early warnings, after all. Or maybe even shift the blame onto someone else. Dara glanced at the unopened envelope on her table. Was it blackmail, then? Would they threaten to reveal something about her unless she cooperated?

"Does this make any sense to you?" Caitlin asked.

Dara chewed on her lip, thinking. "Yes, it does. But only to a certain extent. Anything my audit software picks up would eventually get noticed for some other reason anyway. Shutting me down isn't going to buy anyone much more than a little time if they're trying to hide something big."

"Well, watch out. Tony has a nasty way of getting people to do what he wants. All I know is that he told me I needed to plant the seeds that would get you interested enough that you'd get on a plane. Implicating myself along the way, of course, but that was part of his plan anyway. He wanted you to travel, for some reason. He didn't seem to care where you went, just that you left the country. He wanted you to leave a trail. And I don't know how, but he'll use it against you at some point. If I did my part and confessed enough of my own crimes so that you'd just focus on me, he was supposed to leave me alone. That's how he works. He runs this like it's the spy equivalent of a—what do you call it? A Ponzi scheme. To get out of his clutches you have to bring someone else in to take the heat, only for something bigger. It keeps getting worse and worse. I guarantee that he has something similar in mind for you."

Dara massaged her temples; she had a headache coming on, and she felt exhausted. She was starting to believe that Caitlin might actually be telling the truth this time. Everything at least made more sense. However, she also had the feeling that whatever Caitlin knew was only the tip of the iceberg. Something else was bothering her. "Why are you telling me now? What changed?"

Caitlin smiled sadly. "Because I miss Jonathan. Because they pushed too far. Because I think he might try to kill me next."

Dara frowned at her, still skeptical.

"Let's just say that I've outlived my use to him. And the questions that are going to come up if…" Caitlin paused, her eyes filling with tears. "…if the baby doesn't look like Jonathan don't exactly enhance my chances of getting through this alive."

Dara started to object to this as paranoid, but then stopped herself as the image of the dead man she had found in Barcelona flooded her mind. He had been about the same age as Jonathan Wolff. He'd been killed in much the same way as Jonathan. She hoped that Caitlin was being melodramatic, but she couldn't be sure. She couldn't be sure of anything. "Do you have somewhere safe to stay?"

Caitlin nodded. "I'm going to stay with my parents for a while. They live in Bethesda. If Tony is determined, he'll find me there easily enough, but…at this point I'm finding it hard to care. He can find me anywhere I go, so I might as well spend my last days with my family." Her voice trailed off as she gave another defeated smile. "I'll see you at work tomorrow."

Dara walked her to the door.

Once Caitlin was gone, Dara walked through the house checking all of the locks and the windows. She drew every curtain closed, including the one in the guestroom that she never used for anything but extra storage space.

Then and only then did she take the disc out of the envelope labeled with her name.

She put it into the DVD player and waited for it to start. She assumed that, if she were in fact being blackmailed, it would have something to do with Tariq. Was someone videotaping her when he kissed her in the tapas bar? Did they see her entering or exiting her hotel with Tariq? Worse yet, could they have planted a camera in her room? She shuddered.

But the image that finally came onscreen was none of the above. It was a faint image of poor quality. There wasn't any audio at all. No sound was necessary—the visual told a chilling tale without it.

It was Dara leaning over a bloody corpse.

Dara watched herself as her image scanned the room, looking for surveillance cameras. *There hadn't been any, damn it!* The only way this video could possibly exist was if that shabby, dirty apartment had been equipped with surveillance equipment so small and sophisticated that she hadn't been able to spot it. It seemed unlikely, but there she was, bending down, touching the body. Wiping the blood on her pants.

The pants that Tariq had peeled off of her when she returned to the hotel room. Dara stood up and raced over to the small suitcase she had tossed in the corner of the room as she entered. She pawed through the contents with her heart racing.

The black pants weren't there.

The last time she had seen them, they had been crumpled up on the floor of the hotel bathroom as she stepped into the shower. *Did I leave them there? Did Tariq take care of them for me?* She didn't remember seeing them the next morning, but she had left the hotel in a rush, stuffing her clothes unceremoniously into her suitcase without paying attention to whether anything was missing. If someone had been watching her that carefully, then chances were that they had taken the pants as further evidence tying her to the dead man in the apartment. The weight of this possibility felt like an anvil crushing her chest. It wasn't like her to be so sloppy. This wasn't how she operated!

Dara continued to watch, horrified, as her onscreen image stood up, did nothing to help, did nothing to alert the authorities, and then simply left. This footage would give people the wrong idea, Dara realized all too clearly. Just like Caitlin's video.

But what made her more nervous than anything else wasn't what was *on* the video. It was what was conspicuously missing from the video.

Tariq.

CHAPTER THIRTY-THREE

A sleepless night had done nothing to help Dara find any clarity among her murky suspicions and dreads. She had spent hours mentally playing and replaying the scene from the apartment in Barcelona, picking apart the details, looking for something—for *anything*, really—that could soothe the gnawing ache that engulfed her every time she allowed herself to think the unthinkable. To even begin to consider the mere possibility that Tariq, who alone in Dara's thirty-six years had made her feel whole, could have betrayed her. *No. It can't be him. It can't. There's an explanation. There has to be.* She couldn't seem to distance herself enough from her emotions to sort out the facts, no matter how hard she tried, and her sleep-deprived thoughts kept returning to the same pointless loop.

Fact: Tariq had been tracking her.

Fact: He had followed her to the apartment in Barcelona.

Fact: He had somehow managed to stay out of camera range for the entire duration of the video clip.

Almost as if he knew there was a hidden camera. Almost as if he knew the precise location of the hidden camera.

Almost as if he had placed it there himself.

Just the facts, Dara reminded herself. *Stick to the facts. You'll drive yourself crazy otherwise.* But the facts were grim enough.

Fact: Tariq was a foreign spy who maintained a file on her at work.

Fact: Tariq's presence in Barcelona had been enough of a distraction that she had made some incredibly stupid errors.

Fact: Dara loved him, even knowing the facts.

Fact: Dara trusted him, in spite of the facts. The trust was tenuous, though, and it pained Dara to feel it slipping away like a handful of smoke.

She couldn't shake the competing facts, and they danced around in her thoughts even as she arrived at work and trudged, zombielike, through the halls until she reached her office. She was so absorbed in her thoughts that she almost didn't notice that every single person she passed was staring, mesmerized, up at the TV monitors anchored overhead.

As she threw her coat and purse onto a chair, she finally realized that the usual buzz of hallway conversations was muted and that something unusual had grabbed everyone's attention. She wandered out of her office and joined a group of young officers who were peering silently at the TV screen. "What's happened?" she asked.

A gawky young man wearing a suit that looked two sizes too big for him shook his head sadly. "They killed another one. Another one of us. Look," he pointed. "I think I recognize him. Like maybe I've seen him in the halls or something."

Dara's heart froze in her chest, and her next breath caught in her throat. The worries that had been simmering in her thoughts came to a torrential boil as she stared at the image on the television screen.

Fact: the young man being identified in the breaking news story as a CIA officer killed in action was the very same young man Dara had found in the Barcelona apartment.

Dara staggered backward. "Are you okay? Did you know him?" The young man put his hand out to help, but she waved him off. He gave her one last concerned glance but then turned back to hear the rest of the story.

Dara somehow managed to make it back to her office and close the door. If the story was already on network news, then surely there were internal reports about the murder, which she knew had been reported almost forty-eight hours ago.

She logged in to her computer, cursing at the amount of time it took to get through the various security passwords and protocols. Once in, she clicked through all of the various databases that would have contained such a report.

She found nothing.

"That's impossible!" She checked again. There should have been something in the system. Two days was plenty of time, even with the time difference.

It was *possible* that the news channel had scooped the agency, she supposed, but it seemed doubtful—particularly since Tariq had reported the murder to his official contacts in Spain, who surely would have notified the US government well before they leaked the story to the press. Even as she wanted to doubt the story playing on the television sets outside her office, though, she knew that it was true. *His label-free clothes. His ambiguous ethnicity. A man who could fit in anywhere. Just like the rest of us.*

Shaking, Dara forced herself to go back into the hallway to watch the rest of the news report.

The earnest blonde anchorwoman was still discussing the murder of the man she identified as "slain CIA officer Travis Park, whose body was discovered in a Spanish apartment earlier this morning." The rest of her coverage was vague, but she did have a quote from CIA director Abram Hendricks. "Travis Park represents the finest that America has to offer, and we will leave no stone unturned in our pursuit of whichever groups or individuals are responsible for this reprehensible act."

Dara slumped against the wall, ignoring the young man who was shooting her another concerned glance. So they were already confirming that he was a CIA officer. That in and of itself was unusual; the agency did not like to lift the cover of even its dead officers.

Something wasn't right. Why were they acknowledging Travis Park's CIA connection? Why hadn't her report—Tariq's report—given them plenty of time to cover up Park's identity? It wasn't in Spain's best interest to allow a CIA officer to turn up dead in their country, either, so she couldn't imagine that the Spanish police had tipped off the media before reporting it through official channels.

She whirled around and nearly ran down the hall. She punched the elevator button four times, and when the doors finally opened to reveal a crowd, she nearly screamed with frustration. Puffy-faced employees still wearing their winter coats shuffled on and off on each floor until the slow-moving elevator finally reached Dara's destination. She pushed her way out and then hurried to Dominic's office.

It was only eight thirty in the morning, but there was already a crowd queuing up for their turn to talk to him or to get his signature on the stacks of paper they held in their hands. Dara ignored the people waiting in the hall, as well as the fact that Dominic was talking on his secure phone line even as the hold button flashed on his nonsecure line. She walked in uninvited, ignoring the protests from the impatient hallway crowd as she slammed the door behind her.

"I'll have to call you back, Phil. Yes, *soon*. I don't know how soon, just *soon*, okay?" Dominic looked annoyed as he hung up. "I'm kind of busy in here, Dara, in case you hadn't noticed."

She ignored his attempt to brush her off. "Travis Park. The guy on the news. Was he really one of us?"

Dominic sighed deeply and nodded. "It looks that way, yeah. We're still trying to get details, though. We only found out a few hours ago."

"What?" Dara couldn't contain her surprise. "What are you talking about? It was reported nearly two days ago."

Dominic cocked his head at her. He was either surprised to hear this, or he was a damn good actor, because he genuinely seemed not to know what she was talking about. "Two days? Try two hours. The body was just found by the landlord of the apartment, who called the Spanish police. They notified us the minute they found the US passport in the pocket. We don't know how the hell it leaked so fast to the press. Is there something you need to tell me here? If so, make it quick. Everyone in that line of people you cut past outside is waiting to report to me on this situation."

Dara gave him the thirty-second version of what she had learned in Dubai and then in Barcelona. Her version of events was shortened considerably by the fact that she didn't mention Tariq's involvement.

Dominic looked grim when she told him about the video. "So you think someone set you up?"

"Well, even I admit that it looks suspicious as hell to watch myself poke around in there like I own the place and then walk right on out into the Barcelona night," she answered. *But we reported it immediately*, she almost said. She stopped herself, though. It was Tariq who had made the call to his contact in the Spanish police, and Dara didn't want to admit that detail. "I used a chain of contacts to report the body. I don't know why the message didn't get through," she said lamely, hoping Dominic wouldn't push the subject. "But I can tell you with one hundred percent confidence that there was no passport on the body; I checked every pocket. Someone planted it—or replaced it—after I left."

"And who knew that you were in Spain?"

Dara hesitated before answering Dominic's question. Standard procedure was to notify the CIA's chief of station in each country *before* arriving for any operational purpose. "The Barcelona lead arose in a time-sensitive manner, and I determined that it was most appropriate to pursue it immediately rather than to wait for approvals through official channels." Dara cringed even as she spoke, hoping Dominic wouldn't ask where the lead came from, since she had neither requested approval nor reported her contact with Yousef al-Kuwari.

Her mistakes were piling up. Just as Tony probably intended. He may have pushed her enough to get on an airplane, but she'd managed to screw everything else up on her own. Dominic could crush her career now—this time permanently. *And this time he'd probably be justified*, Dara thought. She'd truly made a mess of things.

Dominic frowned and then glanced worriedly at his closed door. "Look. I don't know what to do with this information. I don't know what it means any more than you do. But…" He paused, as if to carefully weigh his words. "We're minutes away from redirecting every officer in the agency to work on this right now. If one of them comes across your involvement, I won't protect you. I can't. But I know you. And based on everything I know, I don't think you killed Travis Park. So I'll give you twenty-four hours to figure out for yourself what this means. After that, I'm going to have to bring this—bring *you*—into the investigation."

Dara swallowed hard, not knowing whether to feel grateful or doomed. "I'm going to need my old clearances back if I'm going to learn anything at all. Right now I can't even access my own case files." Ever since she had been forced back to headquarters, she had been given only minimal access to classified data. She had effectively been compartmentalized right out of the loop.

Dominic nodded and picked up the phone. He barked instructions at whatever poor IT guy happened to answer his call. "This is Dominic Cahill, calling to authorize universal access to Dara McIntyre." There was a short pause. "Yes, you heard me correctly. Universal access." After another short pause, Dominic erupted. "I will make myself clear exactly one more time. Universal access. To be granted immediately. Immediately. In case you either haven't seen the news, or are just completely brain-dead, then you should know we're dealing with an extremely urgent situation right now. If you want to wait until you get the director's personal approval, I suggest you march your fat ass up to his office and get in line to see him. I'm sure that, between his morning meeting today with the vice president and then lunch with the prime minister of Malta, he'll be overjoyed to get a visit from a GS-9 IT guy. But don't worry—by the time you manage to even open your mouth to ask for an appointment, I'll have completed your termination paperwork and have security on their way to escort you permanently out of the building. Do I make myself understood? Yes? Good."

He slammed down the phone. "Twenty-four hours, Dara. That's all I can give you."

Someone tapped on his door insistently, and Dara took the hint to leave.

She decided to take the stairs back down to her office. She couldn't bear to be trapped in an elevator full of people discussing the murder in hushed tones. The musty, dim stairwell was deserted and a little bit creepy, as always, and only served to strengthen her growing sense of unease.

Something was *really* not right.

First of all, Dominic had been almost...nice. He was being far more understanding about this than Dara had expected, and that alone made her suspicious. And then there was that phone call. For Dominic to have authorized universal access for her was both unexpected and, even Dara had to admit, wildly inappropriate. It was no wonder the IT guy had balked. Universal access to the CIA's computerized files was supposed to be reserved for a small handful of the agency's senior-most officials. It represented the electronic keys to the kingdom, and it meant that she had access to everything. *Everything.* It was unheard of for someone at her level.

Her thoughts were spinning wildly. Either Dominic was so frazzled by Travis Park's death—the second such murder of a CIA officer in as many months—that he had first overlooked her mistakes and then had made a foolish error in granting her universal access when he had actually intended something more limited, or...

Or perhaps there was something he wanted Dara to find. Something so sensitive that only the highest clearance available would allow her to find it. Perhaps Dara's front-row seat in this mess was exactly what Dominic wanted.

Dara picked up her pace, nearly running down the stairs. She only had twenty-four hours to find out.

CHAPTER THIRTY-FOUR

Caitlin had enjoyed her entry ops training, what felt like a million years ago. Picking locks in class had felt like playing with a puzzle—like solving a Rubik's cube. Surprisingly, it didn't feel much different to be doing it now, in broad daylight.

She probably should have been more cautious.

She probably should have just driven to her parents' house, the way she had told Dara she was going to do.

She probably should have been more nervous.

And she probably *would* have been nervous—in fact, she probably wouldn't have even thought to attempt a stunt like this one in the first place—if she had been in the right frame of mind. But it had been one hell of a month. She'd been widowed, threatened, stalked, assaulted, demoted, and—to top it all off—she'd discovered she was pregnant with a child who may or may not have been fathered by her murdered husband. Her life was starting to feel like it was coming straight out of one of those melodramatic, over-the-top telenovelas. It really couldn't get much worse. She smiled ruefully as she wondered if pregnancy hormones had anything to do with her complete lack of fear as she manipulated her government-issued lock-pick gun into place.

To her credit, she really had *intended* to go home and weep like a good little widow. She'd even driven halfway to Bethesda, with an overnight bag packed and tossed into the trunk of her car. But somewhere along the way, something snapped. She snapped.

Tony would find her soon enough in Bethesda. She was certain.

It was better that she find *him* first.

She was happy to discover that the pick gun did its job every bit as quickly and easily here in the real world as it had during training. She waited a moment to make sure no alarms sounded before entering. She had no doubt that Tony had armed his townhouse with some sort of system, but when no bells or whistles erupted, she concluded that it must be a silent alarm.

She entered the house calmly, walked straight to the dead center of the living room, set her bag and coat down on the floor, and raised both arms into the air with the middle finger extended on each hand. She turned slowly, until she could be sure that any security cameras hidden in the room had recorded a 360-degree visual of her one-finger salute. She didn't bother trying to spot the cameras; she was sure they were there. Tony, as she knew all too well, loved cameras. "Honey, I'm home," she called out sarcastically, just in case the cameras were recording audio as well as visual.

She had never been in Tony's home before, but it was small and sparsely furnished enough that she figured finding his hiding place should be fairly simple.

Caitlin hummed as she strolled through the rooms, reaching out every now and then with a flick of a finger to toss a pillow to the ground or to lightly tip over a jar filled with pens and pencils. "Whoops," she breathed as she daintily slid an entire row of paperbacks off a bookshelf.

There was nothing incriminating in any of the obvious hiding spots, but she wasn't discouraged. Tony was a professional;

she knew he wouldn't keep anything under the mattress. She checked the obvious spots anyway. She was in no hurry. "Naughty boy," she clucked as she found a stash of girlie magazines hidden in his sock drawer.

She made her way back to the living room and plopped herself down on the couch. Her pregnancy wasn't showing yet, but she could feel herself getting winded more easily. Soon enough there would be no denying it. Caitlin stroked her abdomen gently, partly as showmanship for Tony's invisible security cameras, but partly because she was actually warming up to the idea of her pregnancy.

"Well, hello there," she said to the empty room. Something caught her eye, and without even getting up off the couch she knew she had found Tony's hiding spot. She had to laugh out loud—only a woman's eye would have picked up the discrepancy between the rest of Tony's furniture, which was pure, cheap, Scandinavian functionality, and the piece she had just spotted.

She rose from the couch and helped herself to a glass of water from the kitchen sink before she got to work. She let the tumbler slide lazily from her fingers when she finished drinking, and she smiled with satisfaction as the glass shattered on the tile floor. Only then did she approach the large teak armoire that housed Tony's television and DVD player.

She ran her fingers appreciatively over the decorative carvings that graced the heavy piece of furniture and then nodded with satisfaction. This piece *definitely* stood out from the rest of Tony's bachelor pad fixtures. It could have, of course, been a hand-me-down piece of furniture, or a rare splurge on quality, but Caitlin didn't think so. She had a good feeling about this.

She started at the top and worked down. She scrutinized every hinge, inlay, screw, and drawer pull, poking and prodding, checking for give. It took her twenty minutes, but she finally found the trigger. Actually, there were two. It really was an impressive piece of workmanship. Only by rotating one of the drawer pulls at the same time as she depressed the center of one of the decorative swirls carved into the wood was she able to reveal the hidden compartment at the base of the armoire. And once the secret drawer slid open, Caitlin realized that its contents were most definitely worth hiding so well.

CHAPTER THIRTY-FIVE

Dominic's threat apparently carried weight, because Dara's new accesses had been granted by the time she closed her office door and sat back down at her computer. She marveled at the list of hundreds of databases now at her disposal; she quite literally had the world's most sensitive information at her fingertips.

One database in particular caught Dara's eye, and she batted away a juvenile impulse to open it. The FIR database was probably the agency's most restricted database of all. It didn't contain information about state secrets, war strategies, or sensitive technology, though. This database contained the secrets of the people who were responsible for stealing all of the *other* secrets possessed by the CIA. FIR stood for Foreign Intimacy Reports. All CIA employees were expected to self-report each and every non-American citizen with whom they had engaged in intimate contact. The FIR database had it all—from one-night stands with a name-unknown prostitute in Bangkok to a marriage proposal to someone living just across the border in Canada. Dara had filled out several of the blush-worthy reports herself to disclose her relationship with Tariq. The idea was that if employees with top-secret access were required to self-report even the most personal details of their intimate relationships while they served abroad, then they couldn't be blackmailed into revealing secret information by criminals or foreign governments who might threaten to expose their off-the-clock activities.

Indeed, the database was a blackmailer's dream. With a single click Dara could have access to truly scandalous information about anyone she wanted. And over the last few months, Dara's list of enemies within the CIA had grown considerably. The idea of collecting dirt on some of the people who had systematically destroyed her career was definitely tempting.

She shook her head and moved on. She didn't have time to waste on petty vendettas. She needed to figure out who was trying to frame her for a colleague's murder.

She started with the obvious choices: the three individuals at the center of Operation Golden Mean. She opened the personnel files belonging to Jonathan and Caitlin Wolff and to Tony Alvaro and manipulated the images on the screen so that she could compare the three records side-by-side. And then she started reading from the top.

Just as Caitlin had told her, all three of the officers were relatively new; they had all joined the agency within the last three years. But that was where the similarities ended. Whereas Jonathan and Caitlin were still in their late twenties, Tony was in his midthirties. Jonathan and Caitlin had met during their year-long training course at The Farm. Tony had been waived from completing the course. Dara had never heard of such a thing, but a brief notation in his file stated that it was "due to significant relevant experience obtained during prior military service." This struck Dara as odd, since the skill set used by even military intelligence officers differed substantially from what was taught to CIA officers, but the agency had been through a series of hiring surges following 9/11 and then the 2003 invasion of Iraq, so for all she knew the training standards could have been relaxed to get more bodies into the field.

Tony's background investigation was also unusual. Whereas Jonathan and Caitlin's files showed records from extensive, in-person interviews with references, neighbors, and various other personal contacts dating back to their grade-school days, Tony's file only reflected "verification of internal references." In other words, someone at Langley had vouched for Tony, and that had been deemed sufficient. That must have been one hell of a glowing recommendation, Dara thought.

Tony's psychological screening was interesting too—if only because the lack of information had troubled the psychologist conducting the evaluation as much as it troubled Dara. According to the report written by Jeffrey Hallford, PhD, "The candidate displays a remarkable lack of disclosure that borders on noncooperation. Although overtly polite, candidate demonstrates a consistent and willful refusal to amplify or expand on information sought by this evaluator. In light of this failure to engage or divulge, candidate is not recommended for further employment consideration."

The electronic file was annotated with a single comment: Overruled. There was no information to indicate who had authorized such a decision, but it had apparently been final, since Tony's processing had continued unhindered.

Out of curiosity, Dara keyed in Jeffrey Hallford's name. *Interesting.* He had been a contract employee, used to conduct mental health evaluations on a part-time basis. Tony Alvaro had been one of his last screenings; after that he had disappeared from the system. The last note in Hallford's file was a simple statement indicating that his security clearances had lapsed.

Dara didn't like to give in to paranoia. She told herself that it could have been a coincidence—perhaps Hallford had simply retired or found other employment. Maybe he was even angry enough about being overruled that he had quit. But the timing struck her as odd. Someone with real authority was obviously on Tony's side. *Get in his way and find yourself out of a job.*

And right now *she* stood in Tony's way.

She shook off the growing feeling of dread. Facts. She needed facts right now; she could react later.

She was still staring at Tony's psych eval when she remembered that she had heard about another instance of an evaluator's recommendation being overruled. She quickly clicked over to Jonathan's polygraph records.

Sure enough, there it was: that single word that was starting to say so much. *Overruled.* Just as Jim, the polygrapher she had chatted up at Red Mercury, had told her, Jonathan's file indicated that the initial recommendation to fail him on his polygraph had been rejected.

Dara scanned first Jonathan's and then Tony's most recent polygraph results. They were both remarkably simple: No deception indicated on any counts. And as Jim had said, that in and of itself was suspicious. Nobody was *that* honest. Particularly no one in the CIA's employ.

She dug deeper into the file, pulling up Jonathan's preemployment polygraph. It had been conducted over three years ago, before he had met either Tony or Caitlin. Unlike the more recent polygraph record, this one was riddled with flags and notes indicating secondary lines of questioning. Jonathan had shown a reaction when asked about his drug use, for example, and then ultimately confessed to his polygrapher that, yes, in fact he *had* tried smoking pot, but just once, back in college…This initial polygraph, with its petty revelations and embarrassing disclosures, was typical. Everyone had *something* to hide—even if it was something as trivial as lying to their third-grade teacher about losing their homework. It was only natural.

Dara flipped back to the more recent record in Jonathan's file—the spotless one—and looked for the standard question about drugs. "Never," Jonathan had answered when asked this time if he had ever used illegal substances. And the polygraph hadn't picked up so much as a trace of a lie. "NDI," No Deception Indicated, was the verdict in the file, even though just three years prior Jonathan had told a different story.

Dara chewed on the end of her pen. Sometime during the last three years, Jonathan Wolff had learned how to beat the machine.

Dara pulled up her own most recent polygraph write-up, just out of morbid curiosity. She grimaced as she saw page after page stretch out before her eyes. She had been accused of lying about everything from prescription drug abuse to accounting irregu- larities to providing classified information to a foreign govern- ment agent. Dara knew that she had responded with the absolute truth to each and every question she was asked, but her results were peppered with accusations of lies. Her blood pressure rose perceptibly as she spotted what she considered one of the more ludicrous polygraph findings—that she had lied about having significant gambling debts. Reading it again, Dara snorted out loud. Other than her government-sanctioned alias gambling queen persona, the last time she had gambled was on a high school bus trip to the Grand Canyon, and she and her friends had been using M&Ms as currency while they played poker. And yet the suspicion remained documented in her file.

The thought occurred to her as she compared her lengthy report to the clean, brief reports in Tony and Jonathan's files that she could have made her life a whole lot easier if she had just used a few countermeasures of her own during her polygraph. But at the time she was hooked up to the machine, she had still believed in the system. Besides, she didn't have the same fairy godmother the two men seemed to have had on their sides; no one would have overruled Dara's polygraph results had she been caught cheating.

Don't get sucked back into it, Dara warned herself. She closed her own file and spent the next few minutes comparing travel records for the three junior officers. As she expected, there was considerable overlap that could not be explained by their reported assignments. Like all CIA officers, Jonathan, Caitlin, and Tony each had complicated and convoluted travel histories, but they had managed to be in the same cities more often than chance would dictate.

It was yet another factor that connected—or would have eventually connected—Dara with the group. At some point, Dara's audit software would have picked up on the similarities in their travel destinations. Part of her job as a counterintelligence desk jockey was to make sure that CIA officers didn't become predictable in their patterns and activities. Various airports that were considered easier to transit in alias, for example, became overused by officers looking to take advantage of lax security. Frequent overlap between officers' travel patterns eventually would have been flagged and then reported to the various officers' supervisors. Not for the first time, Dara realized that she was more deeply involved than she had understood.

On a whim, Dara pulled up Travis Park's file. It was almost more puzzling than the others. He'd been a star during his training. He'd received top marks in everything from land navigation to cryptography. And then, for no apparent reason at all, he'd been benched—parked in a dead-end job that made Dara's look exciting. He continued to apply for foreign assignments while he labored in his data entry position in the Counterterrorism Center. A string of rejections was documented, but unexplained, in his file.

"Kid couldn't catch a break," Dara said out loud.

But he had caught *some* sort of a break, finally. His assignment hadn't changed, but someone had finally allowed Travis Park to go operational. Again, there were no details. Simply a travel record. In the month before his death, Park had traveled three times. It was hardly worth noting for a CIA officer, but it was definitely a change in the pattern.

Dara winced at the last entry in his file: travel to Barcelona, Spain. One way.

She pushed away from her desk to think through her next steps when a sudden realization caused her to freeze. *That bastard. That goddamn bastard.*

She should have known that Dominic was being too helpful. The Dominic Cahill she knew would never have given her a twenty-four-hour reprieve. Instead, he would have cheerfully and immediately thrown her to the wolves, all the while claiming credit for taking her down.

Dara cursed her stupidity as she realized too late why Dominic had given her such extensive computer access. It hadn't been a mistake at all.

In her rush, Dara had completely forgotten to consider that each and every file accessed from her account was tagged with an electronic signature indicating the time and duration of her visit. If someone was senior enough to waive hiring, training, and polygraph requirements for Tony Alvaro, then it would be child's play to keep tabs on anyone digging too deeply into records that were never meant to be seen. And one glance at Dara's recent computer searches would instantly reveal exactly how much she knew.

In her effort to clear her name of any involvement in Travis Park's murder, Dara had just managed to place herself in the center of Tony Alvaro's crosshairs.

She ran her fingers through her hair, adding up the threats that seemed to be popping up all around her. The tally was disturbing. There was Dominic, who had just trapped her into documenting the very suspicions that could get her fired—or worse. It also occurred to Dara that Dominic had been the one to first introduce her to Caitlin. He had also approved the travel that resulted in her ill-fated trip. She shook her head at his ingenuity. He really had given her just enough rope to hang herself, hadn't he?

Then there was Tony, of course, who had waltzed into a job at the CIA with all obstacles and security measures waived and who, according to Caitlin at least, had broken into Dara's home and left her a teasing sample of the incriminating evidence against her.

And now, with said evidence floating around who knew where, even the FBI represented a threat. Slam-dunk video footage of a disgraced CIA officer wandering around the scene of an unreported murder would be damn near impossible to explain.

There was Caitlin, who had most certainly lied in the past, and who may or may not be lying to her now.

There was surveillance, both here and in Dubai. The men following her could have been terrorists or Feds; she had no idea. And, come to think of it, the line between the two was starting to blur as far as Dara was concerned.

And, finally, there was Tariq. Tariq who claimed to have called in the murder to his contacts in the Spanish police, but who now appeared to have called no one at all. Who had peeled off and then tossed aside the bloodstained black pants that could be used as evidence against her, in what now seemed to be a carefully orchestrated pantomime of passion. Who did *not* appear anywhere in the video of Dara wandering through the Barcelona apartment where Travis died. Who always seemed to know exactly where she was, and exactly where she was going next.

Dara hesitated over her keyboard. Her fingers shook as she slowly typed in *Bataineh, Tariq M.* She paused before confirming the query. She was afraid that the electronic trail left by conducting this record search, along with the other searches she had just completed, would be the nail in her professional coffin. And she was even more afraid of what she might find amid the results. She hit enter and then closed her eyes.

When she opened them, the first file she glanced at allowed her to release the breath she hadn't even realized she was holding. It was the file that she herself had created, documenting various intelligence exchanges with Tariq in his official liaison capacity. Then there were the FIR reports that, once again, Dara had authored. But below those reports was a far more disturbing document.

The document was nearly inscrutable. "For classified services rendered." There were few words, and no explanations. It was an electronic copy of a simple financial receipt, with no reason given for the payment. A very substantial payment, signed for by Tariq himself, the very same month that Dara had arrived in Jordan to begin her two-year assignment.

The room seemed to spin around Dara as she considered the meaning of this payout. She calculated the timeline of events: she arrives in Jordan, Tariq gets a payout worth nearly a decade of his salary, Tariq seduces her, and then she is sent home in compromised shame. *Had she been set up all along? Had she been betrayed by both Tariq and the CIA?* She wanted to believe that it was all a coincidence, that there was some sort of explanation, but...she couldn't. There were no coincidences in the intel world.

It made no sense. *It made no sense!* Dara felt herself slipping into tears. A sob choked its way out of her throat before she could cut it off. *Enough.*

She clenched her teeth, willed away the emotions, and forced her mind back to the rational facts alone. *Deep breaths.*

Fact: She was alone in this.

Fact: She wasn't going to let them—whoever they were—fuck with her anymore.

She briefly considered marching herself straight into the J. Edgar Hoover Building in downtown Washington, DC, and throwing herself on the mercy of the FBI, which was officially leading the investigations into the murders of both Jonathan Wolff and Travis Park. It was a different agency, after all, with different politics and a different agenda. If she was going to end up on the suspect list eventually anyway, she might be able to garner some credibility by coming in voluntarily.

Not yet.

Dara wasn't naïve. She knew that anyone with the ability to set her up within the walls of the Central Intelligence Agency most likely had influence outside of Langley as well. There was also the fact that Dara would have to disclose a number of protocol violations—if not actual crimes—that she had committed in the last week. Unofficial meetings with individuals with known terrorist connections and prohibited romantic contact with foreign intelligence agents were not looked upon favorably by law enforcement types. Plus, if they did their jobs, they were eventually going to come across Dara's fingerprints all over the Barcelona apartment, and maybe even the pair of pants covered in Travis's blood that Dara had somehow, stupidly, left behind.

Her credibility was about to self-destruct no matter what she did, and Dara had no intention of making it easy for the FBI to place her under arrest.

But whether she volunteered the information or not, Dara's presence in Barcelona was going to come to light soon enough. She needed to put things in order before her house of cards came tumbling down.

She took a deep breath and turned to her computer one more time. "If you're gonna go, go big," she said out loud as her fingers flew across the keyboard. She hit the print button. Again and again.

CHAPTER THIRTY-SIX

There was a time when Dominic would have instantly heeded the call of the director of Central Intelligence, dropping everything to rush into his office before Hendricks could blink twice. Those days, however, were gone. Fifteen minutes after Hendricks called, Dominic finally made his appearance, and the DCI appeared livid.

"It's about goddamn time!" Hendricks was pacing the floor of his office; he waved toward the door, distracted, and waited for Dominic to close it before he spoke. "This Park thing is a goddamn disaster. I just spent the last hour assuring the FBI director that he would have our full and complete cooperation and that no relevant information would be considered off-limits to the investigating agents." Hendricks looked as if he wanted to throw something. "And the imbecile thinks we're going to let *them* decide what's relevant."

Dominic simply raised an eyebrow, wondering where this was going.

"Obviously that can't happen," Hendricks continued. "But we need to make them think it's happening."

Dominic resisted the urge to roll his eyes. They'd been through this often enough; he didn't need to be treated like an idiot. "We will maintain full compartmentalization, as always. I will personally be reviewing all interagency requests for information. The FBI will get what they need, within certain parameters."

Hendricks snorted. "It's the 'certain parameters' that concern me, Dominic. Obviously I want the murder of CIA officers stopped, by any means necessary. But opening our files to outsiders would be a disaster—the FBI would shut us down for the next century. We can't compromise the rest of our operations in pursuit of justice for a single death."

"*Two* deaths," Dominic reminded him, earning a steely glare from the director.

"Make sure they get only what we want them to get," Hendricks warned. "Let's get this resolved quickly. It's a distraction, and I don't want it to turn into a witch hunt that sucks in innocent people who have more important work to do."

Dominic smirked at Hendricks's choice of words. "Innocent" wasn't a term bandied about Langley very often. He walked over to the windows that lined the wall of the director's office and admired the view for a moment before answering. "I'm taking care of it. We've put in place a virtual trail of breadcrumbs that'll lead the FBI exactly where they need to go without…getting distracted. One way or another, the murders will stop."

"Good. It's a public relations nightmare. Makes us look like a bunch of idiots who can't even keep our own officers alive." With Dominic parked in the director's usual spot at the window, Hendricks didn't seem to know what to do with himself.

Dominic turned and strolled out of the office without waiting to be dismissed. As he left, a slow smile spread across his face. He was getting pretty good at speaking in vague abstractions, if he did say so himself. Doublespeak seemed to be a requirement for senior intelligence officials. All the more reason for him to practice it now.

CHAPTER THIRTY-SEVEN

Dara's heart thumped in her chest as she fumbled with her car keys. The afternoon had turned icy cold, and her gloveless fingers felt numb. When she finally managed to get the car door open, she nearly dove in, throwing her gym bag onto the passenger seat and relocking the door in one fluid motion.

She laughed—a humorless, brittle sound emerging from her mouth—at her own nervousness. She had smuggled everything from false documents to huge wads of currency to the occasional cache of weapons across a dozen borders far more heavily armed than this one. This, however, was the first time she had felt anything like the panic threatening to overwhelm her now.

Walking out the doors of CIA headquarters with a bagful of classified documents was actually quite simple. There were guards in place, of course, but none of them ever gave departing employees a second glance; it was unheard of for an officer's bag to be searched. Still, this was an undeniable felony.

Dara hadn't wanted to break the law. In spite of the accusations that had been levied against her, she had always taken her officer's oath seriously. She'd done none of the things that she had been charged with—until now.

Guilt alone didn't explain her rapid heartbeat, though. It may have been easy to get the documents past Langley's armed guards, but, ironically enough, Dara had very nearly been caught by the department secretary, of all people—a meekly pleasant woman in her midfifties.

Massive secret budget or not, the CIA was still a government entity, and it still tried to save pennies on petty items. Because of this, Dara's office had no printer of its own; like everyone else, she had to walk down the hallway and pull all of her printed documents off of a shared machine. Knowing this, she had raced out of her office moments after hitting print for the last time, hoping to get to the machine before anyone else could see what she was printing. Unfortunately, she hadn't been fast enough. She ran straight into Linda, the secretary, who was walking away from the printer after having scooped up Dara's documents as well as her own.

"I think you have some of my printouts, Linda," Dara had said, trying to sound bored and unconcerned.

"Do I?" Trying to be helpful, the woman had started to flip through the handful of pages to sort through them.

Dara had no choice but to snatch them out of her hand. She peeled the secretary's pages from the bottom of the stack and held them just out of reach. "You should know better than to try to look at documents you aren't cleared to see," Dara barked at her before turning over the woman's pages. Fortunately, the chastised secretary had blushed a deep crimson and scurried away. But it was exactly the type of situation that Dara had wanted to avoid. Now Linda would remember exactly what had happened, if anyone started to ask questions. It was one more breadcrumb in the trail that could be Dara's undoing.

She took a deep breath and then started her car. She couldn't worry about the possible consequences now. It was too late to turn back. She waited until she was well off the CIA compound before pulling her cell phone out of the glove compartment. When she glanced at the screen she nearly rear-ended the slowing car in front of her.

Five missed calls. All from a number she knew well: Tariq's personal cell phone.

"Damn it!" she yelled. He knew not to call her. He *definitely* knew not to call her from his own phone.

It was obvious what he was doing. He was digging her professional grave even deeper. He was intentionally creating an electronic record of contact between the two of them. Contact that was going to strengthen the rapidly growing case against her. Furious, she threw the phone and then cursed when it bounced to the passenger-side floor of the car.

As if to taunt her from its now unreachable position, the phone started to ring. She debated ignoring it. At least up until now her phone records would reflect that she hadn't actually had a conversation, and that all attempts at contact were initiated by *him*. Her temper took over, though. She had a few choice words to deliver to Tariq—none of which were going to be within light-years of civil.

She slammed on the brakes, ignoring the honks of protest from the cars behind her, and leaned over to grab the phone before the call went to voice mail. She screamed in frustration as her seat belt prevented her first reach. "Shit!" She unclipped her seat belt and then dove one more time, hitting the answer button just as the phone rang its fifth and final ring. "You're going to regret this call," she started, her voice low with fury.

"Um...Dara?" It was definitely *not* Tariq.

Dara groaned. "Caitlin? This isn't a good time."

"I tried you at the office first. It's important." Caitlin's voice sounded odd, flat.

"What do you want?" Dara was way beyond small talk.

"I'm in Tony's house. There's something here you need to see."

Dara yanked the steering wheel and pulled into the parking lot of a huge, suburban megachurch. She couldn't drive *and* keep on top of the rapidly growing storm that her life was becoming. "Caitlin, what the hell are you doing there?" she hissed. She paused, wondering how much she should say. She still didn't know how deeply Caitlin was involved. She didn't know who was listening. "It's not safe for you to be there."

Caitlin didn't answer for a moment, but Dara could hear movement in the background, so she knew that she hadn't hung up the phone. "You're probably right. It's not safe. Especially since he just walked in." Caitlin's voice was still strangely emotionless, in spite of this bombshell. The phone clicked and went silent.

CHAPTER THIRTY-EIGHT

TOP SECRET. The classification labels on the top and bottom of every printout served as bold-faced recriminations as Dara shuffled through the pages that she had smuggled out of headquarters. Finally she found what she was looking for.

The biographic data available on Anthony Michael Alvaro had been thin, but a home address was listed. Dara wouldn't have put it past him to use a fake location, but she had nothing else to go by. She had tried calling Caitlin's phone a half-dozen times already, but her calls all rolled straight to voice mail.

She regretted the decision to head to Tony's house before she had even left the church parking lot. "I must be insane," she muttered to herself. She was unarmed—CIA officers didn't make it a habit to bring firearms into the headquarters building. She had no backup, no partner; ops officers almost always worked alone. She had no idea what she was about to walk into, and she couldn't even tell anyone where she was going. For all she knew, this was yet another one of Caitlin's lies, and she was being baited into yet another trap.

But she had to go. If she had any intention of clearing her name or, hell, just getting off the radar screen of the people who seemed to be intent upon ruining her life, then she had to understand what was happening all around her. She needed to know *who*. She needed to know *why*. She needed to go, trap or no trap.

Ten minutes later she pulled up to the aging townhouse. Nothing about the exterior gave any hints as to what drama, if any, was going on inside. It did look like the kind of middling real estate that a bachelor with a government paycheck would buy, though, if that meant anything at all.

Dara parked her car a block away, out of sight. It was one small nod to security under circumstances in which everything else could have come from a manual titled "How *Not* to Conduct Safe Operations"—like buckling her seat belt before driving off a cliff. She hesitated, the car still running and her foot still on the gas. Here was one last chance to drive away, call the cops— anything other than to march right into…into what? A hostage situation? Another murder scene? Another heap of evidence that might ultimately be used against her? She was alone, fumbling, and clueless.

She got out of the car and walked to the townhouse, dread slowing her steps.

She tried to glance in a window, but was thwarted by the tightly drawn curtains. The front door was unlocked and ajar. This fact made Dara even more acutely aware of just how much risk she might be facing. *If it seems too easy, then it probably is.*

Steeling herself for the worst, Dara entered the townhouse as quietly as possible. In spite of her efforts at stealth, her footsteps seemed to creak deafeningly in the otherwise silent home. Slowly, she edged her way down the short hallway and peered around the corner into the living room.

The scene that greeted her stopped Dara in her tracks. "Caitlin! What the hell is going on here?" The situation was the exact reverse of what she had expected to encounter.

She recognized Tony from the ID badge photo she had just seen in his digital file. He was slumped on the floor, looking pale and stunned, and he was grimacing as he clutched his right foot, which was bleeding heavily onto the beige carpet.

Caitlin, on the other hand, was sitting on the couch looking bizarrely relaxed and comfortable. She had only a loose grip on the gun that was pointed at Tony.

"She's insane. The crazy bitch shot me in the foot!" Tony seemed to think he still had a chance of getting Dara's sympathy.

Dara shot a questioning glance at Caitlin. The young woman only shrugged her shoulders indifferently.

"I'll take that to mean he's telling the truth." Dara considered urging her to drop the gun, but the truth was, Dara didn't know who the bigger threat in this situation was. She fought an impulse to simply reverse course, to back out of the room, walk to her car, and drive away from this—*all* of this—forever.

Before she could do anything, though, Caitlin leaned forward and picked up a remote control from the coffee table. "Watch this. I think you'll find it very interesting." She hit a button, and the television screen lit up with the horrible and familiar scene of Jonathan Wolff about to be executed.

"Caitlin, don't," Dara started. "You don't need to see this."

Caitlin repeated her small, apathetic shrug. "Too late now." She settled back on the couch. "You know, I actually never watched it before today. I never watched him die. They played it a thousand times on TV, but I could never bring myself to watch the whole thing. I always turned away at the last second."

Dara stepped over to the table to pick up the remote and turn off the video, but Caitlin leaned over and snatched it out of her reach. The young woman's eyes weren't on the screen anyway.

They were locked on Tony, who was moaning pathetically over his injured foot.

"Watch it," Caitlin said to Dara, more firmly this time.

"I've seen it. I don't need to see it again, Caitlin. I don't *want* to see it again. Ever."

"You haven't seen this version. Watch." Caitlin's voice still had the strange, flat quality Dara had first heard over the phone.

Dara looked at the television reluctantly, wincing as Jonathan Wolff was killed all over again, the knife drawing a slow, fatal arc across his neck and the blood first welling, then spurting in gruesome sheets of red liquid. Jonathan's body dropped in what seemed like slow motion, horribly graceful, as if to show that there was still some life force left in him that wouldn't exit until every last drop of blood had spilled out onto the floor.

It was the same footage that had first aired on Al Jazeera, and Dara's reaction to it hadn't changed since the first time she watched it. Her mouth filled with a metallic taste, and she fought back the wave of nausea. This wasn't like watching someone die in a movie. This was vicious in its undeniable reality.

But as the video continued to play, Dara realized that something *was* different. The video clip she had seen before, the one that had quickly been snatched up and aired by TV networks worldwide, had ended the moment Jonathan's blood-covered body had slumped to the floor. From defiant hostage to corpse in mere seconds, the pithy finality of it had made for sensational news stories, and for several days it seemed to be playing every time Dara turned on her television.

This video, however, didn't end there. In this version, the three murderers stood silently over Jonathan's body for a long moment, almost as if they were praying over the corpse. Or, Dara thought, almost as if they were shocked themselves, as if even *they* couldn't believe it had actually happened.

Then, one of them laughed. It was a cruel, horrible sound that made Dara's stomach turn all over again.

"I almost feel sorry for the poor bastard," the laughing man said as he unwound the scarf that had been covering his face. The smirk stayed on the executioner's face as he walked over to the camera. His looming image on the screen flipped and blurred briefly as he fumbled with the camera, and then the television went dark.

Dara turned in horror toward Tony. She had known he was involved, of course. She had even come to the conclusion that he was somehow responsible for causing Jonathan's death. Until she saw this version of the video, though—actually saw him pull off his blood-spattered mask with the knife still in his hand—she hadn't ever considered the possibility that Tony Alvaro, fellow CIA officer, had murdered his friend and colleague with his own hands.

"Why?" Dara's voice was shaky, incredulous.

Tony ignored her question. "Can I get a little help before I bleed out?" he asked, gesturing toward his foot.

Both women ignored him. "Caitlin, what's the plan here?" Dara knew it was a stupid question the moment it came out of her mouth.

"I'm going to kill him, of course," Caitlin answered matter-of-factly. "Trust me, you want him dead too. I think a *lot* of other people probably do." She gestured toward a drawer that stuck out strangely from the bottom of the armoire holding the television.

Dara headed for the drawer and then hesitated. Sighing, she walked over to the kitchen, puzzling at the broken glass on the floor, and retrieved a dish towel that looked only marginally filthy. "Here," she said briskly as she walked back to the armoire, throwing the towel at Tony. "I don't know yet whether I want you dead or alive, so use this to stop the bleeding in the meantime. If you so much as move after that, though, I'll shoot you in the other foot myself."

He cast a malevolent look at her, but used the towel to fashion a rough tourniquet for his foot.

Dara knelt next to the drawer and peered in, her breath catching in her throat. There were dozens of DVDs, all meticulously labeled with names and dates. She flipped through the discs and recognized some of the names—including her own. Judging from the other labels, Caitlin was right. If the contents of the other videos were even as remotely incriminating as the two Dara had already seen, then there were most definitely a lot of other people who would want Tony dead if they knew what he had on them.

The last two discs in the stack both had Travis Park's name on them. Dara didn't even have to finish reading the label to know that the last one had both Travis's *and* her name listed. She knew without a doubt that this was a copy of the disc that had been left in her own home.

"Look in the envelope," Caitlin directed. Her eyes never left Tony, and her gun stayed on him at all times.

Dara pulled a manila envelope from the drawer and slid out the contents. Birth certificate. Driver's license. Passport. An expired military ID card. Dog tags. And not a one of them mentioned Anthony Alvaro. "Anthony *Russo*," she read from each one.

"Those are fake, obviously," Tony hissed from where he sat. "They're from work."

Dara shook her head. "No, I don't think so. I've never known the CIA to issue alias dog tags. Besides," she looked him up and down, "you look more like a Russo than an Alvaro. Nice try, *amigo*, but you should have paid more attention to the details."

Pieces of the puzzle that her life had become were falling into place, but Dara felt no closer to understanding what had happened. What *was* happening. If anything, it was all becoming even *more* complicated. She tuned out the scene in front of her and tried to sift through the facts.

The lack of background information on Tony Alvaro in the CIA files made perfect sense if his name was not actually Alvaro. The question was, would the files even acknowledge a Tony Russo? Had he somehow managed to con his way into a job at the CIA, in alias? An impressive feat, if so. Or, more likely, she realized, someone *inside* the CIA had set him up to act with impunity. Dara was willing to bet there was no record anywhere within Langley of an employee named Anthony Russo.

If this was true, it made Tony the perfect spy. The perfect weapon. He had all of the CIA's resources behind him, but if anything went wrong, then he had never even existed anyway. He was a living, breathing black op.

Dara could only think of one person opportunistic enough to come up with such an idea. *Dominic.*

The sight of Caitlin rising from the couch, her finger now on the gun's trigger, yanked Dara back from her thoughts.

"Say good-bye, Tony Russo," Caitlin said softly.

"Wait! Caitlin, stop!" Dara hoped Caitlin would listen to her, because she had no intention of saving Tony's life by jumping between him and the gun.

Caitlin didn't back away from Tony, but neither did she shoot him. She appeared only mildly interested in what Dara was saying.

"Caitlin, stop. It isn't just him. It isn't just Tony—Alvaro or Russo, it doesn't make a difference. Look—there are two other people in the video. And trust me, he's had help from above. Killing him isn't going to fix anything. It won't stop anything."

Caitlin narrowed her eyes and then lifted the gun to within a foot of Tony's head.

"Jesus, Caitlin! I'm not saying this to be a do-gooder. I'm not trying to protect *him*. But he has information we need. We have options here. Besides," her voice grew softer, "don't you want to know why Jonathan died? He can tell us."

This seemed to make sense to Caitlin, because her finger finally left the trigger.

"I need to go see someone and maybe make some calls," Dara said, trying to sound confident. "Let's just keep him here for the time being while I figure this out."

Caitlin thought it over and then nodded almost imperceptibly. Then, in a flash of motion, she raised the gun over her head and brought it down viciously against the side of Tony's head. Tony fell over, unconscious, bleeding from an impressive new gash to his temple.

Dara clenched her teeth. "*Alive*, Caitlin. We need to keep him *alive*."

"Then don't take too long." Caitlin settled back down on the couch, her eyes never straying from Tony.

Dara ran.

CHAPTER THIRTY-NINE

Dara was halfway to her car when she noticed the gray SUV. It was parked just far enough away to be nonthreatening, but close enough to have an unobstructed line of sight to her car. Perfect surveillance positioning. It definitely hadn't been parked there before. And it looked…familiar?

Who am I kidding? Dara berated herself for being paranoid—and also for being sloppy yet again. With the events of the last few hours, she had actually managed to turn off the constant vigilance that was drilled into CIA officers until it became second nature. The truth was that she hadn't even been looking for surveillance, since she had thought that she was *chasing* the person who had been following her. Besides, gray SUVs were ubiquitous in suburban northern Virginia; they were about as close to vehicular anonymity as it came. It wasn't as if she could even see the license plate from where she stood, one hand on her own car door. Plus, the last time she had caught someone following her, they were driving the stereotypical American-made sedan that had "government issue" written all over it. This one didn't look government issue.

But something about the SUV bothered her.

"Aargh! I don't have time for this!" Dara shouted out loud as she started her car and pulled out of the neighborhood. She had wanted to drive straight to her destination, but now she couldn't. Not with the nagging little doubt pecking at her thoughts. "Okay, the long route it is," Dara sighed and turned left instead of right— the better choice for surveillance detection.

She was feeling foolish about her decision to take the time for this—time she didn't have to spare—until she glanced in her rearview mirror and saw that the gray SUV was still behind her, several blocks back.

Just twelve hours before, Dara would have dismissed the surveillance as annoying CIA tails keeping tabs on her personal life. It seemed to come with the job these days, at least when your personnel file was as thick as hers was. Now she couldn't be so sure.

Her mind flashed briefly on the two masked figures who had stood with Tony as Jonathan Wolff dropped to the ground. She still had no idea who they were. Had she unwittingly passed them in the halls of CIA headquarters? Or were they Anthony Russo's private mercenaries? She didn't even know their nationalities. They could be anyone. From anywhere. And that could be them in the gray SUV that had tailed her at a distance through the last three turns.

It was time to act. Dara grabbed her cell phone and called a familiar number. The conversation was brief; Dara was grateful that she didn't have to explain. "Meet me in twenty minutes. At the place we first had lunch together." She hung up and then made another left. She had another phone call to make now— one that required a pay phone.

Fortunately Dara wasn't far from Red Mercury. Not many newly established bars bothered to install pay phones anymore, but Naomi had known that they might come in handy for her particular clientele. CIA officers sought anonymity more than most—even during their off-hours.

Dara entered the bar with her head down, avoiding Naomi, who was busy chatting with a small group of drinkers. She headed straight to the back and was grateful to find that the pay phone was free. She lifted the receiver, inserted a few coins, and then hunched over the phone while she punched in the numbers in order to block any prying eyes from trying to see who she was calling.

The phone call was quick—less than thirty seconds—and Dara spoke quietly enough that no one could possibly overhear. Mission completed, she skirted out of the bar before she could run into anyone she knew from work.

Twenty minutes later, Dara was sitting in the parking lot of a small deli less than two miles from Langley. She was lucky that she hadn't been arrested for the way she had been driving since she left the bar, but she needed to be sure that she had lost her tail. Fortunately this was her turf, and she hadn't found it hard to shake off her surveillance.

She smiled with relief as a bright red—of course—compact car pulled into the parking space next to hers. Naomi Macek got out and then shifted her considerable bulk into the passenger seat of Dara's car. She handed Dara a manila envelope before she even said a word.

"You brought a copy of your security camera footage?" Dara smiled wearily in greeting.

"Honey, I did a lot better than that. I'm full service, all the way. What kind of ex-spook would I be if I didn't have my place wired with all the latest and greatest technology?" Naomi tossed her red curls back flamboyantly. "Anyway, I went through the footage myself and spotted your little friend within seconds. You were right—he went straight for the phone after you used it and hit redial. I took the liberty of printing out the screen shot that captured his face best. He's actually kind of a looker, I have to say, if it makes you feel any better. Who did you call, by the way?"

"My favorite Chinese takeout spot. I asked what time they open on Sundays." Dara grinned.

"Clever girl. You know, you're almost making me miss the spy-versus-spy world. I'd nearly forgotten how much fun this stuff can be."

Dara shook her head. "Trust me. You want nothing at all to do with this one. Thank you for the help, though, Naomi. Really."

"Anytime. You just let me know." Naomi slid out and then drove off in her own car.

Dara glanced around one last time before opening the envelope that Naomi had delivered. The parking lot was deserted; the gray SUV was nowhere in sight.

Taking a deep breath, Dara pulled out the single printout. She felt numb as she saw the unmistakable image on the page. The very image that had been so strikingly absent the last time she had been caught on surveillance footage.

Tariq.

CHAPTER FORTY

Ten minutes and two security checkpoints later, Dara took a moment to compose herself before getting out of her car and trekking across the nearly deserted headquarters parking lot. She closed her eyes and willed her hands to stop shaking. This wasn't the time to show any more weakness than she already had to.

There is no shame in this, she tried to tell herself. But there was. There was plenty of shame. Shame, along with anger, betrayal, and grief, was driving her actions now.

The worst part of all of this was the unfamiliar feeling of helplessness. She had always been able to take care of herself, even amidst the explosive hazards of warzones and the more subtle treacheries of international diplomacy. She had always been able to find the right path, to see the right solution. Now, for the first time in her life, she was at a loss. The line between ally and enemy had been blurred and then severed.

She hated that she needed help.

She also didn't know if she would actually find it here, in the marble-floored CIA headquarters, but Dara didn't know where else to go. The fact that her ID card still allowed her into the building was a good sign, she hoped. She had half-expected alarms to sound as soon as she swiped her badge through the guarded entryway's turnstile. There was nothing of the sort, though—just a disinterested glance from the night shift security officer.

Dara struggled against the schoolyard sensation of feeling like a tattletale as she took the long way to her destination. It was late, and she hoped Dominic Cahill had already gone home for the day along with most of the other CIA employees, but she couldn't be sure. It had been her experience that craven bastards like him tended to work late, when no one else could see what they were up to. Avoiding Dominic's office was worth the extra two minutes of walking. She had no desire to bump into him while she was en route to blowing the lid off of the treasonous game he was playing.

For better or for worse, CIA Director Abram Hendricks was also notorious for his round-the-clock hours, and Dara hoped that she had a reasonable chance of catching him alone in his office.

Deep in thought, she was startled when her feet hit the carpeted hallways outside the director's office. In Langley this, and only this, hallway was outfitted with plush floor covering, in contrast to the tiles everywhere else in the building. The carpet silenced her footsteps and served as a physical reminder that she was in unfamiliar territory. After the smooth surface of the rest of the building, walking in this hallway felt like trudging through quicksand.

CIA officers did not just drop in on the director; all pretense of an open-door policy ended where the carpeting began in the CIA building. If fact, most officers actively strove to steer clear of the seventh-floor executive offices altogether, since it was well known that politics trumped operational sense there every time. Occasionally an officer was called upstairs to provide an impromptu debriefing or receive a rare honor, but otherwise the seventh floor was known as a place to avoid.

Dara was glad to see that the lights were still on in the director's office suite. She was even more pleased when she stepped in and found that the secretaries' desks in the outer office were deserted. A single young security officer posted outside Hendricks's door glanced at her briefly to ensure that she posed no obvious risk, but it wasn't his job to ask her business. He remained silent as Dara hesitantly approached the inner sanctum.

Abram Hendricks was sitting at his desk with his reading glasses on, but he wasn't reading a classified document when Dara tapped on his half-open door. Instead he was intently studying a bottle of wine. An open wooden crate next to his desk contained eleven more identical bottles.

"A gift from the French minister of the Interior. We saved their butts big time last week with a little scandal that could have gotten very ugly. This had better be a truly spectacular case of wine," Hendricks said. Dara thought he was joking, but she couldn't be sure.

She was thrown off guard by his casual reception. She had prepared a short speech to introduce herself and explain her problem as quickly as possible; she had assumed that she would need to get to the point quickly or else risk being tossed out of his office as an unwelcome intruder. She had only met the DCI twice, and both times it was in a crowded meeting room, so she didn't think he would even recognize her.

But he did. Or at least he seemed to. "Care for a glass?" he asked her as he opened the bottle and filled a cut-crystal wineglass for himself.

"No, thank you." Dara fidgeted, still standing in the doorway. She just wanted to say her piece and get out.

Hendricks was in no hurry, though. He took a sip of wine and held it in his mouth studiously, his eyes closed. Judging from the blissful look on his face, Dara guessed that he approved of the French minister's selection. Finally, he swallowed and opened his eyes. "I wondered if you might pay me a visit. Dominic said you were bright."

The mention of Dominic's name—and Hendricks's immediate association between Dara's visit and Dominic—felt like a physical blow. Dara's head buzzed, and her legs felt leaden. *He's part of it.* She opened her mouth, but nothing came out. If this... whatever it was...plot? If this plot involving Tony Alvaro-slash-Russo went *this* high, if the director of Central Intelligence himself approved, then what could she do? *I surrender,* she thought. *I give up.* She was outmanned and outmaneuvered, plain and simple. She wanted out—whatever that meant.

Hendricks finally broke his attention from his wine and noticed Dara's shock. He chuckled softly. "Don't look so worried, Ms. McIntyre. I assure you that we are on the same team. We both want the same thing."

Dara felt an instant of relief, but it was quickly followed by anger. She wanted no part of Hendricks's "team." Not after what she had been through. "And what would that be, *sir*?" she asked through clenched teeth.

Hendricks gestured for her to have a seat at the small, round table in the corner of his office. He remained standing, thoughtfully swirling the remnants of red wine in his glass. "Are you sure you wouldn't like a glass? It really is an incredible vintage."

"No," Dara hissed. She wanted to strangle the man. "I want to know what the hell is going on. I want to know who Tony Russo is. I want to know why my career is in pieces."

Finally Hendricks appeared to be paying attention. His brow furrowed. "Tony *Russo*, you said? Well then, if you've learned that name, then you already know most of the story."

"Humor me," Dara said. "Spell it out for me. I've been a bit distracted lately, shall we say. But I suspect you already know something about that."

Hendricks's eyes narrowed, but he otherwise maintained his composure. "I see. You're upset about what happened to your career. I am sorry for that, truly. But it's only temporary. It was just a matter of...*alignment*."

Dara felt her fingernails digging painfully into the palms of her hand, and she forced herself to loosen her fists. She had to listen, even if she hated Hendricks more with every syllable that emerged from his lips. "*Alignment?*" she asked incredulously. She had heard every sort of groupthink, but this one seemed an unbelievable euphemism for the hell that she had been through.

Hendricks didn't seem fazed by her anger. "You were chosen for this operation because you are one of very few officers who possess both the experience required for success and the vulnerability required for failure." He looked pleased with himself for this little riddle. Fortunately, he continued before Dara gave in to the impulse to throw something at his head. "Alignment, you see? We needed to make it look credible that someone of your caliber would be in the relatively pedestrian job we placed you in. We knew that Tony was going to go after whoever was in your job, because your position is one that would have eventually exposed his...irregularities."

"Are you kidding me?" Dara couldn't believe what she was hearing. "This is all about the stupid audit software? You're the head of the goddamn CIA. Couldn't you have just manipulated the data any way you wanted?"

Hendricks sighed. "You'd think so, wouldn't you? Unfortunately, the idiots who designed the software had the brilliant idea of creating a Chinese wall for the system. The company that developed it even used it as a marketing ploy. It's the one piece of software in this place that I can't touch; once the data is in, it can't be altered. Obviously it wasn't my decision to buy the system. The damn fool who was the previous DCI fell for it and authorized the system way before I got here."

He walked over to his bookshelf, where the bottle of wine rested, and refilled his glass. This time he didn't even bother to offer a glass to Dara. "But don't get distracted by the details. The software is only a minor part of all of this, and we all know that there's always a way to bury data in our line of work. One way or another. We didn't tell Russo that, of course. In fact, we had to exaggerate the potential of the audit software more than a little. To be honest, it was mostly just a way for you to attract Tony's attention."

It suddenly dawned on Dara what the director was saying. "You used me as bait?" she asked, horrified. "You stuck me in that job because you wanted him to come after me?"

Hendricks seemed to think that over for a moment before answering. "No, not bait. Bait is passive. Helpless. That doesn't give you enough credit. I think of you as being more of a poison pill. Once in Tony's reach, you have a unique ability to bring him down. Permanently."

Dara was baffled by this whole conversation. Nothing seemed to be making any sense at all. "Aren't you the one who brought Tony inside in the first place? Someone with serious authority pulled a lot of strings for him."

Hendricks gave a stiff, reluctant nod. "Tony Russo did not work out as intended. He was brought in to champion and mentor programs from within. Programs that stood to benefit the agency—the whole country, really—but for a variety of reasons could not be officially sanctioned. I needed to be able to maintain plausible deniability for these operations for obvious reasons, so we needed someone with the appropriate background to help foster and build them outside of the normal channels of approval."

"Operation Golden Mean," Dara breathed, finally beginning to understand. When Hendricks nodded, she pressed further. "Among others," she said, although this was only a guess.

The same stiff nod. "Unfortunately, as you've already seen, Tony Alvaro became a bit of a monster. My own personal Frankenstein, if you will."

"What went wrong?"

"It doesn't matter," Hendricks said, too forcefully.

A sore point, Dara saw. "Actually, *sir*, it does matter. It matters quite a lot. Two officers are dead now precisely *because* things went wrong."

"And that is something I sincerely regret." Hendricks sounded as if he had rehearsed that line more than once. "But those two young men chose to become involved in operations they knew to be dangerous. They chose to go above and beyond the usual call of duty because they were sick of the restrictions. They saw what the constant oversight, the never-ending leaks, and the public scrutiny of our methods was doing to this agency. They were just as frustrated as I am with the status quo."

"More so, I'd say," Dara said drily, "considering the fact that they're dead and you're sipping Bordeaux." Her mind was spinning, leaping. "But how much of their frustration was their own, and how much of it was manufactured for them? You 'aligned' my life for me. You backed me into a corner until I had no choices left. I can only assume you did the same for them."

Hendricks didn't answer. He shoved his wineglass away and stared past Dara.

Dara didn't need him to answer. She had seen the files. Jonathan Wolff's had been filled with far more awards and accolades than most junior officers; he had been promoted far faster than the norm. Now the glowing record took on a darker meaning. Now Dara understood that Jonathan had been stroked and coddled and praised until he was convinced that he was invincible. He'd been patted on the back, given operational carte blanche, and then sent to die. It could not be coincidence that the golden-haired hero's death was a PR bonanza for the CIA.

Then there was Travis Park. Dara had wondered why Travis, who seemed just as promising as Jonathan, had been relegated to a desk job far from the field. He'd received nearly perfect marks during training; he had all the markings of a superb officer, but he was held back while the rest of his peers flourished. *Why?*

Suddenly, Dara saw it. She couldn't help but be impressed by the manipulation involved in Travis Park's case. He was put into a job that would leave him frustrated enough to be vulnerable for recruitment into a shadowy operation. The job itself was a brilliant choice, too. He worked in the CIA's equivalent of the coal mines—digging through and processing raw data alongside people with no operational training or experience. So if he happened to stumble upon choice information—accurate or not, and via legitimate means or not—he could slip it into the coal heap, so to speak, without anyone ever being the wiser. Plus, it was the frustrating kind of job that would make him eager to do just about *anything* to escape it.

Jonathan Wolff. Travis Park. *Her.* Their jobs, their lives, and their fates all handily aligned for them. They were all just pawns in a game of chess that they hadn't even realized was being played.

"So why are they dead?" Dara asked finally, not even expecting an answer. "And, more importantly, am I next?"

"No one was supposed to die," the director said, sounding almost petulant. He brushed a piece of lint off his jacket and then walked halfway to the door, clearly dismissing her. "I told you, Ms. McIntyre. We're on the same side. We both want to get rid of Tony. We both want this to end. I want *you* to win." He gestured to the door. "And now if you'll excuse me, I need to prepare for the Senate hearing tomorrow." His eyes drifted toward the bottle of wine, Dara's question already forgotten.

Dara walked out in stunned silence. What more could she possibly say?

She walked down the hallway silently. It was only when her feet left the carpeted stretch and hit the more familiar marble tiles that her heart stopped thudding quite so violently in her chest. She found the nearest elevator, pressed the call button, and then leaned gratefully against the cool metal frame.

The elevator doors were sliding shut when she realized what she had forgotten to ask. What she should have asked—what she needed to know—if she wanted to get through this alive.

What was Tariq's part in all of this?

CHAPTER FORTY-ONE

Dara had a good guess as to what role Tariq had played; she was no fool. But the thought that a senior, highly decorated Mukhabarat officer would accept payment for seducing her, risking both his reputation and charges of espionage all for about the price of a vacation villa, seemed awfully...tawdry. And it didn't go along at all with what she knew of Tariq's character.

"Wow, he sure sucked you in if you're still defending him," Dara muttered to herself as she pulled open her car door. She slid in and then screamed as she realized that Dominic Cahill was sitting, waiting for her, in the passenger seat. She lunged out of the car, manipulating her keys instinctively in her fist to use them as a weapon.

"Dara, wait! Wait a minute! Hold up. It's just me." He held up his empty hands for her to see. "I come in peace." He winced as Dara stared him down. "Sorry, bad joke."

"Dominic, you're about as trustworthy as the wrong end of a shotgun right now, so say whatever you need to say fast, and then get the hell out of my car."

He offered her a weak smile. "I know. I'll make it quick. But a little bird told me that you were just in with Hendricks, so we really need to talk. I have some information that might change the way you react to whatever it is he told you. Please."

Against her better judgment, Dara sat back down in the driver's seat and closed the door. She kept her grip on her keys, though, and mentally calculated the trajectory between the makeshift weapon in her right hand and Dominic's left eye.

Dominic glanced at her fist and shifted nervously in his seat. "Did he give you his little speech about alignment? He loves that one. He has a bit of a God complex, if you haven't noticed."

"I noticed. And hats off to both of you—and to whoever else is a part of your little planning committee. You played me but good; I never even saw any of this coming. The American taxpayers would be proud if they knew what their top spies were spending their time doing." Dara didn't bother to hide the sarcasm in her voice.

"Oh, come on, Dara. When this is over you'll get your career back. You can name your next posting—anywhere you want. I'll see to it."

Dara shook her head. Did she have to spell it out for him? "Dominic, for the moment my career is about the last thing on my mind. Right now I'm just focused on trying not to end up dead, either at the hands of the sociopath *you* brought into the CIA, or the man you paid to seduce and then humiliate me. I don't give a rat's ass what pay grade I end up in when this is all over; I just want it to be over."

Dominic looked confused. "By sociopath, I can guess you're talking about Tony Alvaro—"

"Russo. Tony Russo," she cut him off.

He raised his eyebrows in surprise. Apparently neither he nor Hendricks had counted on her learning Tony's real identity. They, of course, didn't count on her allying with a slightly deranged pregnant woman with a loaded gun and good aim, Dara thought ruefully.

"Yes, Tony Russo," Dominic confirmed. "But we didn't pay anyone to *seduce* you." He looked almost insulted by the thought.

"Tariq."

Dominic's eyebrows climbed even higher. "You think we paid him off? Really?" He looked genuinely surprised. "Just the opposite. If we could have paid him off, then we wouldn't have needed you in the first place. Trust me, we tried that route. We need Tariq. Money isn't his motivation, Dara. *You* are."

She wanted to believe him. She wanted to believe that Tariq had not been part of any of this. But he was, somehow. Her heart was racing. She needed to know. *Now.* "Would you all stop speaking in your goddamn riddles and just tell me what the hell you want from me?" she begged, humiliated by the sting of tears threatening her eyes. She turned her head so that Dominic wouldn't see.

She needn't have worried; Dominic was oblivious. He laughed—*laughed*—at her question. "You have it all wrong, Dara. Getting Tony to go after you was the only way we could get Tariq to act. We need him—we need the Jordanians—to make Tony disappear."

He sighed when he saw that Dara was still baffled. "Look, our hands are tied these days. The CIA can't authorize any sort of lethal action without presidential approval. Do you know what kind of paper trail that leaves? It's unbelievable. And no one on Hendricks's personal security detail is going to kill a fellow officer. They're all a bunch of fucking Boy Scouts; half of them are ex-cops. And Hendricks obviously isn't going to take anyone out on his own—can you even imagine that yuppie fool getting his hands dirty?"

Dominic was on a roll. "So that brings us to our foreign liaison partners. 'Partners'—hah! After the fiasco in Iraq and then the unraveling of the secret prisons, nobody's stupid enough to agree to take on our dirty laundry anymore. Everything has to be 'transparent' now—fully documented, endlessly scrutinized, and always, always *official*." He said the word as if it were obscene. "There's no back door anymore. The days of the gentlemen's handshake are gone. No offense, meant," he said, glancing at Dara's chest and then blushing slightly.

Her skin crawled. But, finally, things were starting to make sense. *Poison pill*, Hendricks had called her. "So your idea was to sic Tony on me so that Tariq would swoop in to rescue me like some damsel in distress? Seriously? That's the worst damn operational plan I've ever heard."

Dominic shrugged. "It was the only way we could get rid of Tony without implicating ourselves. We created him; we brought him inside. Now we need to get rid of him. But we also need plausible deniability."

Dara snorted. That was another term Hendricks had used. These guys seemed to spend an inordinate amount of energy trying to cover their own butts. She wanted to get away from Dominic—from all of this—but there was something left that she didn't understand. "What went wrong? Were Jonathan Wolff and Travis Park supposed to die? Was that part of some sick, twisted plan?" Dara didn't want to believe that the director of the CIA would have ordered Tony to kill the officers simply as a ploy for public relations or funding, but at this point she wouldn't put it past him.

Dominic grimaced. "No. That was not supposed to happen. They died because things took on an...unexpected momentum." He was choosing his words carefully. Just like Hendricks. "The deaths occurred because Tony Alva—Tony Russo decided he needed an insurance plan. He knew that Hendricks wouldn't back him up forever. The murders were his way of making sure that he'd never take the blame for any of this. Tony killed Wolff to show that he was in control, and to make sure that Hendricks would be *forced* to protect him."

"What are you talking about?" Dara asked impatiently. "That doesn't make sense."

"Sure it does. It was really quite brilliant, actually—" Dominic cut himself off as he saw Dara's look of disgust. "If Tony is ever implicated in Wolff's death, then Hendricks's role in all of this will be revealed. Now, Hendricks not only can't make Tony the fall guy for any of this, but he also has to actually *protect* the son of a bitch from the FBI and everyone else who's trying to solve the murder. If Tony goes down for Wolff's murder, then Hendricks goes down too. The only way out for Hendricks is for Tony to disappear."

Dara struggled to process all of this. It was almost unbelievable in its macabre simplicity. She thought back to Caitlin's description of Tony's Ponzi scheme. The young woman had been more accurate than she realized. Each life taken was to protect someone else's. "What about Travis Park? What about me?" she asked softly.

Dominic shrugged. "Momentum. I don't know, really. Maybe he's enjoying it. Maybe he's just rubbing Hendricks's face in it. Or, more likely—and what keeps Hendricks up nights—is the possibility that he's about to start making demands. Demands neither Hendricks nor the CIA can possibly afford to meet. That's why we need your help. To make this stop."

She had heard enough. "Get out of my car."

Dominic sighed. "Dara, we're on the same team here."

"So you all keep telling me. Well, *teammate*, get the fuck out of my car. Now."

He climbed out reluctantly. She wasn't finished, though. "I'm going to take care of this my own way. But your fingerprints are all over this, no matter what you think. It's going to come back to haunt you."

Dominic's expression turned cold. "Actually, you're wrong about that. I'm smarter than you think, *Sun*dara. Let's just say I've been very, very careful to 'align' my own interests for the long run. I knew from the beginning that something was off about Tony, so I protected myself accordingly. You won't find my fingerprints anywhere. And let's not forget that I've done you a few favors recently. If it weren't for me, you'd have no clue that you were walking around with a big target painted on your back. So before you get any ideas, I have a word of caution for you: pick your battles. You won't win them all here, I promise." He shut the car door gently and walked back to the headquarters building with his hands in his pockets, whistling.

She stared at his back, processing everything he had just told her. In her heart she knew that he was probably every bit as guilty as Hendricks. But he *had* given her a few gifts. He'd steered her toward answers when he could have just waited for Tony to pounce. He'd planted seeds.

And he'd given her back Tariq. Maybe.

She didn't bother waiting until she was off of the CIA compound before she turned on her cell phone and dialed. The phone rang three times, then four; she struggled with the steering wheel to make the left turn out of the secured exit while still holding her phone to her ear. Finally, he answered.

"Dara." His voice was cautious.

"Where are you?" Her voice was not.

"Look behind you."

She glanced at her rearview mirror just in time to see the gray SUV turn right out of a suburban neighborhood street onto the road behind her. She hung up the phone, her heart racing, and pulled into the darkened parking lot of a small car repair shop that was closed for the night. The SUV followed.

She got out of her car, walked halfway to his, and then stopped.

He also got out of his car, but he didn't approach her. He was waiting for something. A sign.

She smiled, and he saw what he was looking for. They rushed toward each other, and Dara buried herself in his arms. "I thought…" she started, her face pressed into his chest.

"You thought what?" Tariq whispered in her ear. His voice carried no guile, no deceit—just concern and warmth.

"Never mind. Later." She just needed to be still; to be near. The rest would come soon enough.

CHAPTER FORTY-TWO

"What have you gotten yourself into, darling Dara?" His light tone matched his teasing smile, but his eyes showed something darker. They were sitting in Tariq's rental car with the heat cranked up, since Dara couldn't stop shivering.

When she didn't answer—she didn't know *how* to answer—he continued, "I realize that you are probably very angry with me. I've been keeping tabs on you. More than I should have, I know, but I didn't like what I was seeing and I've been worried." He looked at her nervously, as if afraid that she was going to spit in his face.

A thought crossed Dara's mind. "Were those your men I saw in Dubai? Did you have me under surveillance?"

Tariq hesitated, but only for a moment. "Yes. But my men saw two other men watching as well. You were a popular pursuit that day. That's when I really started to worry."

Dara frowned. There were no easy answers here. The more questions she asked, the murkier the story became. "And Barcelona?"

Tariq looked stricken. "That I can't explain. I called my contact in the *Guardia* exactly as I told you, Dara; you have my word. He tells me now that he filed the information as an anonymous tip, but that somehow the information was lost in the system.

Maybe he's telling the truth, and it's all just a horrible coincidence, or maybe he's lying and someone told him to bury the information. I honestly don't know." He took her hand in both of his. "I came here immediately when I saw the reports on television. I knew what you must have thought…what you must be thinking. And I worried that you might be in some danger as a result—both from whoever killed your colleague and from your government. That's why I called your phone, even though you asked me not to. I needed to reach you, and I didn't give a damn about anything else. I'm sorry."

Every part of Dara wanted to tell him to shut up and just hold her, but she didn't allow herself that indulgence. Yet. There was one more question she had to ask. Probably the most difficult of them all. "And the money?" she whispered, looking directly into his eyes.

Tariq looked confused. "What money?" he asked, head angled in bewilderment.

"The two million dollars paid to you personally, in cash, less than a month before you first asked me on a date." Dara held her breath and watched for his reaction, every muscle in her body tense.

Tariq's eyes narrowed. Not a good sign. He broke eye contact with her. A worse sign. He ran his fingers through his black hair, which was longer than Dara remembered it. He was stalling.

Her stomach sank.

And then he laughed. It was a bitter, terrible sound that did nothing to help Dara breathe. She felt faint, but no air would enter her lungs. Was this the sound of a guilty conscience? "Tariq?" she pleaded faintly for explanation. She needed something from anything.

"They think they are very clever, don't they?" Tariq asked finally. His face twisted with contempt. "Your people make it look as if I am the dirty one here. Do you think that I wanted everything kept secret?" His voice was too loud for the airless car interior. He seemed to realize that he was shouting, because Dara had to strain to hear what he said next. "If it had been up to me, the director of your CIA would have to stand on a mountaintop and sign his name to each and every one of those unmarked bills with his own blood. Because that's what it is—blood money."

Tariq paused, but Dara didn't say a word. Finally he continued, calmer this time. "My country has been accused many times of human rights violations. And your government looks the other way while we are condemned as torturers. But guess who is willing to pay lots of money—always in cash, of course—for our services? Your employer. Director Abram Hendricks personally delivered the funds to 'sponsor'—that's his word, by the way, not ours—at least a half-dozen detainees in the year before we closed our doors to his requests. Each was considered inconvenient in some way or another, and the CIA wanted them to simply disappear. Any information that we 'extracted'—again, his word—from these detainees, however, was most welcome. The money I was given was the last time my government accepted such payment. Ironically, it was *my* country that decided to end this arrangement, because we didn't approve of *your* employer's methods. And yet we're still the ones considered savage by the world's human rights organizations." He shook his head in disgust. "I took great pleasure in informing your director that our detention services were no longer available."

Dara looked at him. She looked at his dark, pleading eyes. She looked at the lines etched too early into his face by laughter and by stress, the scar on his neck that she had traced on a hundred different nights, and his lips, half open with unspoken words.

She believed him. And she also finally understood why Hendricks had targeted *her*. So many countries had been burned providing Hendricks with secret prisons or torture-for-hire that no one was willing to help him anymore. Unless, of course, it was someone other than Hendricks doing the asking. Someone with a close, personal connection to the very man who could easily make Tony Alvaro disappear forever. Someone like Dara. She was Tariq's vulnerability after all—he had said so himself.

She finally knew what she needed to do to make this all stop. She would ask for Tariq's help. But it wouldn't be quite what Abram Hendricks had in mind.

"I need your help," she whispered.

He caressed her cheek. "Anything you ask."

It took a long time to explain. Some of what Dara told him was theory and some was fact. And some of what she told him was classified. In the back of her mind she imagined the hawk-faced polygrapher gleefully rubbing her hands together. *Unauthorized disclosure of classified data to a foreign agent! I knew it!* the image cackled.

But if Dara didn't do something, she had no doubt that she was next. And then likely someone else after that. Still, she struggled with the words, knowing that she was violating her oath. In spite of everything, her gut still twisted with guilt, and she found herself skipping details. Tariq was smart enough to fill in the gaps for himself, she knew.

When Dara finally described her plan, Tariq smiled and nodded. "Poetic justice. A nice touch."

Dara smiled back. It had been a long time since she had felt someone was on her side. "I figured the request would be better received coming from you than it would from me."

He nodded again. "I agree. Give me an hour. Maybe two. We will fix this together, Dara."

As she climbed back into her own car and watched Tariq drive in the opposite direction, she felt something that she hadn't felt in far too long—with anyone: She trusted him. Completely.

CHAPTER FORTY-THREE

"What the—" Once again Dara didn't know what to make of the scene in front of her.

Caitlin was still on the couch, sitting exactly as she had been when Dara left the house almost three hours earlier. Tony, on the other hand, was looking far worse for the wear. His hands and feet were tightly bound with duct tape, and he was soaked with water. A bucket and several damp towels were strewn around him. He was on his knees, gasping for air as if he had just sprinted a mile.

Dara assessed him quickly. He looked like he was in pain, but the bindings around his ankles at least seemed to have stopped the blood loss from his gunshot wound. "You didn't shoot him again, did you?" she asked Caitlin. There wasn't much more blood than when Dara had left, but clearly *something* had been done to the guy.

"Not yet." Caitlin sounded slightly less robotic than she had earlier, and there was a new determination in her eyes. "Do-it-yourself waterboarding," she said, gesturing to the water soaking Tony and the carpet. "It's surprisingly effective."

"Cra-cra-crazy bitch!" Tony heaved, still struggling to catch his breath. He leaned over and vomited a stream of clear fluid.

"Jesus, Caitlin. What were you thinking?"

Caitlin crossed her legs demurely. "We were just having a little chat. It turns out that Tony has some very interesting stories to tell about all sorts of people."

Tony flopped over onto his side, groaning as his injured foot twisted. "I was just doing my job. If you're looking for someone to blame, you're going to have to look a lot higher up than me."

"Yes, I just had a very interesting discussion with Director Hendricks," Dara said noncommittally.

Caitlin's head whirled around. "The DCI? He knew about all of this? Really? So this piece of crap on the floor was actually telling the truth?" She was suddenly more animated than Dara had ever seen her.

"I told you," Tony whined. "Now can you please loosen the tape? It's killing me."

"No!" The two women shot him down in unison.

Dara and Caitlin quickly compared what they had learned. The stories told by their respective sources were remarkably similar, with the predictable exception of who was to blame. Tony claimed that he had been coerced into his role as an off-the-books assassin and that Director Hendricks was using evidence of his previous acts to blackmail him into targeting Dara next.

Dara suspected that the truth lay somewhere in the middle.

Caitlin, however, didn't give a damn whose version was more accurate. "I didn't see anyone holding a gun to your head when you slit my husband's throat." She stood up from the couch and raised her gun. Her voice wavered, but her firing hand was steady as her finger found the trigger. "I didn't see anyone looking over your shoulder as you manipulated my husband into getting involved, or making him think it was all *his* idea. I didn't hear anyone threatening you when you tried to rape me." She edged closer, the gun inches from his head.

"Caitlin, don't do it," Dara warned her for the second time that day. This time, though, she had no doubt that the young woman intended to shoot to kill. "He'll be taken care of."

"By who, Superman?" Caitlin asked incredulously. "Because it's sure as hell not going to be the CIA. It's not going to be the FBI, either. They're only going to see what the CIA wants them to see. Don't you get it? This is the only way. No one else can stop him."

"They can." Dara pulled back the curtains and pointed at the white van that was just backing into the townhouse driveway. She felt an incredible sense of relief: Tariq had come through. Quickly, too. The men walking up the steps must not have needed much convincing.

Tony's eyes widened in horror when he saw the diplomatic license plates on the van. "No! No, no, no. Don't do this. I have information—it's all on video. You can have it all. I'll help you! Don't do this!" He was begging now, babbling. "I had to kill them, I had no choice! Hendricks was going to set me up. It was the only way to protect myself. And Park had a big mouth; he was going to bring everyone down!" He started to cry.

Caitlin, on the other hand, smiled. She had also understood as soon as she saw the plates. She walked to the front door and opened it before the three burly men in dark suits even had a chance to knock. They entered cautiously, warily eyeing Caitlin, who seemed far too pleased to see them, given the circumstances.

Tariq caught the door just as it was about to close and slipped in behind the three men, none of whom had uttered a word yet. "No formal introductions necessary," he said, to the relief of both Dara and the newcomers. "They're with...security, shall we say, from the Egyptian embassy."

"No!" Tony screamed. He was writhing on the floor, struggling unsuccessfully to free his hands. "They'll torture me! They'll kill me!"

"Nonsense," Tariq said in a voice dripping with insincerity. "They merely have a few questions to ask you. In Cairo. In a prison cell. Using methods encouraged by your own employer— off the record, of course."

Tony started to weep openly.

One of the dark-suited men leaned over and whispered something to Tariq.

Tariq's eyebrow rose, and he turned to Dara. "The gentlemen understand that their detainee may, at some point, claim to be an officer of the Central Intelligence Agency. They are concerned that interrogating a US official would be a breach of diplomatic protocol."

Dara shook her head and spoke directly to the Egyptians. "I can assure you that Anthony Michael Russo is not, and has never been, an employee of the CIA. Any such claim would be completely without merit." She knew that, no matter what, no one would ever contradict her on this.

The man grunted his approval and then gestured at his colleagues. They lifted Tony as easily as a sack of groceries and loaded him, still screaming, into the back of the van.

The man, who Dara assumed was the most senior of the three, turned back to her one more time before leaving. He spoke perfect, British-inflected English. "During the course of our... *discussions*, it may come to light that he is an American citizen, in which case we are obligated to report his detention to the US embassy." He hesitated and seemed to be assessing Dara before continuing. "Of course, sometimes there are language barriers or bureaucratic delays, and the message is not conveyed as quickly as some may like."

Dara understood his meaning perfectly. "Take your time. No one will be looking for him." She glanced back at the drawer full of video discs. "No one will miss him for quite some time."

The Egyptian looked satisfied with this response. "Perhaps we might not get around to asking this question for, say, one week's time?"

Dara agreed that one week would be appropriate. She knew that it would be a very, very long week for Anthony Russo. "I think the US government will be extremely grateful for your cooperation in finding and capturing the terrorist who killed one of their much-loved intelligence officers. I don't think they will fault you too much for the delay. Particularly when you provide them with a full report of his confession."

The man bowed his head in agreement. "And we are grateful to you for letting us have this time with him. Your FBI's presence in our country, and the accusations that it was an Egyptian plot, have been…tiring. We are pleased that this will put an end to both." With that, he disappeared into the van with his colleagues and drove away.

"I'll wait outside." Tariq stepped out of the house, closing the door softly behind him.

"They're not going to kill him?" Caitlin sounded disappointed.

"No. But he's going to have one hell of a bad week." Dara almost felt sorry for him. Almost.

"This is going to kick up a whirlwind of shit for Langley when the Egyptians turn him over to the FBI with a full report, isn't it?"

Dara suddenly felt exhausted. But she couldn't quit now. Not while there was still more work to be done. "I have no intention of waiting that long," she answered enigmatically.

Caitlin fell silent. She looked even worse than Dara felt. The fire was once again gone from her eyes, and the robotic stiffness had left her movements. Now she just looked tired, pale, and lost.

"Why don't I drive you home." Dara put her arm around Caitlin and guided her out the door.

CHAPTER FORTY-FOUR

After two days it still felt surreal to be with Tariq. At least to be with him *here*. In her home. In the United States, where, thanks to her career choice, Dara had considerably less freedom than the average citizen. It felt risky and forbidden, but at the same time, it felt completely right.

The twenty-four-hour window that Dominic had given her had come and gone with nothing more dramatic than the tick of the clock. She hadn't bothered to go back into the office or otherwise make contact. She was certain that Dominic and Hendricks were well aware that Tony Russo was...*unavailable* at the moment. Hendricks may have made enemies out of most of the intelligence services around the world, but he still controlled a mighty budget, and that meant that he still controlled valuable sources.

Dara liked the thought of the director of the CIA sweating, panicking, wondering just how much Tony would reveal. Until he knew what Tony would say, and whether or not anyone would believe him, Abram Hendricks wouldn't be able to plan or react. He was like a rat trapped in a cage, and until someone else made a move, Dara knew that she was safe. She was in control.

"I could stay a bit longer, you know." Tariq brushed her cheek with his lips as he handed her a mug of coffee. "Although perhaps I should buy my own bathrobe."

Dara laughed. He looked ridiculous in her fluffy periwinkle robe. "Your habit of dressing up in women's clothing seems to be a recurring theme in our relationship."

"Well, with legs like mine, can you blame me?" He flashed a bit of ankle, then glanced at the *Washington Post* newspaper spread out in front of her. "Still nothing?"

She sighed. "No. I didn't expect there to be anything this soon, but I keep hoping."

"Hoping that you don't have to be the one to spread the story?"

Dara both loved and hated the fact that he always seemed to know what she was thinking. "I'm still not keen on the idea of being the source of a news leak. No matter how justified it might be, it still goes against everything I'm still trying to believe in."

"Then let's run away together," Tariq said, teasing her. "We can start with Disneyland. I've never been. And then maybe Graceland? Everybody loves Elvis."

Dara rolled her eyes and smiled. "No. I need to get this over with." She reached for his hand. "I might need your help. Again, that is." She paused, suddenly feeling a professional awkwardness about the question she needed to ask. "Were you serious when you said that you keep files on all CIA officers you deal with? Me included?"

Tariq frowned, but he nodded. "I would think that you, of all people, would understand how the system works. It's not personal. It's just the way it is."

Dara cut him off before he could get defensive. "I know, I know. And I'm not asking for personal reasons. Or, at least I'm not asking about my own personal file." She stopped, trying to decide whether she really wanted to do this, to once again mix her love life with her professional life, just when things were finally starting to look up.

She had to, though. Even if it drove a wedge between her and Tariq. She had to ask. She had to finish what she had started.

"Does your little collection include a file on Abram Hendricks?"

Tariq's frown deepened. "Of course. His is thicker than most, for obvious reasons."

"I hate to ask this, Tariq, I really do. I don't want to cause any problems for you at work, but…" She cringed, hating that she had to put him in this difficult position.

As usual, though, he guessed what she needed before she even had to ask. His frown vanished, and he laughed gently as he reached for her other hand. "Ah, darling Dara. You're so nervous about this. So American. For you this is a black-and-white issue, I know. But for me, it falls in that beautiful shade of gray. Don't worry, I have just what you need. And there will be no trouble for me. In fact, in this case I think that your esteemed Director Hendricks might approve, or at least find some irony: my personal life and my professional life are very much in alignment here. I hate the man, for very personal reasons." He pulled Dara into his lap as he spoke, pausing briefly to kiss the side of her neck, running one finger under the neck of her shirt. "And my employer happens to think he's a rotten bastard as well." He lifted her up and carried her into the bedroom. "So you see, Hendricks is right about something. Alignment *does* feel good."

"I don't think this is what he meant by alignment," she started to say, laughing, but she only got the first word out before he cut her off with his lips on hers. "Never mind," was all she managed to get out, and it was quite enough.

CHAPTER FORTY-FIVE

"Turn on your TV."

"Dara? Is that you?" Caitlin obviously hadn't bothered to look at the caller ID before picking up her phone.

"Turn it on. Channel seven." Dara waited until she heard the muffled sound of the news report coming from Caitlin's side.

"What is this? It isn't about Tony. This is something different?"

"No word on Tony yet, but that will come soon enough. I doubt it'll ever go public, though. There are too many people interested in keeping that particular part of the story quiet." Dara hadn't told Caitlin anything about her plan, so what she was about to see was a surprise. A bonus. "Just listen for a minute."

Dara, on the other hand, had already seen the story. Several different versions of the story, in fact. It broke first on Al Jazeera, of course. Yousef al-Kuwari, her Qatari source, had come through one last time for her. This time, however, it was Dara who provided *him* with the video, rather than the other way around. "For you, my shadowy friend, I will do this for free," he had said generously when Dara told him what she needed him to do. "Consider it a gift from me to you."

The story had morphed only slightly as first the European networks and then the American networks picked it up in rapid succession: An unnamed source had provided a damning videotape of a meeting between CIA Director Abram Hendricks and several unidentified but heavily accented individuals, none of whose faces were shown at any point on the video footage. The purpose of the meeting was clearly to discuss the fate of several individuals suspected of involvement in terrorist operations. Several segments had proven to be especially popular with journalists.

In one, Hendricks shrugged nonchalantly; in the shadows of the low-resolution video he looked bloated and arrogant. "The fact that he's an American citizen makes it all the more important that we keep him out of our court system. A jury's not going to convict him. Juries are full of soft, ignorant people. It's my job to protect them from themselves by getting rid of scum like this. This guy needs to spend time in your interrogation rooms, not a courtroom. I trust in *your* system's ability to handle someone like this more than I trust ours, if you know what I mean. I'm not going to tell you what to do with him. I'm just going to leave him in your capable hands and forget I ever heard his name."

It was another segment, which Dara had already noted blossoming across various Internet blogs and news sites, that was the real coup de grâce, though. It was short and concise, and it quite handily ensured that Hendricks would have to deal with the repercussions of the news stories on his own. "The president?" Hendricks laughed dismissively in response to an off-camera question about whether his plan had support from the White House. "He's an idiot. He doesn't have a clue. I spend my days protecting America from his decisions. Let's just say that his support for my proposal is optional, and leave it at that."

Dara glanced at the headline of one of the latest Internet news stories. "CIA Director Abram Hendricks: Protecting

America from Itself?" An editorial cartoon farther down the page depicted Hendricks squatting grotesquely on a toilet, using the Constitution as toilet paper. He was speaking to an audience of grinning caricatures of medieval torturers: "It may be ignorant, but at least it's soft!"

The video that Tariq had provided had no shortage of quotable moments, Dara noted with satisfaction. Whoever Jordan's General Intelligence Directorate had used to set up the hidden cameras that had recorded every word Hendricks had uttered when on Jordanian soil deserved a huge raise. Hendricks would be removed from his position within a matter of hours, and then he'd have to deal with the aftermath of his actions as a private citizen. There weren't enough expensive lawyers or private bodyguards in the world for him to ever come out of hiding—if, that is, he somehow managed to avoid jail time. His life was about to be investigated very, very thoroughly.

But Caitlin was still disappointed. "There's nothing about Jonathan. I want the world to know that Abram Hendricks was responsible for my husband's death. He needs to pay for that. What about the videos in Tony's apartment? Wasn't there anything you could use to tie him to Jonathan's murder? Or Travis's?"

Dara winced. She knew that her plan was far from perfect, and Caitlin had just zeroed in on its main weakness. "I want the same thing, Caitlin. Remember, he tried to ruin my life too. I want him to pay for everything he's done. And this video is going to yank every bit of support out from under Hendricks just in time for the Egyptians to deliver Tony Russo and his full confession back to the FBI a few days from now. That part of the story may or may not go public, but I promise you that Hendricks is not going to get away with what he did." She paused, debating yet again how much Caitlin should know. "I went through every single one of the videos in Tony's apartment. None of them show Hendricks talking specifically about your husband. They don't prove anything."

"I don't care!" Caitlin was crying. "It was bad enough when I thought that Jonathan was killed because he got in over his head. But now I know it wasn't even his idea. It was just Tony Alvaro—or Russo, or whatever his name is—and Hendricks manipulating him, pushing him, pushing *us* into it. Now I want them to suffer."

Dara's stomach clenched, and she leaned against the wall for support. "Caitlin," she said softly. "You're going to have to trust me on this. I have the videos, and I'm going to keep them as insurance. But they aren't going to help you get revenge on Hendricks. He's already dug his own grave, and now we need to just sit back and let everything unfold."

Caitlin didn't sound convinced, but she agreed. "Thank you, Dara," she said softly before they hung up. "For everything."

Dara sank into a chair, rattled by the conversation. Her lie of omission gnawed at her conscience. *Was* she doing enough? The DVDs were scattered on the table in front of her; she picked up the one labeled "Hendricks" and slipped it into her computer to watch it one more time. She hadn't lied to Caitlin when she said that it didn't show Hendricks ordering Jonathan Wolff's death. It was footage of what appeared to be a rare, in-person meeting between the director and Tony Russo. Tony, who had used a hidden camera to record the meeting, was obviously trying to goad Hendricks into being as explicit as possible. But Hendricks didn't bite. His instructions to Tony were chilling, but vague. Other than laying out Tony's new identity as Tony Alvaro and backdoor path into the CIA, the video didn't prove anything. Further instructions, if there were any, must have come later.

Besides, there was another reason why Dara wanted to keep the video secret for now. There was a third person at the meeting shown on the video. The man was quiet, almost as if he suspected he was being recorded, but his presence alone at a meeting like this one was enough for him to want very badly for the video to disappear.

Dara finished watching. She was still convinced that releasing the video now wouldn't help matters. *Maybe later, though...* she thought to herself as she prepared several backup copies of the footage.

CHAPTER FORTY-SIX

Dara was busy tidying the impossible stacks of files in the office, trying in vain to make life just a little easier for whichever poor soul inherited this lousy job and crappy office from her, when Dominic Cahill once again darkened her door.

"Congratulations on the new assignment, Dara," he said with his usual false cheer. "Beirut station chief is quite a step up from this."

Dara gave him an equally insincere smile in return, coldly noting the tension in his voice and the question in his eyes. "Congratulations yourself, Dominic," she said. "To be promoted to deputy director at your age. What's your secret?"

His left eye twitched, and he fidgeted from foot to foot, laughing nervously. "Just the right place at the right time, I guess. Hey, no hard feelings, right? I told you that everything would get sorted out, and now look at us both. You and I survived the purge while a heck of a lot of other folks were sent packing. We're going to run this place before you know it."

Dara dropped the pretense of the phony smile. She wanted Dominic to understand exactly how she felt. To know exactly what she knew. "Yes, I would say that both of our futures are nicely *aligned*, as your former boss would have put it."

His eyes widened, and she could see that he was desperate to know what she knew. She briefly watched him struggle to dissect the meaning of her statement, but then lost interest. "If you'll excuse me, I have a lot to do here before I fly out tomorrow," she told him finally. *Let him wonder.*

Dominic Cahill, quiet third participant in the meeting with Abram Hendricks and Anthony Russo, nodded and walked silently and obediently away.

He was right, Dara had come to realize, about her not being able to win all of her battles, at least not all at once. And there were other people who were getting off without consequence, too. She thought grimly of the other masked participants in Jonathan Wolff's murder. Hopefully either the Egyptians or the FBI would unmask them, but there were no guarantees. There were too many people involved, hiding between too many layers of secrecy and lies. She couldn't identify everyone who had been involved. No one could.

But that didn't mean she would stop trying. She had a growing list of names already, and she had no intention of stopping her pursuit for more. Some of the names were surprises. Some were not. And sooner or later, some of those people would make mistakes. Without Tony around to manipulate, guide, or threaten, someone would talk. And the best way for Dara to stay in the game was to have someone in Dominic's position on her side. Even if it was for all the wrong reasons.

She leaned back in her chair and watched Dominic leave. She had picked her battle, and it was far from over.

ABOUT THE AUTHOR

J. C. Carleson is a former undercover CIA officer. Her near-decade of covert service took her around the globe, from bomb shelters in war zones to swanky cocktail parties in European capitals. A graduate of Cornell University, she lives outside Washington, DC.